GOD'S WEAPONS
of
MASS DESTRUCTION!

Armored And Dangerous

WILHELMENA PRINGLE-GODFREY

PRESS

DEDICATION

I especially dedicate this book in loving memory to my parents, Ezekiel and Missionary Mary M. Pringle. These two godly soldiers have gone on to be with the Lord, but have left a tremendous legacy and example of how to live a totally submitted, dedicated and triumphant life in Christ.

To my three children — Darrell, Kevin and Colette — who continue to show love and support!

To my two remaining sisters, Rebecca Williams, Dr. Celestine A. Pringle; and to my dear niece Gwen who lovingly and prayerfully encouraged my vision in writing this book.

To women of God who cease not to pray for me: Mothers Claudine Thompson, Evelyn Simpson and Annie Hayes; God's end time warriors!

Last, but certainly not least, to Sister Virginia Foster and Brother Michael Semple, faithful servants of God. To all of the saints of God who pray for me to accomplish God's purpose.

TABLE OF CONTENTS

INTRODUCTION

N ow is not the time for Christians to be at ease in Zion. The central theme of the Bible is God's holy warfare against Satan; therefore, it is not a strange thing for God's people to be at war. The idea of warfare may be disturbing; nevertheless, God has declared war against Satan (Gen. 3:15).

God is Spirit, and Satan is *a* spirit; for this reason, we are engaged in *spiritual* warfare. The entire human race is subject to this warfare. The difference is the side one chooses to fight on: 1) God's side; the winning side or, 2) Satan's side; the side that is already defeated.

God made a bold statement of Satan's doom. He declared victory over the kingdom of darkness through "the Seed" (Jesus Christ) of the woman. Genesis 3:15 refers to Jesus' death on the cross where He bruised (mortally wounded) the head of the serpent (Satan).

The Christian life can be described as a battle scene. The Lord Himself is a "Man of War" and He views all things from the standpoint of the spiritual warfare in which we are engaged.

Being a "good" Christian does not mean that you are exempt from troubles. Some wars are short, and some wars can go on for years. The purpose of war, whether long or short, is to help the disciple of Jesus Christ get to know God better, become more like Christ and learn how to endure in hard times. How we react under pressure will reveal the shallowness or depth of our character.

During times of war, the Commander-in-Chief (God) gives specific instructions (the Bible) to His soldiers (believers). When His orders (the Word of God) are obeyed, victory is guaranteed. When His orders are disobeyed, defeat is guaranteed!

Some troubles are sent by God; some are sent by Satan; some by man; and some are imaginary. In the end, they will all work together for good!

Even though the adversary has launched a no-holds barred attack against the Church, we are armed and ready to meet every challenge. We are not fighting *for* victory; we are fighting *from* the standpoint of victory! Jesus is our Champion.

Christ has already defeated every foe! Nevertheless, there are still battles to be fought. Like the Disciples of Christ, some of us have a misconception of the Kingdom of God. The Kingdom of God is not about glitter and glamour. The strongest Church is a persecuted Church! You will have trials in this life, but they come to benefit you in some way; to do you good, not to destroy you, and to give you an expected end. Expect to win!

There are valuable lessons to be learned even from defeat and set-backs. Scripture teaches you how to turn defeat into victory. The Lord wants Christians to profit from their trials. He wants you to have a positive outlook on life, whatever the circumstances. Comfort yourself with the knowledge that God is with you and He has made provision for you to overcome every obstacle.

When Jesus ascended back to Heaven, He did not leave the Church comfortless or powerless. He provided all that the Church needs to be victorious; the "whole armor" of God — *God's Weapons of Mass Destruction!*

CHAPTER ONE

THE BELIEVER'S PROTECTION: GOD'S ARMOR

———————◆———————

E phesians is often described as the *warfare letter* to the Church. It is also referred to as a "prison epistle," because it is one of the letters written by Paul while God's tried warrior was in prison.

This letter to the saints makes it clear that the Church is engaged in a fierce, ongoing battle with the forces of darkness. Therefore, Christians must use all of the spiritual armor at their disposal.

God gave Paul the revelation of these weapons through the inspiration of the Holy Spirit. They are referred to as the "whole" or complete armor of God, provided for the believer's protection.

Christ has already defeated the devil; and so, through Christ we have the victory! The Bible lets us know that warfare is real. It also instructs us how to live the victorious life. There seems to be a problem in our *application* of the Word we have received.

It has always been God's plan for believers to triumph in every area of life. Therefore, rather than trusting secondary sources, we must solely put our trust and confidence in God.

Ephesians focuses on three key points that ensure the believer's victory: 1) his *position*; he is *in* Christ (1:3-4), 2) his *practice*, his lifestyle (4:1-6:9), and 3) his *protection*, God's armor (6:10-18).

The Christian life is one of hills and valleys, ups and downs, tragedies and triumphs. All humans will face adversities in life, whether you are in Christ or not! God sends problems our way for a purpose and they always work together for good. Battles are won as we seek to fulfill God's plan and purpose for our lives.

You may be experiencing a financial battle or an emotional battle; you may be battling cancer or some other illness or difficulty; just know that your battles should always be examined from the Lord's side. The focus should never be on the problem.

God will never allow Satan or man to send a problem that will destroy you. Furthermore, He is never at a loss for a solution to a problem. Jesus is The Way when you can see no way out.

While you are trying to figure it out, the Lord has already worked that situation out! First, God works that problem out in the realm of the spirit; then He manifests the solution in the natural realm, where you *see it* -done!

~The Believer's Position~

Jesus Christ has position power –the right hand of God; the giving hand, the hand of power! His right hand is always active! The believer has position power –*in Christ*. To have "position" power means that God Himself has positioned Christians beyond the realm of defeat!

Losing is not an option for God. Since there is no failure in God, He gets no glory from failure. Jesus is the Winning Man and God has chosen us to be in His winners' circle! Christ did not lose to the cross; He was victorious by it.

When He triumphed over the cross, Christ went from humiliation to glorification. He flipped the barrel for us through His resurrection. We are no longer at the bottom of the barrel, but the top; not the tail, but the head!

To be *in* Christ is to have *on* Christ; to have *on* Christ is to have *on* His armor. At conversion, our position changes from an enemy of God to a friend of God. We become a new creation in Christ, putting off the old man and putting on the new man; having on the whole armor of God!

Position is the key to the believer's victorious living. Because we are in Christ and He is in Heaven, seated at the right hand of the Father, the place of authority, we are *seated with Him in heavenly places* (Eph. 2:6). The believer's fight is from the position of power and authority.

Battles do not come every day, but when they do come we should maintain our victorious posture in Christ, by whom we are blessed with all spiritual blessings.

The Christian's position is that of an overcomer: to "overcome" means 1) to conquer: defeat, 2) to prevail over: surmount, 3) to overpower, 4) to win! Be sure to maintain your winning walk. If you are not in Christ, you need to switch positions!

~The Believer's Practice~

The Holy Spirit indwells believers to help them live godly, victorious lives. Every believer must practice what he or she preaches. It is hypocritical to say one thing and do another. Jesus called the Pharisees *hypocrites*, taken from the Greek word which means *actors*. There are a lot of actors in the Church.

Born-again believers are called to "walk worthy" of their call. We are called to live according to the standards that are set forth in the Holy Bible. Our behavior should emulate Christ's behavior. Jesus walked in perfect harmony with the Father.

It is not enough to know the Word of God; we must obey what it says. No one does everything perfectly, but Christians should make it a habit of doing right toward God and man. Believers have privileges, and with privileges come responsibilities. Paul balanced doctrine and duty by reminding the saints of how they must live in response to all that God had done for them.

The old nature and the new nature are diametrically opposed to each other; therefore, we must be careful of the way in which we live. Somebody is watching you! Somebody wants to be just like you! Can you say, "Follow me as I follow Christ"? If so, continue to follow His example and practice living the new life daily by frequent and diligent self-examination (I Cor. 11:28).

Walking uprightly before God and man will give the enemy no opportunity to attack. He wants to drive a wedge between you and God. If he is successful in tempting you, it will dull your shine.

Practice using your time and spiritual gifts wisely. Serve the Lord with gladness in all that you do. Be an example of the believers in word, conversation, charity, spirit, faith and in purity by modeling your life after Christ. Your conduct is the most effective message that you could ever preach! A Christian's life is a living epistle, read by the world: *"So be careful how you live. Don't live like fools, but like those who are wise,"* (Eph. 5:15, NLT).

~The Believer's Protection~

The whole armor of God is the believer's spiritual protection from God to the Church. Clothed in God's complete armor of protection, you need not shudder or shake at the attacks of the enemy. He will be the one who is doing the trembling, shuddering and shaking!

Regardless of the circumstances, the armor of God is the believer's only foolproof protection; affording no opportunity for misuse, error, or failure.

The enemy of your soul wants God out of your life. Your ex wants you back! Not because he loves you, but because God loves you and wants what is best for you. Satan will try any scheme to make you turn your back on God. The warfare begins when you disagree with him.

As long as you are on Satan's side he won't mess with you much, but as soon as you make up your mind that you are going to live for Jesus, he becomes your archenemy. He is the enemy of God; don't think it strange that he is your enemy also! Be determined to obey God and trust for a favorable result at the end of your battle. For you to doubt God's Word will allow the enemy to sabotage your victory.

Jesus *bruised the head of the serpent* over two thousand years ago. Satan's evil government has been totally overthrown. Christ publicly disarmed evil rulers and authorities by His victory over them on the Cross. As Christians, we have position *in Christ,* from whom we derive all the *protection* and power necessary to defeat all the hosts of hell.

Christ did not have to face the enemy alone and neither do you. It is not enough for you to *name it* and *claim it.* Victory must be achieved in the manner that is stated in the Bible; *put on the whole armor of God,* the only sure means of being more than a conqueror!

Due to a lack of knowledge of the Bible, many of us do not realize *the power* of the resources that God has made available to us. No wonder the devil is having so much of his way!

~Prisoner with A Purpose~

God has a masterful plan for the life of His children. We are positioned *in Christ* for a purpose, for the sake of the gospel! The Great Commission is to evangelize the world with the gospel of Jesus Christ. The enemy will try anything to stop that from happening.

Paul, a special messenger of Jesus Christ, paid the price required for the manifestation of the power of God operating in his life. The apostle was tried, tested and persecuted for the sake of the gospel. Actually at the time Paul wrote this letter, he was in prison. The purpose of this writing was to comfort and encourage the saints at Ephesus and faithful believers everywhere.

Paul was called to preach the gospel to the Gentiles; yet, he preached to Jews and Greeks alike: *"He is a chosen vessel unto Me, to bear My name before the Gentiles, and kings, and the children of Israel,"* (Acts 9:15, SFLB). When Israel rejected his message, Paul "shook the dust" from his clothes and said, *"Your blood is upon your own heads-I am innocent. From now on I will go preach to the Gentiles,"* (Acts 18:6, SFLB).

God's purpose was the driving force behind Paul's actions; therefore, let's not concentrate on the fact that Paul was in prison, but on the reason why he was there. Also, don't focus your attention on your problem; ask the Lord to reveal His purpose for the situation that you're in and to show you how He can get glory out of it. Pray, "Thy will be done!"

The apostle did not meditate upon his physical location—*in prison*. He found contentment in his spiritual position —*in Christ*. God has the ability to bring some good out of the worst situations.

In his final words to Timothy, his son in the gospel, Paul wrote that everyone had abandoned him, *"But the Lord stood with me and gave me strength so that I might preach the Good News in its entirety for all Gentiles to hear,"* (II Tim. 4:17, SFLB). He, who had imprisoned Christians for the sake of the gospel, was now imprisoned for the sake of the gospel! Jesus flipped the script on Paul; the persecutor had become the persecuted!

Paul may have been locked up; but no jailer, no Roman soldier, nothing can lock up the gospel of Christ. It will go forth! He, who once caused some to denounce their faith, was now preaching *to* the Church and praying *for* the Church. Undaunted by his surroundings, Paul preached things pertaining to the Kingdom of God; teaching those things concerning the Lord Jesus Christ.

The enemy is relentless in his quest to stop the gospel. However, being empowered by the Holy Spirit, Paul was unmoved by threats and attacks from the opposition.

Paul understood the resources that were available to him. It was that knowledge that called forth these powerful words, *"For the weapons of our warfare are not carnal, but mighty through God to the pulling down of strongholds,"* (II Cor. 10:4, KJV).

Being protected by God doesn't mean you will not experience hardships. God does two things to push you into your purpose, 1) He *sends* trouble and 2) He *allows* trouble to come into your life. In either case trouble, after it runs its course, achieves what pleases God.

Paul was a dynamic preacher. *"And my speech and my preaching was not with enticing words of man's wisdom, but in demonstration of the Spirit and of power,"* (I Cor. 2:4, KJV). However, neither his title nor his credentials prevented the attacks upon his life.

Jesus was the Son of God and Satan knew it, but that did not stop him from attacking Jesus! Satan is no respecter of persons. You are also on his hit list and he will use everything in his arsenal to try and prevent you from accomplishing your God-given assignment.

Paul was under arrest, and yet the only crime that he committed was to preach the Gospel. It was for this reason God *allowed* the tried warrior to be imprisoned. Even those who are in prison must hear the Good News. Christ cannot come again until the Gospel is preached to all men everywhere; it is the power of God unto salvation! The Scripture must be fulfilled.

Being thrown in prison did not make Paul abort his mission; he didn't threaten to stop preaching! The apostle was not idle during his imprisonment, neither did he whine or throw a pity-party for himself. On the contrary, Paul remained firm in his conviction that God was in control of the situation. He even boasted about being in prison! With the picture of a Roman conqueror in his mind, leading his captives in triumph, Paul likened himself to one of Christ's captives being led into triumph! One could almost visualize his chest sticking out with pride as he wrote, "I Paul, a *prisoner* of the Lord Jesus Christ!"

Not once do we read that Apostle Paul sulked, cried or begged for deliverance. In the past, God had sent an earthquake to deliver him from prison. He was confident that God could deliver him again if He chose to do so.

Paul was a born thinker. Would we have been so blessed by the apostle's creative mind, with so many *spiritual nuggets,* had he not been totally surrendered to the Lord?

During his imprisonment in Rome, Paul received revelation knowledge from the Holy Spirit concerning the whole armor of God for the Church. This information could not have been acquired sailing on a ship or preaching in a synagogue in Jerusalem.

In Rome, Paul could observe the soldiers up-close and personal! Before he reported for duty, the soldier would take up his armor and put on each piece until he was completely dressed. Not even one piece was ever omitted or discarded. Every day, this routine was followed to the letter.

Paul's understanding of the armor of God was drawn from the life and weaponry of the first century soldier. Seeing a fully clothed soldier in his battledress was a visual aid; a pictorial illustration. When God wanted to teach Israel about His absolute sovereignty, He sent the prophet down to the potter's house to watch as he shaped and molded his clay (Jer. 18:1-10).

The potter never began with a lump of clay that was perfectly formed into the image he desired. Bringing that piece of clay to perfection required taking it through a process.

First, the potter had an idea (spirit realm): then he took the piece of clay into his hands and beat it, twisted it, shaped it and reshaped it until he achieved the desired result (natural realm). The potter took the imperfect piece of clay into his hands and worked it until he was satisfied.

It was the end result that was important to the potter, and so he shaped and reshaped it until the clay turned into his idea. He may have gone through this process over and over again until he was completely thrilled with the end result. As long as the clay was pliable, the potter never threw it away.

Throughout the shaping and molding process, the clay never said, "Stop! You are hurting me." It was totally at the mercy of the potter and the end result was greater than the beginning.

Jeremiah learned that, just as the clay was in the hands of the potter, Israel was in God's hands. The Church is in God's hands. To be all that God wants us to be, we must remain pliable and allow Him to shape and mold our lives into His idea. We are God's handiwork. Every day, we are being shaped and molded by God into something great!

Behind the plan and purpose of God is a heart of love. He *allowed* the enemy to imprison Paul as part of His plan and purpose for the apostle's life. Nowhere in the Bible will you read that Paul addressed himself as a prisoner of Rome. However, he did refer to himself as the prisoner of Jesus Christ "for you Gentiles," (Eph. 3:1).

Paul's heartbeat was to follow Christ's mandate for the Church: "make disciples of all nations" (Matt. 28:18), and "preach the Gospel to every creature" (Mark 16:15). Even in prison, he ran revivals under the watchful eye of the Holy Spirit. As John Wesley, the Christian theologian said, "The world is my parish."

God's Suffering Servant: (II Cor.11:23-28, KJV)
- *"I have worked harder, been put in prison more often, been whipped times without number, and faced death again and again. Five different times the Jewish leaders gave me thirty-nine lashes. Three times I was beaten with rods. Once I was stoned. Three times I was shipwrecked. Once I spent a whole night and a day adrift at sea,"* (vs. 23-25).

19

- *"I have traveled on many long journeys. I have faced danger from rivers and from robbers. I have faced danger from my own people, the Jews, as well as from the Gentiles. I have faced danger in the cities, in the deserts, and on the seas. And I have faced danger from men who claim to be believers but are not,"* (v. 26).
- *"I have worked hard and long, enduring many sleepless nights. I have been hungry and thirsty and have often gone without food. I have shivered in the cold, without enough clothing to keep me warm,"* (v. 27).
- *"Then, besides all this, I have the daily burden of my concern for all the Churches,"* (v. 28).

Experience is married to purpose. Face every problem knowing that God's ultimate plan, in spite of your situation, is for you to share the Gospel with the world and to live a victorious Christian life! You are a "prisoner" of the Lord Jesus Christ with a purpose!

CHAPTER TWO

THE LOCATION OF YOUR STRENGTH

"Finally, my brethren, be strong in the Lord, and in the power of His might," (Ephesians 6:10).

When a man and a woman who are in love marry, they sometimes feel as though all of their problems are solved and that marriage is going to be one big honeymoon. As soon as the honeymoon is over and reality sets in, many marriages fall apart and some end in divorce.

At conversion, some folks are on such a spiritual high and they feel as if all of their problems have been solved; no more suffering, no more pain and no more bills. Much of what they are taught focuses on the material and temporal rather the spiritual and eternal; therefore, when the problems don't go away the convert becomes discouraged and disappointed.

Young converts think that everybody in the household of faith is madly in love with each other (they should be), and that they won't have a care in the world. Alas, they soon find out that this is far from the truth. More often than not, this is when all hell breaks loose! The reason for this is that God wants to teach them from the outset to look to Him as their Source.

Being a Christian does not mean you will live a carefree, trouble-free life. You will still have struggles; however, if you put your trust in God you will emerge victorious every time. Jesus made it very clear to His disciples from the beginning that they would endure hardships; that some would die, and some would be put in prison *for His sake.* Knowing this, Paul admonishes the saints to be strong *in the Lord and in His mighty power!*

The strongest person gets weak at times. We are human, but Jesus never gets tired and He never slumbers or sleeps. All power is given unto Him in Heaven and in earth! Jesus is our Source of help and strength. God's power never diminishes. His strength never weakens. He is never too busy or too frail to help in the time of trouble. The Lord is the Source of strength to sustain us during tough times.

The entire life of the believer from beginning to end is one of warfare. Besides our struggles with the common cares of life, we also have a spiritual enemy to fight who wants to keep us from God and Heaven. The devil is on the warpath against the people of God and he will continue to war with us until "death do us part" or until he is cast into the lake of fire and brimstone.

Only after death is the believer out of Satan's reach. Meanwhile, when you feel as though life has a stranglehold on you and you cannot go another step, you can draw strength from the Lord who is *ready and able* to deliver you. God allows trouble to come into our lives to show us and the world His power; that with Him, nothing is impossible!

Because of Christ, we fight from the vantage point of victory! The enemy is well aware that God will not fail to rescue those who depend on Him; however, that doesn't stop Satan from attacking you. He does not care that you are a Christian, that you are anointed, or that you are determined to stay saved. Satan does not care that you are a powerful preacher, that you are rich or poor, young or old. He is coming after you and he fights dirty!

With every problem, difficulty, trial, and assault of the enemy comes God's provision for total victory. Behind every set of circumstances in your life, there is a specific and meaningful reason. God is preparing you for a *take back* and a *take-over!* The enemy has some stuff that belongs to you and it is time to take it back. There are some new territories that God has given us and it is time to "possess the land" (take over); we must take it by force.

Trying to fight in your own strength is like a soldier fighting on the battlefield with a water pistol! Don't freak out. God's protective gear makes you a deadly and dangerous opponent to whatever is working against you. By the mighty power of God, stumbling blocks become your steppingstones to breakthrough deliverance and victory!

When Paul told the saints that they were *blessed with all spiritual blessings* (Eph.1:3), they must have been ecstatic! Nearing the end of his letter, however, he writes, "Finally, my brethren..." It is as though he was saying, "Wait! I'm not finished. I said all that to say this." After he inspired the saints, Paul proceeds to warn them that they also had an enemy to fight; that they were now engaged in a ferocious combat with an evil spirit.

One can imagine after reading this "battle letter" that some of them might have said, "No way! I didn't sign up for this!" Paul, knowing their frame of mind, said, *"[My brethren,] be strong in the Lord."* To be armed with God's armor is to be *army strong!*

Satan does not have all power; Jesus does. Our time on earth is limited; therefore, we must be strong and use our time wisely. To murmur and complain, to worry and become stressed out is a waste of time. The Word of God admonishes us to *redeem* the time, make the most of time for the end is near. There is an expected end for you; expect to win!

A final word, my brothers: Be strong in the Lord. God is the Source of our strength and supply; not the job, the bank account, the family, business or investments. Put no confidence in these things or in your own abilities. The location of the strength that we need in every situation is in the Lord. *"You have armed me with strength for the battle; you have subdued my enemies under my feet,"* (II Samuel 22:40, NLTB).

While Paul was in custody his movements were restricted, but his mouth was not. God is not bound or limited, and since God is not bound or limited, the Word of God is not bound and the Church is not bound or limited either! The Church was not born weak and anemic; it was born in power! Actually, it is the most powerful vehicle on earth.

Try to imagine how the Roman soldiers felt who guarded Paul day and night. They heard him talk about Jesus on and on, incessantly. The more Paul witnessed for the Lord, the bolder he became. As he preached and prayed, the resurrection power of God rested upon him mightily.

That which was meant to destroy Paul made him strong. The supernatural favor of God was upon his life. As you introduce Christ to others, you will find your inner man growing stronger and maturing by leaps and bounds.

Paul was a superb orator, and long-winded if you will; for he had much to say concerning Jesus' death, burial, resurrection, Headship over the Church, spiritual gifts, and the Holy Spirit. This may have gotten under the skin of some who heard him preach, but many believed and received Jesus Christ as Lord and Savior.

Prisoners were not given three nutritious meals per day to sustain them. Paul was no exception; however, the Lord was the *Source* of his spiritual and physical strength. That's why he was able to say with such conviction, "Be strong in the Lord." Paul had divine help; otherwise, he could not have survived.

The Lord Jesus strengthens His children who are weak, because He cares for them. He forever reaches out and helps those who are in need. No trouble can outlast God; He is eternal. You can outlast your trouble! When God stretches out His mighty hand to bless you, nothing and no one can prevent, restrict or stop Him from doing that which pleases Him.

The saints at Ephesus were going to suffer many things because of their testimony; however, their life experiences would offer them opportunity to learn more about God and themselves. Paul was concerned that some of the saints might be tempted to turn back into idolatry, and so he encouraged them to put all their faith and trust in the True and Living God, not sculpted images.

Problems come into our lives to teach us that God is our Source of help, strength and deliverance. You will find that your prayers are much more fervent and sincere when you are experiencing hardships! Distress will turn your attention to God when you find that there is no help elsewhere. The Lord does not endorse trouble; however, He uses it to fulfill His plan and purpose.

Instead of waiting upon the Lord to come to our rescue, we often give in to pressure and rely upon our own ability to free us from that situation. Look to Jesus. He will supply (fill-full) all our *need* according to His riches in glory! God desires that you prosper in every area of your life!

Be strong in the Lord and you will overcome adversities, Satan and the world. Long before the apostle wrote this spiritual warfare letter to the Ephesians, Jesus had already warned His disciples of satanic opposition; but *the gates of hell would not prevail* (succeed) against the Church.

Reject anything that would lead you away from the Lord. Do not pattern your life after the world; it will make you weak. Paul's durability was drawn out of his relationship with Christ. Likewise, our strength is derived from having on the armor of God.

"Be strong" is a command. The word "strong" in this verse is taken from the Greek word *endunamoo,* which means, "be strong," "to make strong" and "to strengthen."

Endunamoo is a compound of the two Greek words *en* and *dunamis*. The word "en" is our English word "in" and "dunamis" means "power." In other words, power (*dunamis*) is in (*en*) the Lord and He wants to *infuse* that power in you!

Do not lose sight of your own weakness. Depend upon the Lord to empower you and give you strength to fulfill any mission and to victoriously fight every battle. Your true Source of power is in the Lord, not in human beings or in any amount of money you may have. God's full power operates through yielded vessels.

The Greek word *dunamis* is where we get the word "dynamite;" a powerful explosive, composed of nitroglycerin or ammonium nitrate combined with an absorbent material. It is usually packaged in sticks and is used to blow something up.

Since the first part of *endunamoo* means "in" or "into" and the second part describes an *explosive power,* this *explosive power* is going *in* (*en*) something. It needs to be deposited *in* something or someone. In other words, this explosive, *endunamoo* power is located *in* the Lord, and He wants to deposit it *in* you! Christians are the vessels *into* which God deposits His explosive power!

To be strong in the Lord is to be filled with His *explosive power* to blow the enemy away every time he attacks you! He will come against you, but he *will not prevail* against you, because you have the *dunamis* in you. You have been injected with supernatural power and strength.

The same power at work in believers is that of the self-same Spirit that raised Jesus Christ from the dead! When we are born again, we become the receptacles for God's Divine Power. The same power that was in Jesus when He walked this earth — His resurrection power — is in us. Be strong *in the Lord in,* not *under,* any circumstance.

When your knees are shaking under the cares of life and you do not feel strong enough to push on to victory, the power of God will strengthen your feeble knees. In the same manner that

He guides the eagle in its flight to ascend far above mountains and storms, He will cause you to soar, like an eagle, above every problematic situation, every crisis, and every trial!

Look to Jesus and you will be so much stronger than you could ever be on your own. When troubles come, depend upon the Lord to infuse you with His *dunamis* power. Pain, poverty, oppression and persecutions come to bring us down, but the Lord will lift us up!

The Kingdom of God is not just fancy talk or rhetoric. It is living every day by God's power! Some preach so eloquently on the subject, but their lives do not really show that God's power is working in them! They fall apart at the drop of a hat. When trouble hits some believers, right away they cry, "Woe is me!" Yet, they will be the first to preach to others, "Be strong!"

The Early Church was born in power and remained a powerful witness for the Lord Jesus Christ, because they practiced what they preached!

To "be strong in the Lord" is an ongoing process. Because the cares of life tend to drain the inner man, very often the battle has to be won inwardly before it can be won outwardly. The verb "be" speaks of *continuous* action. We must, without interruption, go to the Lord daily for strength.

This phrase also means to "be made strong in the Lord," which suggests that we can do nothing in and of ourselves, but we can do all things through Christ who gives us inner strength by the Holy Spirit. The strongest person in the world is weaker than God and is in need of His help, even if he doesn't realize it. We must "be made strong" by the Lord.

Infused with the power of God, we have the ability (the bold confidence) to deal victoriously with the devil. The people that know their God will be strong and do exploits. When others give up, they stand and bravely resist the temptation to retreat. They take action that will make the devil wish that he were dead!

27

God will not *put any more on you than you can bear.*
Whining will erode your faith in God and encourage thoughts
of giving up.

To grumble against God when things are difficult, to doubt
God's ability to deliver us, and to try to make our own way
through life are the kinds of attitudes that lead us to make horrible choices. This negative attitude is a sign of weakness that
will block the flow of your blessings from God.

Christians must go through hardships in life. The devil
isn't always the one who is picking the fight. God sometimes
sends trials to discipline His children. Stand strong. Stay tuned;
it's just a test. Through the cloud of your adversities, showers
— not a trickle, but a torrential downpour — of blessings is
coming your way.

The Lord may be sending you a deeper anointing, a greater
understanding of His Word, healing in your body, or a financial breakthrough. Miracles, signs and wonders are, because
God is! He is a miracle working God! When He seems to be
doing nothing and seems to have forgotten you (as others may
have), hold on; your miracle is imminent. It's about to happen
any minute! As in the case of Peter (Acts 12:12-17), it's at
your door!

Wherever you are in your spiritual fight — round one, two,
or round nine — stand strong in the Lord and endure to the end.
Have total trust and confidence in God. Be determined that even
though the situation is severe, you will not lose hope. God has
a plan of escape for you.

Do not quit on God and He will not quit on you. The longer
you fight, the more you experience your personal breakthrough
of power from the Father. Oh, you may lose a skirmish every
now and then, but you will always win the war! When God
allows us to lose a battle, it is to teach us something. Some of
life's lessons are only learned through defeat.

If you seem to be losing the battle, it may be that you
are depending upon your own strength. The supernatural,

strengthening power needed for your breakthrough comes from an outside Source, the Lord Jesus Christ, through the indwelling of the Holy Spirit.

Anchor your faith in Christ; not in an office, a title, status, possessions, or an individual. Face every problem trusting in the Lord. It is foolishness to put your trust in flesh. Spiritual weapons are needed to fight an evil spirit. Try shooting or stabbing the devil and watch what happens!

Finally, my brethren, be strong in the Lord. No one can give you the strength you need to be victorious. You must "be made strong" by the Lord. Satan is no match for God!

The devil wants to cut the pipeline to your power source. He will use whatever strategy that is at his disposal to try and disconnect you from God. If you feel like a spiritual and emotional wreck because of your problems, don't give up. Go back for a fresh infusion of God's power!

I recall the saints praying, *"Father, I come before You as an empty vessel before a full fountain."* If you are spiritually, physically and emotionally tired, weak, and lethargic, go before the Lord as an empty vessel and He will fill you up!

Take a moment to think about all that Christ endured at the hands of sinful man so that you could come out of every situation a winner. There are two sides to the Cross: 1) tragedy and 2) triumph.

Jesus' sufferings were tragic, but after His death and burial He rose from the grave in Triumph! He arose from humiliation to Glorification; from the cross to the Crown! No longer a victim, but a Victor! Our position in Christ seals our victory. You're going to win!

All of us have to go *through* trials of life. The Israelites had to go *through* the Red Sea to get to the Promised Land. David walked *through* the valley of the shadow of death before he became king. Your circumstances are designed to help you to completely trust God. As a matter of fact, the fight is already fixed in your favor; you have already won, because of the precious blood of Jesus. If that does not boost your confidence in God to deliver you, what will?

While you are going through that crisis, give God praise! Stop feeling sorry for yourself and get busy doing the work of the Lord. You are not rejoicing *for* the problem; however, you should rejoice in the Lord God who governs all things, and has positioned us beyond defeat to victory!

Furthermore, the Bible says that God's ways are not our ways. He doesn't have to respond to our needs in a manner that makes sense to us. When you feel that you cannot go another step, get ready — something good is about to happen for you! Do not let the enemy make you think, even for a second, that God is not going to come to your rescue. If you have been depending upon Him for dear life, do you really think that the True and Living God you serve is going to let you down?

When you are at your weakest, God comes in right on time and deposits a supernatural surge of power into your spirit that gives you strength and ability to step over every obstacle that lies in your path. Paul said, "For when I am weak, then am I strong," (II Cor. 12:10).

~In His Mighty Power~

God saved each of us for a purpose. His eternal purpose for your life requires strength. We do not serve an ordinary God and He did not redeem us to be ordinary people, doing ordinary things.

To be made strong in the Lord and "in the power of *His might*" brings the focus of our attention to another kind of power. The word "might" used here in verse ten is taken from the Greek word *kratos* which specifically refers to His *mighty*, invincible, *demonstrative* power.

In some translations of the Bible the word "might" is substituted by the word "strong." The Greek word *krataios*, which means strong or mighty, is closely related to the Greek word *kratos*, which means, *strength,* or *relative manifested* (demonstrated) *power.* When God releases this kind of power, something is always clearly revealed.

Kratos brings about a visible display of God's power. That miracle moves out from the spirit realm into the physical realm. Man lives in a natural (material, human, temporal) world, while simultaneously living in a spiritual (unseen) world! In other words, the mighty, *kratos* power of God brings that miracle out of the spirit (unseen) realm, into the natural (seen) realm!

You cannot see the *kratos* power of Almighty God, but you will see the results of this power in action. Something will be seen with the natural eyes. God's power is like the wind; no one can *see* the wind, but they can *see* the leaves moving! Leaves do not move in and of themselves.

The *kratos* power of God empowers you to accomplish something you thought was impossible for you to do. It will force you out of your comfort zone.

The *mighty* power of God is what enables you to do the unpredictable, the extraordinary and the unexplainable! It is the strongest flow of power that exists. This *mighty* power was in operation when Christ was crucified. There were many signs accompanying Jesus' death.

In His final moments, with all His bones out of joint and His battered body in excruciating pain that He might identify with human suffering, Jesus cried with a *loud voice* and gave up the ghost. When a mere man is dying his voice always becomes weaker, not stronger. This was no mere man. He was the God-Man! Surely this was the Son of God!

Jesus' *shed* (on purpose) blood (not *spilled,* which implies that it was an accident) would set men free from the penalty of sin.

Satan and his host thought that they had won the victory over Christ by nailing Him to the Cross, but this was His method of triumphing over the kingdom of darkness. The cross was to Jesus what the briar patch was to the rabbit! The rabbit said,

"Don't throw me in the briar patch! Throw me in the well." The rabbit knew that he could not survive in the well, but he was right at home in the briar patch; from there he could easily hop to safety!

The cross was Jesus' destination. All of His time here on earth, Jesus was headed to the cross. He was born of a virgin (incarnate), to die, on the cross. The trickster (Satan) was tricked!

Man (not an animal) had sinned, and a sinless Man had to die; for the wages of sin is death. Knowing that man would be set free from the penalty of sin, Jesus hung on the Cross and died.

After His death a rich man named Joseph of Arimathea, one of Jesus' followers, went to Pilate and asked for His body. Joseph wrapped His body in a clean linen cloth.

Linen in Scripture represents righteousness. Jesus wore the *breastplate of righteousness*, first. After dressing His body, Joseph laid it in his own new tomb and a stone was rolled to the door of the grave. All this was done that the Scriptures of the prophets might be fulfilled.

God permitted the powers of darkness to do all that they were going to do to His Son. The devil would not be allowed to interfere in this Divine transaction between Father and Son. Christ's enemies were permitted to do their worst, to prevent His resurrection, but on the Third Day the supernatural, indomitable, unstoppable, *kratos* power of God came down from glory and flooded the grave where Jesus' dead body lay!

Divine life made contact with Christ's dead, human body, and immediately the *mighty power* of God brought Jesus' dead body to Life and He got up out of the grave!

The origin of the power that brought Jesus from the dead is not found in anyone else but God! This *same power* is available to Christians! As a matter of fact, the Bible commands Christians to *be strong in the Lord* and *in His mighty power*. When we are tried and tested, we can draw strength from the Lord (by the indwelling Holy Spirit) who is our Source of strength!

There was a time when it seemed that the enemy had won the battle over Christ, but Satan only bruised Christ's *heel* (that is, wounded Him, Gen. 3:15) when they nailed Him to the cross! With Christ in the grave, Satan thought that the fight was over. But thanks to God who gives us the victory, on the Third Day Christ bruised the serpent's *head* (mortally wounded him).

To kill a snake, you must aim for the head. A snake can live without its tail. The deadly poison is in the head. If the snake is allowed to live, he will try to inject his poisonous venom in you to kill you! Jesus finished him off!

Death swallowed up death in victory! Through Jesus' death we can put to death all of our fears and anxieties! Because of Christ, in whatever trial you are facing victory is yours today! There is no power that can stop the mighty hand of God! It was impossible for death, hell and the grave to hold the Savior down! *"I am He that liveth, and was dead; and, behold, I am alive for evermore, Amen; and have the keys of hell and of death,"* (Rev. 1:18, KJV).

His enemies would come to *see* that no rock, no stone, no grave, no soldier, not even an army of soldiers could stop the Son of God from coming out of that grave!

No enemy, adversary, trial, problem, boss, financial difficulty, temptation, famine, power or authority can stop God's mighty outstretched hand when it is stretched out to bless you!

God wants to show the world His mighty power through you; but there must be some battles. How can there be victory without war? How do you know that the mighty power of God is operating through you unless you experience some difficulties? We are being made strong in the Lord through the things we suffer. Fight valiantly, regardless of the circumstances!

Paul experienced firsthand what it meant to have the mighty power of God operating in his own life: *"Therefore I take pleasure in infirmities, in reproaches, in necessities, in persecutions, in distresses for Christ's sake: for when I am weak, then am I strong,"* (II Cor. 12:10, KJV). As you wholeheartedly depend upon God, His power operating in your life will be evident by the way you live!

Evidence of God's mighty *kratos* (demonstrative) power: The Risen Lord was *seen* by Mary Magdalene in Jerusalem (Mark 16:9); *seen* by Peter in Jerusalem; by the disciples in Emmaus (Luke 24:32, 34), and *seen* by eleven disciples in Jerusalem (Mark 16:14). After that, He was seen by more than five hundred of His followers at one time (I Cor. 15:6).

Many who witnessed the manifestation of God's mighty power, the Resurrection of Jesus Christ, became believers! Many will give their hearts to the Lord when they see the results of His power operating in your life, especially during the worst of times.

At this moment, God has already worked that problem out in the spirit realm on your behalf and you will *see* it manifested in the natural realm in due time! We have *seen* the lame walk, and the blind receive their sight. The world needs to see more of God's power working through us!

We are engaged in spiritual warfare with Satan. Natural battles come about as a result of spiritual wickedness. Jesus' Resurrection, the mother of all miracles, is proof that He dealt a death-blow to Satan. He stripped principalities and powers naked and embarrassed them publicly. Christ has ascended back to Heaven and is out of Satan's reach. The focus of his attention is you; however, we have position power (in Christ), from *there* God always leads us to triumph!

With the power of God at our disposal, the devil is no match for us. God gives us strength to meet challenges, not a promise to eliminate them. Instead of giving up, trust God's all-conquering power which gives you the ability to say to that mountain, "You are nothing but a hill. Get out of my way!" Don't be influenced by the way you feel or by things you see in the natural.

Never permit your life to be governed by your thoughts and emotions. Do not allow the natural man to override the spiritual things of God! Our rhythm of miracles begins in the spirit realm; the part of Christians that has been redeemed by the blood of Jesus. In the spirit realm is where believers are guided, governed and controlled by God, the Holy Spirit!

The mighty power of God is available to all who try to achieve something that is sure to fail unless He steps in. God doesn't give us power to sit idly by and do nothing in life. He has an eternal purpose and a plan for your life. *"But you shall receive power when the Holy Spirit has come upon you; and you shall be witnesses to Me in Jerusalem, and in all Judea and Samaria, and to the end of the earth,"* (Acts 1:8, SFLB).

Years ago, the Lord allowed Satan to attack one of my sisters. She had a major stroke, was almost totally paralyzed, unable to speak, and the fluid on her brain was drying up. The doctors gave her months to live. There was nothing more that they could do for her.

Several weeks went by and my sister remained in that state. Then she began to show signs of improvement. Her speech returned. Even the doctors were amazed and baffled!

We prayed, yes, but it was the *mighty power* of God that brought life and healing to her body. Although we knew that it was the power of God at work, no one truly understood that it was the *same* mighty power of God that flowed through Jesus' dead body and resurrected it. That same resurrection power flowed through Rebecca's body so that the dead cells, muscles, bones and tissues came alive! Even if you can't explain it, you just know that God did it!

Incredibly today, more than forty years later, Rebecca prays, walks, talks, sings, and worships the Lord with all of her heart! My sister's battle was more spiritual than physical. The enemy (sickness) had a plan; but God overruled Satan's plan (to kill my sister) with His own. He has a plan and a purpose for everyone. We cannot die until God's purpose comes to pass!

There are no major, visible signs from any of the strokes that she has suffered. Only her speech is slightly slurred. We believe that this residue left by God is evidence designed to be a reminder and a testimonial that God is merciful and compassionate; that with God all things are possible. This is not a fairy tale or a Cinderella story. There are many witnesses to this miracle. Her life is the evidence. Even the doctors had to confess that it was a miracle. They could not help her. God did it! We must say, "Look what the Lord has done!"

Trust God for the season and the situation in which you find yourself. You will not die until God's plan and purpose for your life are accomplished. If He so desires, the Lord can deliver you and there will not be a hint of a struggle. You will come out of that situation without a scratch. You will come out of that furnace of affliction and you won't even *smell* like smoke. Sometimes He leaves a reminder, however, lest we forget.

My sister and I come together often in prayer, petitioning God on behalf of others. Her testimony has become the devil's worst nightmare! So many others have been encouraged and blessed by her praise report! The doctors who gave up on her and said she would be dead within months have long since passed away, but my sister still lives to share her testimony.

Suffering as a Christian makes you grow stronger and keeps you growing deeper in God. The Lord has already deposited *in you* the power that you need to get your breakthrough! While we are wallowing in self-pity, there is a world out there that needs Jesus; needs to hear the *Good News* of the gospel!

The Early Church was not born weak, impotent, powerless, or anemic! In the Upper Room the disciples received more than tongues; the Church was born in demonstration of power by the Holy Spirit. As vessels, God has deposited His power in us to do His will; to be witness of the Lord Jesus Christ so that people can come to know the Savior through what they hear and see!

We were born-again to experience God's mighty (*kratos*, demonstrative) power each and every day of our lives! Be strong in the Lord and in His mighty power! Arise! Take your eyes off your struggles, problems, failures and weaknesses. Think about those who have no hope, who do not know Jesus. Put on the whole armor of God and go forth to fulfill His will in the earth!

CHAPTER THREE

THE ENEMY OF GOD AND THE CHURCH

The aim of this book is not to draw all your attention to the enemy. The intent is not to pay homage to him in any way. This is not a study of Satan, demons or demonology. It would not be wise to obsess with that. Neither is it wise to ignore Satan or to pretend that he does not exist. Actually, he loves when people brush him off as lint.

To ignore Satan — to pretend that he is not real, that he is the figment of the imagination — is to give him a personal invitation to come in and run things your life.

Scriptures reveal that Satan is an evil spirit that hates God and His Church. He is not a mirage or an illusion and must not be treated as such. He is an evil spirit whose desire is to have the great honor and glory that belongs to God only! Through Satan, sin, sickness, poverty, destruction and death have entered the world!

The Bible lists numerous names, symbols and titles in the Old and New Testaments by which Satan is called. Each name or title is descriptive of his godless character, corrupt nature, and his *modus operandi*; the way he operates. Satan hates the Gospel, perverts truth, detests the Church, and works relentlessly to discredit the message of Jesus Christ.

Jesus Christ was commissioned by God to destroy the works of the enemy. God has not planned any defeat for the believer. The only sure way to beat the devil is to fight him with the weapons that God has provided. Rather than run or hide from our opponent, we must look to the Word of God and learn what He has to say concerning Satan as well as our salvation.

Knowing what the Bible says will help us not to downplay the work of Satan in the earth. The enemy cannot outsmart you when you are familiar with his evil nature. Our enemy is called:

~Adversary~

Satan is also referred to as your *adversary* (I Peter 5:8). An "adversary" is one who opposes with animosity. Since the New Testament was translated from the Greek language, let us take a look at its original meaning. The word "adversary" is taken from the Greek word *antidikos,* a compound of the two Greek words *anti* and *dikos.*

The first part of the word *antidikos* is the word "anti" which means "against." In the ancient Greek language it was also used to denote the *mental condition of a man or woman who was on the edge of insanity.*

"Anti" carries the idea of deep-seated hostility, hatred or opposition. Keep this definition in mind as you think of the nature of Satan, and the way he feels about you serving God.

Satan has a *deep-seated hatred* and *hostility* against God. The very thought of you worshipping Him drives Satan *to the edge of insanity.* Want to drive the devil crazy? Stop complaining and start praising God! Now do you see the importance of knowing the enemy? More importantly, do you now realize the importance of knowing the True and Living God?

The adversary opposes the Church with deep-seated hostility and animosity. Satan hates God, the Church and you. No other religion or cult has that effect on the adversary, except Christianity! An unrestrained person with this mental condition would do someone great harm. Being restrained by the power of God, the adversary can only do what the Lord allows him to do.

The second half of the Greek word *antidikos* is "dikos," which means "righteousness."

When the two words *anti* (against) and *dikos* (righteousness) are compounded, they portray one who is *against righteousness*. Scripture makes it clear that Satan is *against righteousness*.

By definition, righteousness drives the adversary crazy; drives him to the brink of insanity! The Bible says let a man examine himself. Is your lifestyle driving the adversary nuts? Is it driving him to the edge of insanity? Are you the devil's worst nightmare?

In calling him the "adversary," we learn that Satan is *adamantly opposed to righteousness*. He lives up to his names! You can see the adversary feverishly at work in today's society where wrong is being called right, and right is being called wrong.

We live in a society wherein, if it makes you feels good — do it! Satan will not be upset at all if you fall into this category. However, if you decide to live a godly life, one that is pleasing to the Lord, he is going to be *against* you. By your righteous living you are driving Satan insane! Hallelujah!

~Angel of Light~

Satan is also described as an "angel of light." In dealing with the problem of Satan's servants — false prophets, false teachers, false apostles, and deceivers who were trying to worm their way into the Church — Paul wrote, *"And no wonder! For Satan himself transforms himself into an angel of light,"* (II Cor. 11:14, SFLB).

The word "transform" used here does not mean inner change of character. Satan can never truly be transformed. He is an imposter; he pretends to be something he is not. He is not an angel of light, but of darkness. Masquerading is what the devil does well. He wears a disguise, a mask, so as to deceive. Satan is unable to fulfill the deepest meaning of the word "transform," which means to *change character*.

Can a leopard change its spots (Jer. 13:23)? If you shave all the hair off a leopard, the spots will still be there, grown into its skin. Neither can Satan change his character! There is no salvation for Satan. Evil is permanently in him and he is utterly doomed.

Satan disguises himself as an "angel of light" to deceive watchful believers into following the wrong path. He knows that darkness has no power to overcome light and so he even pretends to be the voice of God by speaking a perverted version of Truth. Watchful believers aren't fooled by Satan's disguises; those who are not grounded and rooted in Truth, however, will be easily deceived by this master manipulator.

The appearance of the beast (Rev. 17:8, 11) will not be repulsive. He will be handsome and charming, but will have a putrid nature. Satan *appears* to be *an angel of light,* but do not be fooled by the way things look. He is the prince of darkness. The deeds of darkness are dreadful.

~Beelzebub~

The name "Beelzebub" (Matt. 10:25, 12:24) literally means, "Lord of the flies." Originally it was spelled Baal-zebub (II Kings 1:2, 6). Baal-zebub was an arch demon of North Palestine and Syria.

The Jews added a twist to this name and changed it to Beelzebub which became an epithet for Satan's vile nature, describing him as *"lord of the dunghill or lord of the manure."* The Jews were saying that just like nasty flies are attracted to dunghills and places where rotting, stinking things are, Satan and his demonic force of evil are attracted to ungodliness. They thrive in mess.

Beelzebub is a heathen deity that was recognized as the prince of evil spirits. He was the "dung god," which was an

41

expression intended to designate Satan as the prince of all moral impurity.

God is not in mess such as gossip, slander, backbiting and such, none of which brings glory to His name. If you find pleasure in any of these things you may have been bitten by Beelzebub, *the lord of the flies*!

Christ's enemies accused Him of being possessed by Beelzebub (Matt. 12:24-29). To accuse Jesus of being possessed by this demon spirit was nothing short of blasphemy. The name is appropriately assigned to Satan, its rightful owner!

~Liar~

Jesus called Satan a liar and a murderer in the same breath (John 8:44). Lying comes naturally to Satan because that is his nature. There is no truth in him at all. He is the father of lies. Liars are just like their daddy, the devil. Folks who love God know that He hates a lying tongue (Proverbs 6:17). It is an abomination to God. Lying comes naturally to some folks due to their relationship with the devil. Satan and his followers cannot tell the truth.

For over a year, King David lied about his sin with Bathsheba and nothing went right for him. Until he confessed his sin, he could find no peace.

> *"When I refused to confess my sin, I was weak and miserable, and I groaned all day long. Day and night Your hand of discipline was heavy on me. My strength evaporated like water in the summer heat. Finally, I confessed all my sins to You and stopped trying to hide them. I said to myself, I will confess my rebellion to the LORD. And You forgave me! All my guilt is gone,"* (Psalm 32:3-5, LASB).

A "little lie" is like a little leaven. Once a little lie gets into the life, it spreads. One lie leads to another lie to cover the first lie. A lie doesn't care who tells it! Satan is a liar and he twists his lies to sound like the truth. The only remedy for a lie is Truth.

Satan said to Eve, *"you shall not surely die"* (Gen. 3:4); that was a lie. God said, "But of the tree of the knowledge of good and evil, thou shall not eat of it: for in the day that thou eatest thereof *thou shall surely die,"* (2:17). His lie was so subtle that Eve didn't detect it! Since the beginning of human existence, he has been lying and has blinded the eyes of man from seeing the Truth.

This master manipulator leads believers into disobedience by lying to them. Satan's lies are very subtle. When you are familiar with the Word of God, he cannot deceive you with his lies. Why do you think he lulls you to sleep every time you decide to read your Bible? He whispers in your ear, "The Lord understands. You worked very hard today. Remember, the Bible says that the rest of the laboring man is sweet. Hiss, Hiss, Hiss!" Before you know it, you're sleeping like a baby!

Jesus is the Source of Truth. Satan is the source of untruth. He wants you to believe that some lies are harmless. The devil also wants us to believe that lies come in sizes. He will tell you, "It's only a *little* lie." Then he wants you to believe that lies come in colors. "It's only a *white* lie." He even wants you to think that some lies are useful at times. God does not overlook any lies, black ones, white ones, big ones, or small ones. This sin originated from the father of lies, the devil!

The devil is a liar: *"But...all liars, shall have their part in the lake which burneth with fire and brimstone: which is the second death,"* (Rev. 21:8).

~Murderer~

"You are of your father the devil...he was a murderer from the beginning..." (John 8:44).

43

Satan became *homicidal*, a manslayer, at the beginning of his apostasy when he abandoned God.

After the fall of man Satan, the manslayer, used man to murder man. The Jews called him *the angel of death*. Genesis 4:8 states that while Cain and Abel (his brother) were in the field, Cain murdered Abel. This is the first murder recorded in the Bible.

Murder is taking a person's life by bloodshed. Blood represents life, *"the life is in the blood,"* (Lev. 17:11). If the devil had not been strong in Cain he would not have done such an unnatural thing as to murder his own brother. Prior to the fall, it was not in man's nature to kill.

Only God can create life, and only God should take it away. Parents are murdering their children, and children are murdering their parents. Then there is self-murder. Folks of all ages have tapped into this dark addiction. Many have committed self-murder thinking that was the only way to fix the problem. The devil surely whispered, "Suicide is your only way out! You deserve to die!"

Regardless of the situation you are in right now, there is hope! God cares about you. Face that problem head on. Tell the enemy, *"I shall not die, but live, and declare the works of the Lord,"* (118:17, SFLB) and he will flee from you!

There is an on-line chat room where individuals are actually encouraged to kill themselves, and are told *how* to commit suicide. The manslayer whispers to them, "You are worthless anyway, so why not kill yourself?" Satan can be very persuasive. Unfortunately, people have heeded his suggestions and as a result, they have aborted the plan and purpose for which they were born.

Satan wants folks to die. He is a murderer, but the time will come when all murderers, as well as all liars, will be cast into the lake which burns with fire and brimstone (Rev. 21:8).

~Satan~

Satan is the enemy of God and man; a created being, originally fashioned with beauty and wisdom. His name is taken from the Hebrew word *satanas* which means "adversary." The name carries the idea of *slander* and *false accusation*.

> *"And I heard a loud voice saying in Heaven, Now is come salvation, and strength, and the kingdom of our God, and the power of His Christ: for the accuser of our brethren is cast down, which accused them before our God day and night,"* (Rev. 12:10, KJV).

Satan has limitations. He cannot be everywhere at the same time. He works through evil spirits who carry out his commands. He is not all-powerful! Satan is not as bad as some may think.

Originally, Satan was called Lucifer, "the bright one." He was the highest, the most powerful and wisest creation of God. By creation, Satan was perfect (Ezek. 28:15) until his heart became lifted up in pride. God created good and good became evil. Lucifer wanted to be equal with God, and to be worshipped as God. Satan wanted to rule Heaven and all the angels.

Pride was Satan's sin and his downfall. Jesus said, *"I saw Satan falling from heaven as a flash of lightning,"* (Luke 10:18). *"How art thou fallen from heaven, O Lucifer,"* (Isa.14:12). He was kicked out of the paradise of God forever! Satan is the devil!

The personal pronoun "I" means "ego." Satan was on an ego trip. He used the phrase, "I will" five times in only two verses! In Isaiah 14:13-14 he said, 1) *I will* ascend into heaven, 2) *I will* exalt my throne above the stars of God, 3) *I will* sit upon the mount of the congregation, 4) *I will* ascend above the heights of the clouds, and 5) *I will* be like the Most High.

The very next verse (v.15) is God's response to his "I wills." The Lord said, "But instead, *you will* be brought down to the place of the dead, down to its lowest depths." God officially declared Satan's devil's doom.

Satan tempts folks today with the same bait of aspiring to be equal with God. Be very careful of your use of the personal pronoun "I" –you may be ego tripping! Be watchful and pray, lest you fall into the same temptation. It is enough for one to aspire to be like Christ.

~Serpent~

A serpent is a snake, a creeping thing; a reptile. When Scripture refers to Satan as a serpent it speaks to its *venomous nature*. When a snake bites, he secretes poisonous venom.

As the serpent injects his poisonous venom into people to kill them, the devil wants to inject his venomous nature in you to kill your dreams, your ministry, and your purpose. He wants to kill you! Satan wants to inject his venom of malice, envy, lust, hatred, adultery and pride into you.

The enemy will also try to make you think that God has forgotten about you; that He does not love or care about you. To suggest such a thing is venomous.

Check out the nature of the serpent. The Bible says that he is *more subtle* than any beast of the field which God had made (Gen 3:1). The word "subtle" means difficult to detect or analyze; barely perceptible, skillful, crafty, cunning, sly, and marked by or having keen discernment.

The serpent was the shrewdest creature of them all. God created the serpent this way, which was fine *before* the fall. After the fall, these attributes became corrupt. Satan is not literally a snake; he is an evil *spirit* metaphorically described as a serpent, because he has all the characteristics of a snake. He uses the attributes of the serpent for evil, not for good. This snake cannot be seen, but he is real nonetheless.

The Bible calls Satan the "old" serpent (Rev. 12:9), because he has been around a very long time. He knows all the tricks. The old serpent has had a lot of practice hurting and deceiving people.

The malice (desire to do harm to others) of the wicked is compared to the venom of a serpent. Christ teaches us to love one another. No malice can be found in a heart of love. *"You were cleansed from your sins when you obeyed the truth, so now you must show sincere love to each other as brothers and sisters. Love each other deeply with all your heart,"* (I Peter 1:22, NLT).

The serpent is a figure for hypocrites (Matt. 23:33). The Greek word *hupokrites* is the same as our English word "hypocrite." The Greek definition for hypocrite is *actor*. Satan is an actor. There are a lot of actors in the Church today; folks act like they are Christlike!

Satan is like a serpent that creeps upon his target until he gets close enough to strike. If you allow a serpent to get within striking distance, he will bite you and inject his poison in you, so that you die! Satan doesn't want to merely hurt you; he wants you spiritually, physically and emotionally dead. He will spit his poison into you like a deadly snake!

Put a muzzle on the enemy, or he will bite you. If you are constantly murmuring and complaining, lying, speaking evil of folks, have a negative attitude, or cannot get along with others, you may be suffering from snake-bite! Thank God, there is a remedy, an antidote, for snake-bite –the blood of Jesus! The blood of Jesus makes us immune to the serpent's bite!

Jesus said, *"Behold, I give unto you power to tread on serpents and scorpions, and over all the power of the enemy: and nothing shall by any means hurt you,"* (Luke 10:19, KJV). God has given us power over serpents and scorpions; symbols of spiritual enemies and demonic power. No voodoo, no witch's brew, nothing will by any means hurt you!

After God dealt with Satan in heaven, He sent His Son Jesus to deal with him on earth.

Jesus, the Seed of the woman, bruised (crushed) the enemy's head by His death on the cross. Christ battled Satan and the kingdom of darkness for mankind and won! Now He sits at the right hand of God, the place of honor and sovereign power. The blood of Jesus has barred Heaven's door permanently against the enemy!

~In the Name of Jesus~

Now the Church, the focus of Satan's attention, must rise to the occasion! We must battle the enemy in the strength and power of Almighty God! He has provided the same armor Jesus used to break the power of the enemy! We have *God's weapons of mass destruction* at our disposal!

In addition to having access to all the armor Jesus utilized in battle, we have another advantage; the *Name* of Jesus! It is only fitting to end this chapter with the Name that is above every name; Jesus! Jesus is superior to the prophets, to the angels, and to Moses. All power is given to Jesus in heaven and in earth, and all the power and authority Jesus has is in His Name. To us He said, "Whatsoever you ask in My Name, I will do it!"

When you know what is in the Name, the power that is behind His Name and authority that is in the Name "Jesus," you may invoke that power to bring about all that is legally yours; to bring about all that you need. As Christians go to God the Father, our Provider, in the Name of Jesus Christ His Son, you can believe that it is done!

At the Name Jesus, every knee shall bow and every tongue shall confess that Jesus is Lord, to the glory of God the Father. In the Name Jesus, there is eternal life and healing. At the Name of Jesus demons tremble. *"Neither is there salvation in any other: for there is none other Name under heaven given among men, whereby we must be saved,"* (Acts 4:12, KJV).

The Name Jesus is a strong tower, the righteous run into it and they are safe. In the Name of Jesus, "what's-his-name" doesn't stand a chance! Dear heart, call on the Name Jesus often!

CHAPTER FOUR

SUIT UP FOR WARFARE!

*"Put on the whole armor of God, that ye may
be able to stand against the wiles of the devil,"*
(Eph. 6:11).

I n the most famous section of this letter to the saints at
Ephesus, using military terminology, Paul tells them to *suit
up* for warfare! In writing, "Put on the whole armor of God," he
describes the spiritual armor Christians are required to employ
in the spiritual warfare against sin and Satan.

Just before going into any battle, you must have on the complete armor of God. To omit even one piece of armor is to be
unprepared for battle. God's armor is designed for the protection of His Church. God is Spirit. Our enemy is *a* spirit. Spiritual
battles must be fought with spiritual weapons. Clothed in God's
full armor, you are more than a match for any adversary.

Satan's evil strategy is to set up roadblocks to prevent the
Church from moving out in power and victory! The only battle
plan that we need or have been given to resist the enemy is, "Put
on the *whole* armor of God." Before going out onto the battlefield, however, you must first of all know what the weapons are,
their purpose, and how to utilize them.

We need spiritual weapons to overcome wicked spirits. The
whole armor of God is designed for the Church to overcome and

prevail over every attack of the devil! Although the weapons of our warfare are not visible, they are real and they are powerful, nonetheless!

Only one side can win the war, and that's the Lord's side! Choose which side you are on. God's armor (the Word of God, prayer, faith, the Name of Jesus) always prevails! It is created to work together to break through the wall of resistance that the enemy has built. He wants to block your blessings; hinder your walk with the Lord!

Satan, the chief of evil powers, holds the highest ranking seat of an army of exceedingly wicked spirits. This old dragon has many tricks up his sleeves. He has an organized army of diabolical spirits at his command who carry out his orders without hesitation. These evil spirits hover over our communities, our cities, and the entire world.

No man-made weapon has the power to defeat demonic spirits; for this reason, God has provided His spiritual *weapons of mass destruction* to deliver His people. Remain clothed in your spiritual armor, or even the day-to-day common cares of life will wear you down! God's perfect plan is for you to deal with every situation that arises, every circumstance in His unlimited, mighty power!

Since the enemy is always poised to attack, ready to pounce on you, never take God's spiritual equipment off! Our chief adversary doesn't take a break; never takes a nap! To remove a part of your spiritual equipment will make you susceptible to his assaults.

Live every day like you're strong, powerful and invincible! God has done His part. Jesus has done His part. He has destroyed the works of the devil. Now we must do our part to fulfill the plan and purpose that God has for our lives.

Christ is our example and we must follow in His steps. When Jesus walked this earth, His divinity was wrapped in humanity (His deity was veiled). Jesus was completely God, and truly man; this does not mean that He was a freak. It means that Christ took on the limitations of humanity.

Christ was "made in the likeness of men," (Phil. 2:7) to show us that we too could overcome trials, temptations, and adversities the same way that He did; clothed in the whole armor of God. There is absolutely no other provision made for you to be without your armor.

From the very beginning of man's existence, Satan has been employing every trick and diabolical conspiracy to obstruct God's plan, purpose and will from being fulfilled on earth. For this reason, we have been provided weapons that will counterattack every attack of the enemy. No weapon formed against us will prosper. On the other hand, our weapons are mighty through God to the pulling down of the devil's strongholds!

Our Lord and Savior Jesus Christ did not face the enemy in His own strength. He depended upon His Father for guidance and strength in every situation. Through Christ you have come to trust in God, and anyone who trusts Him will never be ashamed or disgraced!

Stand firm and be strong in your faith. In spite of what you are going through, you do not have to face the enemy or the cares of life alone; neither in your own strength. Through Christ, God is involved in every aspect of our lives; however, every believer must suit-up himself. Only fully clothed Christian soldiers are invincible and unconquerable!

To omit even one piece of your spiritual armor means that you are not prepared for battle! When you were a child, someone else had to dress you; put your shoes on your feet and comb your hair. Now that you are an adult, you should dress yourself and comb your own hair. At forty, your mother should not be treating you like a two-year-old. It is time for you to grow up!

You do not want to be one of the devil's casualties! Your victory or defeat depends upon whether you are *suited up* in your armor or not. The same power that was available to Jesus — that spoiled principalities and powers, defeated hell and death

— is available to you! God's power is accessible for your use; to work *in* you, *through* you and *for* you, no matter what comes *against* you.

The armor of God is not to be put on display, or for show. A soldier puts his armor on because he is going to war and he wants to win. Even when it doesn't seem like it, Christians are always at war with the enemy. Never go onto the battlefield unprepared! To omit even one piece of your armor could cause your defeat. Whether you are on the mountaintop or in the valley of despair, remain suited!

God desires for His people to prepare themselves to walk with Him, and to war with Him against the kingdom of darkness, and win. Utilizing the complete panoply of God causes you to triumph! It will protect you from: 1) the lust of the flesh, 2) lust of the eyes, and 3) the pride of life (I John 2:16). All of the enemy's strategies fall into one of these categories.

Paul instructs the Ephesians to "take unto you;" reach out and take the armor and put it on, then you will be able to "stand firm" against all the *wiles*, that is, tricks of the devil.

Christians must put on the whole armor of God and 1) remain clothed, 2) familiarize themselves with the weapons God has provided, and 3) use the armor against the opponent. A weapon (Bible) that is placed on the shelf cannot raise itself up and fight the enemy for you.

God is truly amazing; therefore, He does amazing things, like orchestrating the events in our lives to accomplish His purpose. If Paul had not been thrown into a Roman prison, he would not have received the revelation of the armor of God for the Church. He could not have obtained this teaching had he been in Jerusalem. Jews were not known for their weaponry.

Roman soldiers had a distinct advantage over their enemies, because their weapons were second to none. In the ancient world, Roman soldiers were equipped with the best made weapons man had to offer. The weapons of our warfare are superior to any manmade weapon! We have a distinct advantage over the enemy. The armor that God provided for the Church is unequaled.

Since we are engaged in spiritual warfare, God wanted us to understand the significance of the armor provided for the Church. In prison, surrounded by soldiers who were often at war, Paul was able to describe the various attributes of Christ which make us innocuous to the wiles of the devil. As a soldier prepares for natural warfare, Christian soldiers must be prepared for spiritual warfare against sin and Satan at all times.

In Ephesians 6:10-18, the Holy Spirit revealed to Paul the significance of the whole armor of God, using the illustration of the *full battle attire* of the first-century Roman soldier.

His girdle, breastplate, shoes, shield, helmet, sword, and his spear (lance), all had some *spiritual* significance that the Holy Spirit revealed to Paul for the Church. Each piece of armor exemplifies a particular attribute of Christ; therefore, to *put on* the whole armor of God is to *put on* Christ.

Roman soldiers never ever went to battle without *putting on* each and every piece of armor. For the enemy's weapon to hit any exposed area of his body could potentially be deadly. This military metaphor is used to show us that we are to be fully prepared for spiritual warfare at all times. The Spirit-filled believer should never try to work out a problem without utilizing his spiritual armor. God's armor must be tried.

Your victorious living as an end-time spiritual warrior depends upon your knowledge and use of the weaponry that God has provided for you! The Lord's armor is bullet-proof. Go ahead devil, take your best shot!

Satan hates the very ground that the believer walks on. This is clearly seen in his various names and titles. His focus is always on you, looking for a weak, unguarded area where he can attack. He will strike when you are at your most vulnerable state; when you are ill, bills are pouring in, your back is up against the wall, unexpected expenses, and so forth. Satan will kick you when you are down! Just remember, you have the same weapons Jesus used to defeat the enemy.

The Bible describes warfare and bloodshed as reality, not fantasy. From the time sin entered into the human race, warfare became real. For this reason, we must consciously keep our war clothes on. Read the Bible to recognize, appreciate, and interpret the nature of God's divine protection.

The constant attacks of the enemy can wear you down mentally and emotionally, especially when you have been under a great burden for a long time. You may weaken under discouraging conditions and feel like giving up. In your own strength it is not always easy to pull yourself up under heavy pressure, but you can always trust the armor of God to lift you up!

We suffer for various reasons. Some suffering is the result of our own doing; some is the result of living in a fallen world; some is from sin, man, the enemy; and some suffering is from God. There are even times when you suffer for doing well. Whatever the reason, our reaction to the trials of life will reveal whether or not we have on the armor of God.

When we are tested, we are found out. The Spirit-filled believer will not cave in to pressure. They may *bend,* but they will not break! I vaguely remember a line from a song that says, *"The devil can't do me 'no' harm."* Yes, he can if you are not suited up.

Follow God's instructions and He guarantees you victory. Don't follow His instructions and you will experience the agony of defeat. *"For examples of patience in suffering, dear brothers and sisters, look at the prophets who spoke in the name of the Lord. We give great honor to those who endure under suffering,"* (Jam. 5:10-11, NLT).

"But rejoice, inasmuch as you are partakers of Christ's sufferings; that, when His glory shall be revealed, you may be glad also with exceeding joy," (I Pet 4:13, KJV).

Sometimes you may feel as though the devil is always "breathing down your neck," or that he is always on your case!

During stressful situations, rely upon your armor. Don't be discouraged and take your armor off, because at the end of every battle, victory belongs to those who trust God.

Suffering as a Christian (not an evil-doer) produces great results! Trials will reveal whether your faith is genuine or not. When your faith remains strong through trials and persecutions, it brings glory and honor to God! Sufferings are designed to perfect Christians' faith and purify their souls (the seat of their emotions).

So hold on! Something good is about to happen for you! Daybreak always comes after the darkest hour! Weeping may endure for a night, but joy comes in the morning. Trouble may last for a short while, but God's favor lasts forever. When problems come into your life, look for supernatural favor to come with them!

You can face every trial, every situation, every circumstance, knowing that your problems are no problem to the Lord. God's protective gear will not allow adverse circumstances to hinder you from being all that the Lord has redeemed you to be.

Problems are God's servants. They serve to push you into your purpose. Yes, the righteous fall seven times and they get up (Proverbs 24:16), but why continue falling when the Lord says that He is able to *keep you from falling* (Jude 24)? Could it be that you have omitted a piece of your spiritual weaponry? Maybe you need to put your war clothes back on.

A Roman soldier was a sight to see when he stood fully clothed in his battle clothes. Not one piece of armor was ever left to the side. Each had its specific function to protect a particular part of the soldier's body.

The helmet was not designed to protect the feet, and the shoes were not designed to protect the head. However, all had the same purpose; to protect the soldier. Not to wear his helmet meant that his head was exposed. Not to wear his shoes meant that his feet were not protected. After the soldier put on all his war clothes, he was ready to go to war!

Every single piece of God's armor has been provided for a purpose; to overcome adversities, and to whip the devil's butt! He will not flee unless you resist him, and you cannot resist him if you are *unarmed*. One of the wiliest tricks of the devil is to have you so busy *doing good things* that you neglect *the best thing* —reading the Word of God.

If you do not read your Bible or pray, you are unarmed. If you do not have faith in God, you are unarmed and cannot resist the evil one! Without your armor, expect to be clobbered!

Suit up! Pick up your armor and put it on. To put on Christ is to put on the whole armor of God. Never fight *against* God, and if you want to be victorious, never fight *without* Him; you will not win. When the Holy Spirit has complete control over our lives, we will react to situations the way Jesus did; He always drew strength from His Father.

Christians draw strength to do battle from God. You do not need a back-up or "just-in-case" plan. God wants you to live a victorious life, but victory is not automatic! We must surrender our lives to the Lord and do His will. Jesus broke the power of sin and Satan, but how will lost souls know this unless Christians share this Good News with them?

Paul was undeterred by the fact that he was in a Roman prison. The only crime he committed was to preach the gospel. Satan sought to turn Jesus away from the cross, and he sought to turn Paul away from Christ. Satan's scheme backfired in both cases! Jesus endured the cross, and is now sitting at the right hand of the Father.

As for Paul, suffering only enhanced his devotion to God. He totally surrendered his will to the will of God, in spite of his hardships and suffering. Paul proudly called himself a "prisoner of the Lord Jesus Christ." He said, *"Yea doubtless, and I count all things but loss for the excellency of the knowledge of Christ Jesus my Lord: for whom I have suffered the loss of all things, and do count them but dung, that I may win Christ,"* (Phil. 3:8, KJV).

When Paul took inventory of his life, pedigree, accomplishments, education, and his worldly possessions, he considered them worthless when compared with the priceless gain of knowing Christ. To know Christ and to belong to Him was priceless! The apostle Paul treated everything he possessed as garbage so that nothing could hinder his relationship with God.

God's full power only operates through yielded vessels like Paul. Because of his commitment and obedience to Christ, the Holy Spirit gave the apostle the revelation of the whole armor of God for the Church. As Paul meditated upon each piece of the Roman soldier's military gear, the Spirit *opened up his understanding* and *illuminated his mind* concerning what the Lord had to say to the Church concerning His provision for spiritual warfare.

Manmade weapons can malfunction, but the weapons that God has provided are one hundred per cent effective, one hundred per cent of the time! *"For the weapons of our warfare are not carnal, but mighty through God to the pulling down of strongholds,"* (II Cor.10:4, KJV).

The soldier's manmade outfit required fittings and alterations. The believer's *spiritual outfit* is God-made and does not require taking them off for fittings or alterations. The whole armor of God must be worn at all times *that ye may be able to stand against the wiles of the devil.*

If you are not in right standing with God (not suited up), however, you cannot stand. If you omit even one piece of God's armor (the Word, faith, prayer) we will not have the ability to stand firm when the winds of life (pain, sickness, unexpected expenses, family problems) start blowing!

Not having God's armor on makes the enemy's job easy. If you omit even one piece of armor, you may fall down. When you fall, it makes you vulnerable to the enemy's attack and gives him an advantage. To be invulnerable to his attacks, be sure to remain completely suited up at all times and you will by no means succumb to the wiles of the devil.

The enemy will attack you at an opportune time, when you are at your weakest point; when you are frail, depressed and discouraged. He attacks after you have had a bad day; after the doctor has given you a bad report; when the bills are pouring in and you cannot make ends meet; when your back is up against the wall or when that promotion does not come through and you feel like a failure. Having on the whole armor of God will cause you to bounce back, stronger than ever!

Satan is tenacious and untiring. He is forever looking for a way to be re-enthroned in your heart. He will not pass up even the slightest opportunity to strike careless, unwatchful Christians who are commanded to be *suited up for warfare* at all times. Put on the whole armor of God and you will be immune to the enemy's attacks against your life. There is a wall of protection around you that is impregnable to the enemy!

~Armored and Dangerous~

Take unto you the whole armor of God that you may be able to withstand in the evil day, and having done all, to stand. Each piece of armor is vital to your victory!

You do not have to understand everything about the enemy to defeat him; but you must know, trust, and be clothed in the armor of God which gives you the ability to stand against not *some*, but *all* the tricks and antics of the devil.

The word *able* is derived from the word *dunamis* which describes *explosive ability* and *dynamic strength and power.* Having on the full panoply of God is to be armored and *dangerous.*

With the definition of the word "able" in mind, this verse (v.13) could read, "Put on the whole armor of God so that you may have *explosive ability and dynamic strength and power* to stand against the wiles of the devil." The devil cannot overcome this kind of power! It enables you to stand, confident that God is going to come through for you.

The phrase "to stand" literally means to *stand ready for battle*. You're not simply standing, you're firmly standing, ready (prepared) for battle; armored and dangerous to the devil and his demons!

The picture of a fully clothed Roman soldier, standing upright with his shoulders firmly thrown back and his head held high, prepared for war, gives off an attitude of confidence, not arrogance. Losers do not look like this; winners do! Fight with confidence! There is nobody greater, more powerful or more loving and compassionate than our God; therefore, "big up" your perception of God. He is greater than you think!

When a believer has on the whole armor of God, he or she can say with confidence, *"Come on devil, bring it! Shoot your best shot! I can take it!"* Never go into battle thinking, "I cannot win!" God wants you to live a victorious life until Christ returns!

Suit up! The devil is always outnumbered when he comes against a fully armored believer. One with God is the majority. There is no need to be afraid what the devil can do to you when God is fighting for you. The Church is the chariot of triumph and the reins are in Jesus' hands! Praise the Lord!

God is a Warrior fighting for His people, with His people as His soldiers fighting His battles, under His command. The title "Captain of the Host of the Lord" (Joshua 5:14) refers to armies. It is significant to note that this title of the Lord was used immediately after Israel crossed the Jordan and was about to attack the fortified city of Jericho.

By introducing Himself as "Captain of the Host of the Lord" or "Commander of the Army of the Lord," God was telling Joshua that He had come *into the fight* to give them the victory. Under His command, the walls of Jericho fell down flat! God's people were given the city!

The whole armor of God brings God *into the fight*. He is our Commander-In-Chief, and we are His soldiers fighting His battles here on earth. As His soldiers, we receive our instructions from Him which are found in the Bible, the written Word of

God. Never enter a battle without first consulting God! Follow His battle plan or lose the war.

Victory over every situation requires use of *His* strategy for battle. Not to consult the Lord is to give the devil advantage.

"Put on the whole armor of God that ye may be able to stand against the wiles of the devil."

- Suit up. Put on God's armor. Do not omit even one piece. We are God's soldiers, fighting God's war; therefore, we must fight with the weapons He has provided for us.

- That you may be *able;* so that you, the believer, may have "explosive ability" and "dynamic strength" and "power" to stand.

- To *stand*–firmly stand; body erect, head held high, and shoulders thrown back. This is a look of confidence, not doubt. A hung down head and slouched shoulders are pictures of despair and defeat. Never throw in the towel of surrender to the enemy. Soldiers do not retreat, no matter how heated the battle gets. If you resist the devil, he will retreat.

- Against – The word "against" comes from the Greek word *pros*, which indicates a *forward position, bold confrontation*, or a *face-to-face encounter*. By using the word *pros*, Paul is describing a soldier on the battlefield, not running from his opponent, but looking his enemy directly in the face. Just as David ran *toward* Goliath to boldly confront him in the Name of the Lord, we can boldly face whatever comes against us.

A fully armored Roman soldier is dangerous. So confident is he in his armor that, when he marches onto the battlefield against the enemy army, he knows that he will be victorious!

Even though you may be standing against incredible odds, trust your armor of protection.

There is no emphasis placed on protection for the back. Believers are equipped to have a *bold confrontation* and a *face-to-face encounter* with the adversary. To be hit in the back implies one is running away from a problem. Never turn your back on the enemy; face him head on! The devil should be the one being chased, not the believer!

~The Wiles of the Devil~

Devil should only be applied to Satan as a proper name. By definition, the devil is the "malicious enemy" of God. There is one devil who is the ruling chief of demons. When referring to Satan as the devil, it speaks of his temptations. He tempts man to do evil.

The devil does not have all-power (omnipotent), and he cannot be everywhere at the same time (omnipresent); the Greek word for "devil" is *diabolos* which means an accuser; a slanderer.

Beware of the wiles of the devil. The word "wile" means crafty, fraud; schemes, a stratagem or trick intended to entrap or deceive; a disarming or seductive manner; deceitful, cunning; guile. Wiles are tools of the devil's trade.

Prior to the fall, the human mind was the purest expression of God's creative wisdom. Through man's disobedience, the mind became depraved, evil and corrupted. Good news! God has made restoration and renewing of the mind possible through obedience to the Word.

The mind is the center of change or transformation. "Renewing" speaks of a continual process that brings about change from the inside out! Read your Bible every day! Mediate upon it and obey what it says. God guards the minds and actions of those who obey Him. No demon can stay on a path toward your mind when it is stayed on Jesus!

The mere fact that the word "wiles" is used in its plural form warns us that Satan has many ways to deceive folks. Warning!

His bag of tricks is never empty and, like a crooked card player, he always has something up his sleeve.

Wiles are *schemes sought out.* The Greek word *methodia* further explains how efficient Satan is in the methods that he uses to achieve his goals. The first part of *methodia* is *meta* which means *after.* The second part is *hodos,* which means *a way.*

By using the word "wiles," Paul is saying that the devil is always seeking after (*meta*) a way (*hodos*) to get into your mind, and he is methodical in his attacks. The enemy uses carefully *sought out schemes* and methods to get into your thoughts.

Wiles denote craft. Satan chose the serpent because he was crafty. Being crafty is his craft and he is good at what he does. If he can get you to think that you are a loser, you will act like a loser; *"for as he thinks in his heart, so is he,"* (Prov. 23:7).

Paul wrote, *"Casting down imaginations...and bringing into captivity every thought to the obedience of Christ,"* (II Cor. 10:5). Satan can be compared to a great painter like Picasso. He paints mental images of death, failure and impure thoughts in your mind. His aim is to make you see yourself as a loser. Negative thoughts will block the flow of God's power in your life. See yourself as God sees you: a winner, a son or daughter of God. That's who you are!

Negative thoughts are wiles of the devil and are not just going away! Paul says Christians must take human thoughts captive! "Bringing into captivity" is a phrase that comes from a harsh Greek word *aichmalotidzo* which means, "to take one captive with a spear pointed into his back!"

The idea is to cast down, throw those thoughts down forcefully; fling them away from you as a vile thing! Throw away those imaginations. The word "imaginations" is taken from the Greek word *logismos,* where we get the word *logic* as in "logical thinking."

Do not build yourself on logical thinking or man's reasoning. God has chosen the foolish things of the world to confound the wise. Humans are not smart enough to win the battle of the mind. Let go your own thoughts and imaginations that are not founded upon the Word of God. His thoughts are not our thoughts. The Word of God helps us to think like God thinks.

Satan never stops thinking, plotting and scheming of a way of attack! True to his destructive nature, the devil never seeks after peace, but destruction. He will strike again and again with a barrage of attacks, trying to find a way to break through the wall of your mental resistance.

The devil wants to be the boss of you. Keep on resisting him to the point that he flees from you. When his wiles don't work on you, he will leave for a season and find someone else to try them on who has not been laboring in the Word of God and prayer!

The devil is very methodical. His wiles are his methods. The Greek word *methodia* is the equivalent of our English word *method*. There is a *method* to his madness! He uses *methodical stratagems* to get what he wants. Satan gives his method of attack much thought before he acts.

The purpose of Satan's well *sought out schemes* is to try and influence you to turn your back on God. Some of us may say, "Oh! That would never happen to me!" *"For false messiahs and false prophets will rise up and perform great miraculous signs and wonders so as to deceive, if possible, even God's chosen ones. See, I have warned you,"* (Matt. 24: 24, 25, NLT).

The Devil is always seeking *after* a better *way,* or another *method* by which he can manipulate you into believing his lies. His wiles are his ways. Satan watches your every movement. He plots schemes that he feels will work best on each individual. He knows that you will not steal — he's tempted you with that and it didn't work! So he tries to entice you with something else.

Satan knows that you will not denounce God, but you may have a weakness for gossip. He will bring some juicy tidbit to you concerning your neighbor or co-worker. If your ears perk up, he's got you! Rebuke that spirit of gossip or your lamp will gradually be without oil; your light might not shine so brightly. Gossip will dim your anointing.

God's armor of protection renders the devil's schemes null and void. Through His blood, Christ has cancelled Satan's assignment against you. This doesn't mean that the devil is going to leave you alone. It means he will not prevail against you. Being clothed in the whole armor of God gives you the supernatural ability to withstand every one of Satan's temptations! It is your fault if you unbar the door of your mind and let the devil in!

Be strong in the Lord (your armor). Do not let the enemy talk you into giving up on God. That's what he really wants. His *wiles* explain how the enemy operates and the methods by which he *goes after* the believer.

Wiles of the devil can be deadlier than his armies! The tricks, schemes and methods that he uses to seduce and deceive the people of God can be so subtle that we sometimes do not realize that it is the enemy at work.

The devil plays mind games, and that is exactly where he is always heading; to your mind. *"But I fear, lest by any means, as the serpent beguiled Eve through his subtlety, so your minds should be corrupted from the simplicity that is in Christ,"* (II Cor. 11:3, KJV). His bag of tricks, his wiles, will not work on the believer who is *suited up* in God's armor!

Satan looks for ways to set up *roadblocks* to your blessings. If one scheme does not work, the devil *seeks after* another. There is no shortage of ways to try and deceive you. Maybe you have not heard from him lately. The reason is he wants to choose the *method* that will work best on you next time, but if you keep your armor on his tricks will not work on you.

Terrible things can happen when we take off any piece of our armor, even for a second. It helps the devil reach his destination; your mind. His aim is to stop you from reaching yours –Heaven!

Although the devil is most deceitful, if you are suited up he won't stand a chance! With your thoughts and emotions controlled by the Holy Spirit, you will have the supernatural ability to detect, reject and foil all the tricks of the evil one!

~The Mind: The Devil's Battleground~

From the inception of the Church, Satan has been in a frenzy working hard against it. The enemy has unleashed an all-out assault against the people of God. His mission is to prevent Christians from moving forth in the power and supernatural anointing of the Holy Spirit and to turn their hearts away from God. The only means of preventing him from achieving his goal is to have on the whole armor of God.

Satan wants to feed your heart and mind with the cares of this world. He wants to distract you from your divine purpose. The Bible says to set your affections on things above, not on things on the earth. *"Think about the things of heaven, not the things of earth,"* (Col.3:2).

We must win the war that is waged against our mind! Let us examine what the Bible says <u>concerning Christians who have their minds protected by the armor of God</u>:

- *Then we will no longer be immature like children. We won't be tossed and blown about by every wind of new teaching. We will not be influenced when people try to trick us with lies so clever they sound like the truth* (Eph. 4:14, NLT).
- *Instead, we will speak the truth in love, growing in every way more and more like Christ, who is the Head of His body, the Church* (v.15, NLT).

The serpent was more subtle (expert and skillful) than any other beast of the field which God had made (Gen. 3:1). The serpent was not Satan. Satan used the serpent for his own evil purposes. In its un-cursed state the serpent was a beautiful, harmless creature; skillful, clever and crafty in a wonderful way...*before* the fall. For these reasons, Eve was not afraid when he approached her.

The woman did not realize that she was being set up. Satan, an intelligent creature, was playing mind games on Eve. He knew that the woman would influence the man to disobey God. Scripture says that the serpent *beguiled* Eve. He took a mind that was perfect and totally in harmony with God and corrupted it through deception. Don't let the devil play tricks on your mind!

To test man's obedience, God ordered him not to eat of the tree of good and evil (Gen. 2:17). The serpent was a real smooth talker! The wiliest trick of them all is to have you doubt God's Word! The serpent planted a seed of doubt in the woman's mind by asking her, *"Did God really say you must not eat of the fruit from any of the trees in the garden?"* (Gen. 3:1, NLT)

Today, the enemy is still tampering with God's Word; he is still asking "Did God indeed say?"

Every time the Lord tells you He is going to bless you, the enemy takes that promise and turns it into a question to make you doubt God. Did He really say that? To counteract Satan's lies, you must saturate your mind with Truth. As we fill our thoughts with the knowledge of God's Word, the Bible will become the controlling factor of our lives; not the world's way of thinking!

Satan *shrewdly* used a perverted version of God's Word to attack Eve's mind, and planted a seed of doubt. Your mind is the devil's battleground for spiritual warfare.

First, Satan deceived the woman to doubt God's Word, you *will surely* die (Gen. 2:17). Then he tricked her into believing his words, you will *not* surely die (Gen. 3:4)! Warfare in the mind is ongoing. Let not your imagination run wild, as some suggest. Don't be motivated by the way you think, unless your thinking is based upon "thus saith the Lord."

Man was given freedom to choose. Unfortunately, man chose to disobey God and believe Satan's lies, with sad consequences. Man fell into sin. The enemy's wiles worked on the woman, and the woman's influence worked on the man. Satan's charm doesn't work on Christians who have their minds stayed on Christ!

Satan wanted what he could not take from God; dominion. He wanted to be God, worshipped and in control. His underhanded methodology (wiles) is to disguise himself into something he is not to get what he wants. He is a master of disguises, but he cannot fool the person who "walk not after the flesh," but after the Spirit (Romans 8:1).

If you remove your covering, the armor of God, you will become a sitting duck for the enemy! Put on the whole armor of God (God's weapons of mass destruction), so that you may be able to stand against the wiles (tricks, schemes, stratagems) of the devil. Satan, the master strategist, is called the "old serpent" (Rev.12:9), because he has been around a very long time. He is experienced in the art of deception.

The devil tempted man to sin, and man gave in to the temptation. There was no power *in* the temptation to make man sin. We have as much power to choose to obey God as to disobey Him.

The mere possibility of sin has never made anyone succumb to it. That is a choice that we make for ourselves. The saying, "The devil made me do it," is just an excuse to blame someone else for the wrong choices that we make. Nowhere in Scripture do we read that God created evil. God created everything good; good became twisted or perverted –good *became* evil!

Though he was solicited from without, Adam made a personal decision to disobey God, and he was held accountable for his sin. Man freely chose to disobey God, and to obey the deception of the deceiver. Adam willingly handed over his dominion to the devil! Through Adam, paradise was lost; through the Lord Jesus Christ, paradise was regained (Luke 23:43). To disobey God and to distrust His armor of provision and protection is akin to handing our birthright to the devil!

Satan targeted Eve's mind (his destination), the battleground for spiritual warfare. His method was to distort and pervert the

Word of God. His aim was to plant *the seed of his word* into Eve's mind in a manner that suggested to her that God was selfish, because He would not allow them to eat of *every tree* of the Garden. He deceived, then persuaded the woman to question God's honor and His goodness. Question anything else, but never God's goodness. The Lord *is* good!

Eve foolishly let Satan reach his destination, her mind, by conversing with him. She became comfortable in his presence, and *succumbed* to *the wiles of the devil*. Eve was duped by the devil and ate of the tree of "the knowledge of good and evil," (Gen. 2:17) then influenced her husband to disobey God also. No one really wants to sin alone.

Why did she do it? Why did Eve eat that piece of fruit? Why did Adam listen to her? Why did Adam disobey God? If they had obeyed God, we would not have to deal with the devil! These are some of the thoughts and questions that run through our minds from time to time, and yet the enemy is *still deceiving* people who think like this, every day. They may not eat a piece of fruit, but one way or another they disobey God. Did God indeed say? What's in your mind?

The devil will try to trick you into doing something that seems so innocent, and yet it totally goes against God's Word. You may not even recognize it as being out of order unless someone points it out to you. For example, the Bible says, *"Enter His gates with thanksgiving, and into His courts with praise: be thankful unto Him, and bless His Name,"* (Psalm 100:4). However, we do not see anything wrong with entering God's house with a bad attitude!

Remember, the enemy wants to control your thoughts. He who controls your mind controls you!

Gird your mind with truth! If you allow yourself to think the devil's lies, you may believe his lies, then you may never, never, never! You may never get out of debt. You may never be healed, and your children may never get saved! Do not entertain his lies;

never say "never!" This kind of loose thinking will come back to haunt you later on in life.

Everyone has intervals of unbelief, but don't let those moments of doubt linger. Paul tells us to bring our thoughts under obedience to Christ, quickly! Believers must think saved thoughts. Our greatest strength comes from storing-up the Word of God in our hearts (mind); being surrendered to the Lord Jesus Christ and Holy Spirit controlled!

God loves you. There is evil, but there is a greater Good! That problem you're facing will not last forever. Your trial is going to catapult you right into your purpose and your destiny!

The devil knows that Jesus is the only One who can make your dreams come true. If you doubt His promises, you may never see them come to pass. Dreams originate in the mind. Do not permit the wiles of the devil turn your dreams into a nightmare!

~Into the Minds of Madmen~

The Behavioral Research and Instruction Unit (BRIU) (originally the Behavioral Science Unit [BSI]), located in Quantico, Virginia, studies behavior to construct detailed profiles on the most deleterious, hurtful, evil and villainous criminals in the world; all characteristics of the devil.

FBI profilers have written books on criminals such as (note the recurring theme); "Criminal Minds" by David Owen; "Mind Hunter" by John Douglas; "Dark Dreams" by Roy Hazelwood and "Into the Minds of Madmen" by Don DeNevi.

Mind hunters want to apprehend these murderous psychopaths to try and obtain an understanding of their thought process. They realize that the key to a criminal's evil deeds has its root in the way they think! The profilers are on the right track; however, behind every evil act is a sinister *spirit*.

The person that is controlled by Satan obeys his instructions. He is the commander-in-chief of an army of demons whose orders are to commit extremely cruel acts against other humans. On the battlefield of the mind, Satan (the first murderer) coaxed Cain into murdering his brother, Abel. John List was a Church-going man who killed his entire family. Satan gained access to his mind! Every deed, good and evil, has its inception in the mind.

The Word of God will safeguard your mind. *"Let this mind be in you which was also in Christ Jesus,"* (Phil. 2:5, KJV); it will prevent the battleground of your mind from becoming a polluted playground for the devil!

~Experience Your Personal Spiritual Breakthrough~

Anything that comes against you to hurt you may be considered an adversary; pain, poverty, sickness, depression, oppression, trials, and afflictions are tools of the adversary; he uses them to inflict as much misery upon your life as he can.

Life is a battlefield for the spiritual warfare between God and Satan! You can experience your personal breakthrough clothed in the armor of God. Strength and stamina for spiritual warfare comes from the Lord. The outcome of every spiritual battle depends upon the knowledge and usage of your spiritual weaponry!

Victory begins at the cross of suffering. No cross, no Christ, no crown! Regardless of what anyone says, read the Word of God and know for yourself what it says concerning you!

Only as we operate in the power of the Holy Spirit, utilizing the means God has provided for the Church, can we experience our personal spiritual breakthrough and victory!

A "breakthrough" as an act of *breaking through a restriction or obstacle; a major achievement or discovery that permits further progress.*

Since the fall of man, Satan has been placing *restrictions* and *obstacles* between God and man; nevertheless, God has provided spiritual *weapons of mass destruction* to break through

71

all of the enemy's barricades. No roadblock that is set up by the devil can stop God from reaching you!

Trust the Lord and watch Him turn those *stumbling blocks* into *steppingstones* so that you might experience your personal breakthrough of blessings! Satan knows that nothing can separate us from the love of God, but that does not keep him from trying! Christians must be determined to do the will of the Lord regardless of the cost!

Trouble is designed to draw us closer to our Heavenly Father.

"And we know that God causes everything to work together for the good of those who love God and are called according to His purpose for them," (Rom. 8:28, KJV) has always been one of my favorite Scriptures to meditate upon. Everything that happens to me, from birth to death, works together to fulfill His good purpose for my life!

The power of Christ resting upon our lives is more important than the things that we suffer! God has an eternal plan for your life. This does not mean that you will never experience difficulties, or that you will become a millionaire. All things work together according to *His* purpose, not ours! Thy *will be done* in earth.

Through afflictions, God pushes us into His purpose. The plan that God has for you is already set in motion. Behind that problem is a purpose. Everything we experience — good and bad, ups and downs, the crooked and the straight — are employed by God to work together for our good, and for His glory!

The life that is surrendered to the Lord is dominated by the strong influences of God so that all things work together. For the phrase "working together," Paul uses the Greek word *sunergeo*, which is the same as the English word "synergy."

A "synergy" can be described as the *interaction of multiple elements in a system to produce an effect different or greater than the sum of their individual effects.*

Any single occurrence in my life (i.e., death of my dad) causes me to pray and seek the face of God, but that one heartbreaking event alone cannot accomplish or produce the effect made by the *combined action* of all the events in my life (from birth to present); death of father, mother, siblings, other family members; sickness, problems from within and from without.

The synergy of events — the *combined action* of them all, good and bad — caused me to experience a close spiritual walk with the Lord that without them would not have occurred!

Every problem, crisis, trial and circumstance that we experience *work together* as a team, not to destroy us, but to achieve the greatest good! The life that is totally surrendered to the Lord is governed by Him so that all things work together!

Through adversities, you learn to utilize every piece of armor that God has provided. No one has to tell you to pray when your back is up against the wall. No one has to force you to read your Bible when the devil is breathing down your neck!

God has provided all that we need to accomplish His will. Our ultimate purpose is to obey God's revealed will. His will is whatever His Word requires or commands us to do. Obey the Word of God and you will feel the hand (blessings) of God!

Christ came to earth to die for the sins of man. He came to save humanity. The Holy Spirit led Jesus into the wilderness to prepare Him to do the will of His Father. Christ faced and defeated the enemy using the *weapons of mass destruction*; the Word of God and prayer!

Christ prayed: "My Father! If it is possible, let this cup of suffering be taken away from Me. Yet I want Your will, not Mine," (Matt. 26:39, LASB). To fulfill His purpose, Christ had to die the humiliating death of the Cross. The road Jesus walked to Calvary wasn't a piece of cake, either!

The synergy of events that occurred in Christ's life worked together for our salvation. That Christ might be crucified, He was despised. Unless Christ had been despised and rejected of men, He would not have been crucified. If He had not been crucified, He would not have shed His blood, the price for our redemption from sin.

Everything, from Christ's incarnate birth to His resurrection, worked together not for His good, but for our good. Every circumstance of your life *collectively* works *together* (synergy) for your good. *"He that spared not His own Son, but delivered Him up for us all, how shall He not with Him also freely give us all things,"* (Rom. 8:32, KJV). Behind every problem, there is a purpose!

There are times when you must struggle through your doubts. During those times, the Holy Spirit will teach you how to fix your faith on the immutable Word! The more we trust His Word, the more our confidence in the Lord increases. God sends His Word out and it produces fruit. It will accomplish the good for which it is intended! God's Word prospers wherever He sends it!

Paul wrote, "And we know" —so if we really *do* know God, and *we know* that He is in control, we do not need to know why He allows us to experience hardships. All of the disappointments, trouble and difficulties that have ever come upon humans are because of man's disobedience to God! However, our Heavenly Father still loves us and always wants what is best for us.

During Paul's day, trials and persecutions were par for the course for those who followed Christ, but he saw the big picture! He said his suffering was well worth it. People were persecuting him, but the Gospel was being promoted and proclaimed. Paul's experiences were married to his purpose — preach the Gospel!

The warfare that we fight is between God and the devil, but your life is the battleground! Satan cannot get to God, so he attacks the one closest to Him — you! So, what should you do? Trust His Word, stand still; let the Lord fight your battle. Christ is already positioned for victory!

When you are in the eye of the storm, trust God. Have a bold, fearless attitude, no matter what you are going through or you will *succumb* to the tricks of the devil. Overcomers don't run from, back up or retreat from the opposition; they confront it. Winners move steadily forward with their eyes fixed on Jesus! Satan cannot throw them off course, no matter how hard he tries!

The Bible is our anchor: *"Many are the afflictions of the righteous: but the Lord delivers him out of them all,"* (Ps. 34:19, SFLB). Paul said "stand" against the "wiles" (plural) of the devil. When fear and doubt do not work, Satan will try another tactic. He is an evil spirit; he doesn't need rest.

Satan's aim is to turn you away from God! He wants Christians to think that God does not care about them. Job's wife tried to convince him to curse God and die. Similarly, Satan wants us to denounce God and die; first spiritually (he wants your soul), then physically!

Follow hard after God; the enemy plays mind games! Clothe your mind with the Word; it will increase your spiritual and physical strength and stamina. As a spiritual warrior, your ability to stand *against the wiles of the devil* depends solely upon your knowledge of the Word; the lack thereof will cause your defeat! *"So be truly glad. There is wonderful joy ahead, even though you have to endure many trials for a little while,"* (I Peter 1:6, NLT).

Wiles are tricks the devil uses to try and influence your way of thinking. The enemy wants to put your mind under demonic control. Satan will try anything to hijack your thoughts! To hijack something is to force it to *go in another direction.* Do not let the devil hijack your mind! How to prevent this? Put on the whole armor of God!

Cement the Word of God into your heart. You will not always physically have the Bible at your disposal; therefore, the Word must be stored up, like Joseph stored up corn for the famine.

Nothing is going to thwart God's purposes. If you love the Lord, all of the events of your life are pertinent to the purpose for which you were born. We do not exist on earth just to take up space.

"According to God," means everything that happens is coming from God's hand in one way or another; either He *causes* them to happen, or He *allows* them to happen. All things are regulated by Him! God was and is always in control of the affairs of our life, not the devil. According to God, not man, our problems are going to work together for good, not evil.

Do not go AWOL. Strong, godly character develops as we struggle through tough times. It is always too soon to abandon God. It's always too soon to quit, for quitters never win. Nothing could serve the enemy's purposes more than for you to leave God! Don't even think about it! Giving up will keep you from being all that God wants you to be and from experiencing your personal breakthrough of miracles and blessings!

Trials and difficulties are good for us in that they help to shape and mold our character. They also expose character flaws. Nonetheless, God does not see us as we are; He sees us for what He can transform our lives into! Trouble helps to perfect you.

Problems are not pleasant and enjoyable; however, instead of complaining and feeling sorry for himself, Paul said that he would rather *glory in his afflictions* that the power of Christ might rest upon him. He also said, "I take pleasure in infirmities," (II Cor. 12:10).

No one is going to have a problem-free life! The Christian life is not a bed of roses or a paved road to wealth and ease; it consists of hills and valleys. We must take the bitter with the sweet.

Difficulties remind us that we need God and He wants to be needed, because it gives Him the opportunity to show how much He loves us. Sometimes the Lord even allows us to lose a battle or two so that we may learn to depend solely upon Him. It is not that we doubt God's ability to deliver us; our problem is that we just don't think He is doing it fast enough!

Trouble is actually a servant of God; it goes where He sends it and it accomplishes what He wants it to accomplish. When a particular trouble has finished its job, it leaves; then another comes to work —on you!

Before sin came into the world, suffering was unheard of. Man started trouble when he disobeyed God in the garden. Because of sin *"man is born into trouble."* In spite of that, we can experience our personal breakthrough and victory over every situation through Jesus Christ our Lord!

Laboring in the Word of God and prayer during times of trouble teaches us to cast our cares upon God. Perseverance, strength and courage come from feeding upon the Scriptures. Everything else is simply doping or stimulating, which may last for a while, but will not work during trying times when real endurance is required. When you trust and obey God, you will run without stopping; you will walk and not faint.

Instead of going to secondary sources for help (family, friends), or seeking your own means of deliverance, take your burdens to the Lord in prayer. Sometimes sharing problems with others is fine, but it is not always in your best interest to tell folks what you are going through. They have their own troubles. Maybe they need your prayers or your shoulder to cry on more than you need theirs. Sometimes people really don't want to hear about what you are going through.

The greater the difficulty we face, the greater the opportunity there is for the Lord to do mighty things in our lives. Folks don't always understand the reason why God is taking you through that situation. They do not see the big picture, or what the Lord has shown you concerning your set of circumstances. For *this* is the will of God concerning *you*, not them!

Jesus' time on earth and the things He endured at the hands of men should be a constant reminder of just how much He loves us. He was hated, scourged, reproached, and nailed to the cross where He died! The Just (Jesus) suffered physical and emotional scars for the unjust (sinful man). He was rejected by those closest to Him. His biological family, even His disciples (those of His inner circle) deserted Christ when He needed them most. Let us not be guilty of doing the same!

Jesus came to His own world, but the world He created didn't recognize Him. His own people rejected Him (John 1:11), yet Jesus remained faithful, steadfast, undaunted and undeterred in His mission; accomplishing all that His Father sent Him to do. Regardless of the circumstances He faced, Jesus moved steadily forward with His eyes on the goal; dying on the cross!

Without trials, we cannot appropriate the victory of Calvary. We can only be defeated if God can be defeated. We can only fail if Jesus failed. The enemy thought Jesus failed when He died on the cross, but the cross was the bridge from humiliation to glorification! The devil is the one who was defeated! The cross is our bridge to victorious Christian living! While you are waiting for your breakthrough, do not look for others to encourage you. Encourage yourself in the Lord.

Every Christian's circumstances are not exactly the same, and so the method of deliverance will not be exactly the same. However, the outcome is always the same; *we win!*

Regardless of the time that has passed — one, five, ten years or more — even if your situation hasn't changed, instead of asking, "How long?" tell Him, "Lord, have Your way!" As soon as your attitude changes from questioning to trusting, God's response changes from, "I will do it," to "It is done!" The adversary works feverishly when he is about to lose his prey!

Going through the rough places of life helps you to grow and mature spiritually and emotionally. Spiritual warfare teaches you how to really depend upon the Lord, and teaches you how to trust Him for your personal breakthrough. All that we experience in life is designed by our Heavenly Father to transform us into the image of His Beloved Son; His unspeakable Gift to the world!

I will never forget the day I approached my husband and asked him if he would like to receive salvation. He had always rejected even the idea of attending church, but this particular day was different. Prompted by the Holy Spirit, I witnessed to him again.

That wonderful day, my husband surrendered his heart. He said "Yes" to the Lord! Victory! God had promised that He was going to save my husband and He did. When it actually happened, like Rhoda and the other believers in Acts (12:13-17), I hardly believed it for gladness! My purpose had been to introduce Jesus to my husband and the Holy Spirit did the rest.

He repeated the *sinner's prayer* and received Jesus Christ as his personal Lord and Savior. That day, he experienced *his* personal spiritual breakthrough! The wait was worth it! A soul was saved, snatched out of the hands of the enemy, and all of Heaven rejoiced! Christians must be willing to suffer; to do whatever it takes to win the lost for Christ. See the big picture; it's not all about you!

Satan did not want to be dethroned from my husband's heart, the place that rightfully belongs to God! Maybe you have heard it said, or read, that there is a God-shaped hole in man's heart that only God can fill. That means nothing can take the place of Christ; husband, wife, children, not any amount of money. Nothing can take the place of God!

God has the ability to instantaneously change your situation, but He chooses to bring about the answer gradually. He is by no means on man's time schedule. A thousand years are as a day to the Lord. Jesus healed a man that had an infirmity thirty-eight years. He healed a woman who suffered with an issue of blood twelve years. Jesus remained in the grave for three days before He rose in Resurrection power! Each experienced their own personal spiritual breakthrough!

Weeping may endure for a night (only God knows how long a night can be); but joy is coming in the morning. Your morning may be sooner or later. Just hold on. Victory is doubly sweet when we know it is coming from the Lord!

Satan wanted me to cancel my assignment as a godly wife and abort the Lord's plan for me to introduce Jesus to my husband. At the end of that chapter, the plan and purpose of God for my family was fulfilled and understood. *Life is better understood looking backward, but it must be lived forward.* God's plan was to save my household. Mission accomplished!

Though it seems a hard way, God's way is the best way (lesson learned). A few months after my husband gave his heart to the Lord, he passed away of a massive heart attack! Guess what? Satan lost again. Absent from the body, present with the Lord. He now has a glorified body in Heaven. Winner! Jesus gave us power to penetrate Satan's territory and, like a conquering Roman soldier, take the victory! To the Lord belongs the spoil (soul)!

You may not know why you are experiencing so much pain right now, but if you trust God, you will understand it better in God's set time. That problem is not meant to destroy you, or make you turn your back on God; even though that is the devil's intent. If you trust God, you will be less susceptible (easily influenced, moved or affected) to the wiles of the devil!

Trouble can be a blessing in disguise when you begin to see that problem as an opportunity for a miracle! To experience your personal spiritual breakthrough of miracles and blessings, always view your situation from the Lord's side, the side that always wins! Be confident that *God is in control* and that you are in His hands; the place of power, love, safety, and security.

Trouble doesn't last always, but when it comes the aim is to make us pray harder and to spend quality time reading the Bible. During times of trouble we learn how to face each day trusting that God's ultimate plan is to do us good, not evil. We are taught how to conquer the negative force of self-pity and that obedience for victorious Christian living is of paramount importance!

Each trial is a means to an end; each experience is an opportunity for a miracle! So don't ask *why* you are going through that crisis, ask *for what purpose* God will use this crisis.

God is still on His Throne, giving orders and calling the shots. He is the devil's Boss! All of the circumstances of our lives are part of God's loving plan. He will not allow you to become an emotional wreck or emotionally stretched beyond that which you are able to endure. He will, *with* the temptation, make a way of escape.

Through trials and disappointments, we are made strong in the Lord and in His mighty power. Your faith in Christ will grow stronger; however, it takes the synergy of events to get us where we need to be spiritually and emotionally.

With God's mighty power operating through you as a Christian vessel, you can experience your personal spiritual breakthrough, miracle and victory each and every day of your life!

~Bad Things Happen to Good People~

One day, the angels came to present themselves before the Lord, and Satan the accuser came with them. *"Where have you come from?"* The Lord asked Satan. And Satan answered the Lord, *"I have been going back and forth across the earth, watching everything that's going on."* Then the Lord asked Satan, *"Have you noticed My servant Job? He is the finest man in all the earth-a man of complete integrity. He fears God and will have nothing to do with evil,"* (1:6-8, LASB).

God picked the fight, not the devil! It was God's idea for Satan to attack Job.

Job was not an ordinary man. He was faithful, a man of integrity; a pious man who feared God, avoided evil, and walked uprightly before the Lord. He was married, had ten children, was a very wealthy farmer, herdsman and land owner. Job was the richest of all the men of the East (1:3).

When God is in it, something great is coming out of it! Behind every difficulty, every crisis, trial or problem, there is a meaningful lesson to be learned.

In spiritual warfare, we may not understand the reason why we are experiencing such horrific attacks through our natural senses, and so we must trust God to do what is best for us.

After God urged Satan to attack Job, true to his evil nature, the devil immediately began to slander Job's character. *"But take away everything that he has, and he will surely curse you to your face,"* (1:11, LASB). God would prove and test Job's character by allowing the enemy to tempt him through an onslaught of attacks on his life. The oil will not come out of the olive unless you crush it! Satan was about to crush Job!

In a single day, raiders stole all of Job's livestock and killed all the farmhands; a freak firestorm burned up all the sheep and the shepherds; other raiders stole his camels and killed his servants, and on that very same day, a great windstorm destroyed the house where Job's ten children were gathered and killed them all!

When Job heard the news, he stood up and tore his robe in grief, shaved his head and fell to the ground to worship God. He said, *"I came naked from my mother's womb, and I will be naked when I leave. The Lord gave me what I had, and the Lord has taken it away. Praise the Name of the Lord!"* (1:20-21, NLT)

In spite of all of the awful things that happened, and although he was not able to comprehend the meaning or purpose for these vicious assaults on his life, the Bible says, *"In all of this Job did not sin by blaming God"* (1:22, NLT)!

Job was having his battles in the natural realm, due to a conversation between God and Satan in the spirit realm. He was totally unaware of what was going on behind the scenes; that God had been bragging about him. We have the entire story in front of us, written in the Bible. We know the end of his story. Job did not have that privilege. He had to put his total trust in the Lord.

Undeterred by Job's steadfastness, Satan went back to God and requested permission to attack Job's body, and it was granted. Suddenly and tragically, Job lost his health; sores erupted all over his body from head to foot. Nevertheless, his faith in God could not be shaken.

As he spoke from what must have felt like the brink of death, Job said, *"But as for me, I know that my Redeemer lives and He will stand upon the earth at last. And after my body has decayed, yet in my body I will see God! I will see Him for myself. Yes, I will see Him with my own eyes. I am overwhelmed at the thought"* (19:25-27, NLT)!

Job's heart was fixed. His mind was made up. He would not yield to Satan's temptations! Every attack of Satan against Job failed. He tried everything that he could think of to make Job curse God, and failed in every attempt. Did that stop him? No! The enemy is tenacious and persistent.

Satan used Job's wife to further tempt him. Then said his wife unto him, *"Are you still trying to maintain your integrity? Curse God and die,"* (2:9, NLT).

Apparently, Job's wife wanted God to put Job out of his misery. This is equivalent to the modern-day practice of euthanasia: the act or practice of killing a suffering individual painlessly for reasons considered merciful. To curse God meant sure death!

Neither Job nor his wife was privy to the conversation God had with Satan in Heaven; how Satan had predicted that when his back was up against the wall, Job would curse God (1:11; 2:5).

Job's wife was being used by Satan and she didn't even know it. The accuser of the brethren tried everything, but nothing worked! Job refused to turn his back on God. He would not curse God! So the enemy turned his attention toward Job's wife. Through her, he would further tempt him. Job's wife tried to persuade him to...you guessed it...curse God! Satan is not picky! He will use even those who are near and dear to you to accomplish his goal.

Job had lost all his possessions, his servants, and all of his children! Now his wife was telling him to curse God and die! What testing! Job said to his wife, *"You talk like a foolish woman. Should we accept only good things from the hand of*

God and never anything bad?" So in all this, Job said nothing wrong. (2:10, NLT).

When Job's friends heard of the things he suffered, they got together and traveled from their homes to comfort and encourage him. Brace yourself for this! Instead of consoling their friend, they *accused him* of committing some great sin.

They advised Job to repent, thinking that God was punishing him. Pain is not always the penalty and punishment for sin. Bad things do happen to good people! Job's friends believed that God shields good people from trouble; therefore, he must have sinned. "In all this did not Job sin with his lips," (2:10). The devil thought that he would switch sides, but Job never lost faith in God.

Could it be that God is bragging on you right now? Has God negotiated those attacks of the devil upon you? You may have a problem, but God has a plan. Something good is going to happen for you! You are going to receive double for your trouble; more than you can ask or think!

The secret to Job's success was his steadfast faith and endurance. Job trusted the Lord and kept his integrity in spite of all that the devil did to him. Job did not curse God; he worshipped Him (1:20). If you stop trusting God, you will stop worshipping Him. God is in control of all of your affairs. The power of God shows up strongest when you are weak! God's promised victory is found in His Word: "I AM the Lord and I will bring you out!"

Before God honored Job, He humbled him. This is a perfect example of bad things happening to good people to bring about better! God boasted that Job was a man of integrity, a righteous man who loved and feared God, shunned evil and showed compassion for his fellow man. The fact that Job, a good man, went through so much, teaches us that *bad things do happen to good people!* Suffering is not designed by God to make the believer bitter, only better!

How could a loving, caring, kind and compassionate God permit such a faithful man to suffer so much? Through the things Job suffered — the loss of cattle, camels, sheep, build-ings, servants, and his ten children, being cross-examined and falsely accused of sinning by his friends — God would reveal that there was much room for *spiritual* growth and development.

Job's afflictions worked in his favor; it helped to elevate his devotion to the Lord and made him a better man. He would come to recognize God as Sovereign! His sovereignty means that God is subject to no one. He does as He pleases. God always writes the last chapter.

God declares, *"Only I can tell you the future before it even happens. Everything I plan will come to pass, for I do whatever I wish,"* (Isa. 46:10, NLT). How comforting to Christians to know that even in the severest of trials, God is controlling and orchestrating all the events of our lives!

In his weakness, Job got up in God's face and began his appeal: *"I am disgusted with my life. Let me complain freely. My bitter soul must complain. I will say to God, Don't simply condemn me-tell me the charge You are bringing against me. What do You gain by oppressing me? Why do You reject me, the work of Your own hands, while smiling on the schemes of the wicked?"* (10:1-3, NLT) The one He bragged about is whining, complaining and questioning God!

God sometimes answers a question with a question. When Job demanded answers and accused Him of being cruel, God challenged Job with a barrage of His own questions: *"Brace yourself like a man, because I have some questions for you, and you must answer them,"* (39:7).

Some of God's probing questions are: "Where were you when I laid the foundations of the earth?" (38:4) "Can you direct the movement of the stars?" (38:31) "Are you as strong as God? Can you thunder with a voice like His?" (40:9)

Job got the message: *"I am nothing-how could I ever find the answers? I will cover my mouth with my hand. I have said too much already, I have nothing more to say,"* (40:4-5, NLT). In other words, "Let me shut up!" *"I take back everything I said, and I sit in dust and ashes to show my repentance,"* (42:6, NLT). Job learned that knowing God was more beneficial to him than having the answers to his suffering.

We should not assume that people are suffering because God is punishing them; neither should you think that He is punishing you because of some wrong that you did. Why does God let bad things happen to good people? To show you and Satan what you're made of –He already knows!

From the beginning, Job *did not know the ending*. He did not understand the reason for Satan's fierce attack upon his life, but he continued to exercise tremendous faith in the Lord, and in the end (*after he prayed for his friends*) God ended Job's captivity (42:10) and doubled his salary!

For their misrepresentation of the Lord, even Job's friends had to pay him punitive damages for emotional distress (42:7-9). Job received double for his trouble! His latter end was much greater than the former!

Oftentimes we do not understand the reasons behind Satan's harassments, but we do know that God is in control. Trust God's spiritual provisions for victory (His armor), and like Job you will not break under pressure. Job did not have the Bible, the written Word as we do today; however, he learned about God through the things he suffered.

The Bible says, *"Even though Jesus was God's Son, He learned obedience from the things He suffered,"* (Hebrews 5:8, NLT). God blesses the sufferer through suffering.

If you want to be blessed just like Job, you will have to suffer just like Job suffered. You will have to *be* Job. Your story will not end the same as Job's did. All sufferings are not the same. Everyone is not placed on earth by God for the exact same purpose!

We are all unique, and the problems that we face are uniquely designed according to the purpose and plan that God has for us as individuals. Trust God who writes the end from the beginning.

He has an eternal purpose for your life and the devil cannot prevent you from reaching that goal.

Meanwhile, should we accept only good things from the hand of God and never anything bad?

God doesn't cause bad things to happen. Nevertheless, He does allow bad things to happen to good people for testing, proving, disciplining, maturing and transforming them into the image of His Son. The Christian life involves hard work, trials, difficulties, persecution, deprivation and at times, deep suffering. Do not fix your eyes on your circumstances.

Think about Jesus and all that He has done for you! Think about the Resurrection, the mother of all miracles, which came after the Crucifixion! God helps those who suffer as Christians (I Peter 4:15-16), that they in turn might help others. Bad things *do* happen to good people; however, all things work together for their good!

~Resist the Devil~

God is doing something of eternal significance in your life. In the power of the Holy Spirit, stand firm and resist. Actively oppose the devil, and he will flee from you. The devil is trying to make you switch sides. Tell him, "I would rather fight than switch!" Be determined to serve the Lord.

Think of what the Early Church had to go through. In their eyes, it must have looked as if they were no match for the Roman Empire and its demonized dictators. Christians were ruthlessly pursued, hunted like wild animals, killed and treated like dangerous criminals.

Believers resisted to the death! Standing firm on their belief, many were martyred when forced to fight gladiators and lions to the death. Others were chased and if they fell, they *kept on getting up*, knowing that they would be killed for Christ's sake. These were good people, and bad things were happening to them! Spectators thought that Christians were losers!

To some folks you may look like a loser. To man, Christ did not look like the King of Kings as He walked the earth. He did not look like the Savior of the world. When Christ died on the cross, it looked as if He had lost to the enemy, but the cross was Christ's victory! Things are not always what they look like! On Christ's side there are only winners! He is our Champion!

We are *in* Christ, and have been delivered from the power of Satan unto God. Being *in Christ*, we are overcomers and may experience victory every day right here on earth. The war between Good and evil, God and Satan, will end when God casts him into the lake of fire and brimstone where he will be tormented day and night forever and ever (Rev. 20:10).

God is going to make the devil pay dearly for messing with His children! Until that time comes, we have an enemy to fight. God requires one hundred per cent commitment in His army. It's a *win-win* situation for those who are in Christ Jesus! Absent from the body, present with the Lord.

How do you resist the devil? Submit yourself to God. Remain fully clothed in your armor. Do not war in the flesh, but in the spirit, by reading the Word, prayer and fasting. Carnal weapons cannot get the job done. Satan is bullet-proof, but he is not God-proof!

The wiles of the devil will not work against Christian soldiers who are suited-up! Use every piece of armor that is available to you so that you may have the *explosive ability* to *actively oppose* and *bravely resist* the devil. Stand firm against him and he will flee from you!

CHAPTER FIVE

HAND-TO-HAND MORTAL COMBAT

"For we wrestle not against flesh and blood, but against principalities, against powers, against the rulers of the darkness of this world, against spiritual wickedness in high places," (Eph. 6:12).

B e strong in the Lord, for we wrestle. "We wrestle" speaks of a continuous battle. This verse is written in a tense that indicates the urgent need to be fully equipped with God's weaponry at all times to face the enemy. The problem with many Christians today is that we wrestle *not*.

We are not in a gloom and doom situation. We wrestle, but the outcome is always the same; we win! Unfortunately, some of us would rather run from confrontations rather than face them.

To ignore the devil and think he will just go away, is precisely what he wants you to do. Ignore him; pretend that he doesn't exist. Pretend that the problem doesn't exist. He wants you to think that life should be a bed of roses and everything should be peaches and cream!

The Bible says, *"As sure as sparks from a fire go upward, man is born for trouble,"* (Job 5:7). Job said, *"I was not in *safety, neither had I rest, neither was I quiet; yet trouble came,"* (3:26). Trouble will come, but God has made a way of escape!

God's battles are fought by believers, so *we wrestle*! Because of sin, man is born for trouble. Before the fall, man was born to pleasure. Now it is what it is and we must deal with it, but not on our own. God has created weapons for our warfare to thrash the enemy!

We are engaged in an ongoing, hand-to-hand combat with the forces of darkness. The Church is "not of blood, nor of the flesh, nor of the will of man but of God," (John 1:13).

With many of us, when attacked by the enemy in the natural realm, we rely upon man-made weapons — teachings on positive thinking, CDs, tapes, social media, and so forth — instead of leaning on the everlasting arms (armor) of the Lord.

Our weaponry gives us the supernatural ability to war in the natural as well as the spiritual realm! We must fight poverty, sickness, unemployment, marital problems and so on, with the spiritual armor God has provided for the Church.

The Church is made up of believers who are in a continuous wrestling match with evil. By using the word *wrestle*, the apostle is saying that we come up-close and personal with the enemy every day, in one way or another. For this reason believers must be skilled in all the spiritual weapons of warfare as they wrestle against the powers of darkness. God's armor is vital to your victory!

Wrestle–to fight by grappling and attempting to throw or immobilize one's opponent, striving, to struggle, to deal with, or overcome.

Wrestling–competition between two contenders (good and evil) who strive, struggle or attempt to immobilize each other by struggling in hand-to-hand, up close and personal combat. To "strive" means to "wrestle" to the point of death (in prayer)! You cannot naturally kill a spirit, but you can kill its intent. For this purpose, we wrestle!

The word *wrestle* used here (6:12) is taken from the Greek word *pale* and is used figuratively of the spiritual warfare in which believers are engaged. We are not literally wrestling someone we can see and touch physically. The illustration of wrestling in the natural realm merely describes how we are fighting an enemy in the spirit realm; up close and face-to-face in hand-to-hand combat.

The word "wrestle" is used as a verb and speaks of a *continuous* action. Continuously, every day of our lives, *we wrestle* against evil spirits. We have to deal with issues every day of our lives. By definition, we *fight by grappling and struggling with the enemy every day,* and we overcome.

We are not consumed, because of the goodness of God. It is of the *Lord's mercies that we are not consumed, because His compassions fail not* (Lam. 3:22). Every day, we wrestle. Every day, His mercies are new. God's weapons of mass destruction give you the supernatural ability to *deal with* (wrestle) the devil.

Unlike boxing, which has *distance* between two opponents, wrestling brings the opponents *up close* and personal; face-to-face in hand-to-hand combat. Do not be afraid to boldly confront the devil. He is bold. He will get right up in your face.

With God on your side, you are invincible. Being clothed in the whole armor of God means that you *wrestle* in His dynamic, explosive, unstoppable, supernatural power! God's armor is like Himself — all-powerful!

There are three contenders involved in this spiritual wrestling match: God, you, and the devil! Clothed with the whole armor of God, overwhelming victory is yours! The armor *brings God into the fight* and renders the devil immobile so that you can have at him. Put him under your feet, break his spinal cord and shut him down. Resist the devil and he will flee; he will run away from you licking his wounds, with his tail tucked between his legs!

When Paul wrote, "We wrestle," he was visualizing the Grecian games. The athletes who wanted to *maximize* their athletic abilities were totally *dedicated* and *committed* to their craft.

The athletes trained vigorously every morning, afternoon and night, to be the best that they could be at their game. The most determined athletes could be found working out and training each and every day. Those who were well-trained always won! Sadly, losers were seldom found in the building! Weak believers are seldom found in prayer meetings.

Believers ought to be totally dedicated and committed to the study of God's Word and prayer, for our victory depends upon it. Be skilled in the use of and application of God's Holy Word. Not to do so will impede your spiritual progress and cause you to lose a battle.

"Don't you realize that in a race everyone runs, but only one person gets the prize? So run to win! All athletes are disciplined in their training. They do it to win a prize that will fade away, but we do it for an eternal prize. So I run with purpose in every step. I am not just shadowboxing. I discipline my body like an athlete, training it to do what it should..." (I Cor. 9:24-27, NLT).

The rules for wrestling were -*there are no rules*! The contest was between two contenders who attempted to throw each other down and immobilize each other. In order to achieve this, one might stick his fingers in the opponent's eyes. Satan's rules are: there are no rules! He fights dirty. His aim is to kill (your dreams, vision, ministry) and destroy *you!* Wrestling was a bloody, hand-to-hand, toe-to-toe and struggle-to-the-death sport.

With the spiritual armor God has provided, you will triumph over all principalities, powers, and the rulers of the darkness of this world. When a wrestler, by any means, succeeded in throwing his opponent down on the ground, he would hold him down with his hand around his opponent's neck until he was officially declared the winner!

We have spiritual authority over the devil. Christ has given the Church the *neck of the enemy* and we are declared the winner! Having *the neck* speaks of dominion over someone. In spite of your circumstances, in spite of how dismal things may look to you right now, God has given you the victory! The *neck of the enemy* is in your hand.

~We Wrestle *Not* Against Flesh and Blood~

Do you know why some Christians are still suffering defeat? They have not acknowledged Satan as the destroyer who *uses* people, problems, difficulties and trials as a weapon to defeat them. It's not what you *see* or *feel* with the five senses that are behind your problems. It's what you *do not see* that should concern you. We do not fight *flesh and blood*. The battle is spiritual, not natural.

The source of most of our grief is Satan. Behind the arguments, poverty, the spirit of oppression, depression, rebellion, every cutting word and misunderstanding is an evil *spirit*; the devil. Our warfare is with him. Many Christians are influenced by what they see, hear, feel and think.

Paul told the saints that they were not fighting the Romans (humans); the enemies they fought were much more powerful. To help them understand that spiritual warfare is real, Paul tried to get the message across by using word pictures from the Roman battlefront: *"For though we walk in the flesh, we do not war after the flesh,"* (II Cor. 10:3, KJV).

We are not wrestling against human enemies, but against wicked spirits in high places! Use your spiritual eye to see beneath the surface. If you are fighting flesh and blood, you are wrestling in the wrong area. Battling a carnal war can literally wear you out, while evil spirits roam free to vex people. The real battle goes deeper than what we see in the natural; behind the dishonest mechanic is the evil spirit of greed. Believers must learn to zero in on the enemy.

There are natural wars and there are spiritual wars. We are engaged in spiritual warfare with evil, maniacal, demonic spirits, not humans; however, God has provided all that you need to overcome attacks of the enemy. The devil only wins if you let him. He doesn't stand a chance against a fully armored believer!

You can win every spiritual battle if you put your confidence in God. To trust the Lord is to trust your armor. Trust Him for the salvation of your family, your finances, to heal your body; trust Him to meet all your needs.

Natural battles are won in the spirit realm, first. *"We are human, but we don't wage war with human plans and methods. We use God's mighty weapons, not mere worldly weapons, to knock down the devil's strongholds. With these weapons we break down every proud argument that keeps people from knowing God. With these weapons we conquer their rebellious ideas, and we teach them to obey Christ,"* (II Cor. 10:3-5, LASB).

Like the apostle Paul, we are also weak humans, flesh and blood; and, like the apostle, we do not use human plans and methods to win our battles. God has provided the weapons of our warfare and they are mighty to the pulling down of the enemy's strongholds.

Paul uses wrestling as the sport to describe our warfare against Satan, because wrestling is a one-on-one combat sport. Christians are fighting a one-on-one, *spiritual* combat with the devil and he has no rules! He does not fight fair. Satan will sneak up behind you and body slam you! His aim is to prevent you from attaining your goal.

Satan does not want you to fulfill your purpose and your destiny. The enemy wants to bring you down, immobilize you, and bring you under his control. You are not wrestling with weak people made of flesh and blood, but evil spirits in heavenly realms. We must recognize that behind every *hurtful* situation is an evil spirit. The devil hates man and wants to destroy him, because man is made in the "image and likeness" of God (Gen. 1:26), and Satan hates God and His Church!

We wrestle not against flesh and blood. Your battle is not with another person or religion, atheists, another denomination, human cults, your employer, family members, and so forth. We must stop blaming folks for our problems. Behind your warfare lie demonic spirits that sometimes work *through* humans.

That individual sitting next to you is not the enemy. Your boss is not the enemy. Behind that person's bad behavior there is an evil spirit at work. If you are having problems with your spouse, if your child is being rebellious, it may be the enemy working through them to get to you. Sometimes he even works *through you* to get to someone else! The source of that evil is satanic, not human. On the other hand, some of the issues we wrestle with are imaginary and silly.

Stop arguing with folks! Stop worrying about how someone hurt you, used you, stole from you, borrowed from you and did not pay you back. You will not sit next to that person in Church because they don't like you. Do not allow your emotions to sabotage your blessings.

The weapons that God has provided are spiritual and they are mighty, to the *pulling down of strongholds*. The problem that most Christians have is that when they are confronted with a situation they tend to pick up weapons that are temporal instead of spiritual. The weapons of our warfare — the Word of God, faith, prayer, love — are mighty, through God, and effective!

"We wrestle" clearly means that this warfare will continue until Satan is cast into the lake of fire and brimstone. Christ's defeat of the devil in the wilderness was not His final encounter with the enemy. Satan challenged Christ throughout His ministry.

Through Christ's resurrection power, every enemy that we face here on earth is defeated. As you wrestle with the problems of life and the powers of darkness, keep in mind that the enemy is invisible. The one you see standing in front of you is not really your foe. Your enemy is a *spirit*.

Our Father, God, is Spirit. The secret to having overcoming power and strength is centered in Jesus Christ, the Great Prevailer. Whenever believers lose a fight, it means they are not relying upon the complete spiritual armor of God that is required to defeat unseen, belligerent, evil forces.

Christians are equipped with everything Jesus was equipped with to fulfill their purpose. Nothing can thwart God's plan and purpose for your life, not even Satan and his entire army of demons!

The weapons of our warfare will frustrate the devil's plots. Clothed in God's armor, we have the ability to wrestle with unseen evil powers until — under the mightiness of God's supernatural weaponry — the enemy staggers and falls in defeat, unable to achieve his goal. He wants you to turn your back on God!

~We Wrestle Against Principalities~

After the apostle tells us who we are *not* wrestling (flesh and blood), he goes on to write about what we *are* wrestling. The finger points at Satan. Paul makes it crystal clear that our warfare is not against human beings, but against invisible powers: against evil rulers of the unseen world, mighty powers in this dark world, and against spiritual wickedness in high places that have clearly defined levels of authority.

There are organized satanic forces, evil spirits — spirits of violence, confusion, greed, hate, murder, fear, lust, perversion and spiritual wickedness — in our work places, hovering over our cities, our communities and nations.

Demons are in a real, though invisible sphere, and they are actively opposing (wrestling against) the children of God. They are in hand-to-hand mortal combat with the people of God (Church).

Satan's objective is to destroy all that is holy, all that is pure, all morality, and sense of decency. His aim is also to destroy families, to sow seeds of rebellion in the hearts of teenagers, to weaken governments through immoral leaders who pervert justice, and establish atheistic and ungodly laws. Most of all, the enemy wants to discredit Church leaders and weaken any godly influence they may have in our communities, cities, and nations.

In order to maintain a battle stance against the enemy, every piece of God's weaponry must be utilized. These are not fleshly, carnal weapons that can fail; these are God's *weapons of mass destruction*, weapons that are mighty through God and have the ability to stop any other power.

This subject of spiritual warfare is not very popular. No one wants to hear that they are involved in a war. It may not be as exciting to you as hearing that the "riches of the wicked are laid up for the just," or "money cometh," or "I wish that you would prosper."

You will not hear enough preaching and teaching on the matter of warfare, but the Bible teaches us that Satan is real, and warfare is real. Satan's militia is well organized and ranked in a special order. His aim is to stop the Church from coming into its inheritance; to stop people from being born-again and keep folks in broken fellowship with Christ. He wants you to turn your back on God!

We do not wrestle against flesh and blood, but against *principalities*, against *powers*, against *rulers of the darkness of this world,* against *spiritual wickedness in high places* (6:12). These spirits are all under Satan's command, operating in and through the children of disobedience.

Satan's militia is ranked in this order:
- Principalities
- Powers
- Rulers of the Darkness of This World
- Spiritual Wickedness in High Places

At the very top of Satan's administration are *principalities*. Satan has many principalities at his beck and call. There is always another wicked spirit that is willing to obey his command to steal, kill and destroy you! So *we wrestle,* for, *"Through*

Thee will we push down our enemies: through Thy Name will we tread them under that rise up against us," (Psalm 44:5, KJV). Only by God's power can we push our enemies down on the ground and trample them under feet!

Principalities refer to fallen angels who are always ready to obey their master (Satan). Notice the plural form: principalities. Satan's *principalities* are well-organized and ready to attack without hesitation and without mercy. These forces are dispatched by Satan to commit exceedingly evil, savage, malicious, destructive and abominable acts upon the children of God.

Lucifer was not created evil. God is not the Creator of evil. Everything God created was very good. "And God saw everything that He had made, and, behold, *it was* very good..." (Gen. 1:31). Good *became* evil, through pride, disobedience and rebellion.

Principalities are different orders of angels, good or bad. Through pride, Satan fell from Heaven and took a host of angels with him. Satan was called "Lucifer," *the bright one*. He desired to sit upon God's throne, be worshipped, and to rule Heaven and all the angels. Even though he hates God, Lucifer wanted to be God! Instead of "the bright one" he is now called, "the dark one" or "the prince of darkness."

The devil was cast out of Heaven into the earth and his angels were cast out with him (Rev. 12:9). Those good angels that rebelled against God and fell with Satan became bad angels. Good angels gone bad are called *principalities*.

Satan could not rule in Heaven; however, in earth there is a group over which he does rule. This satanic government is made up of a militia that is well trained and organized, with levels of authority. Its aim is to *try* and put the Church of God, the most powerful vehicle on the earth, out of action!

If you are not being challenged in life, be very concerned. When there is no godly character, the enemy will allow you to run the course more or less without opposition. As long as you are walking in spiritual power, Satan is going to attack you and all that pertains to you. He does not care who you are, what your name or title is, or the amount of money you have in the bank.

Satan wants to sabotage your relationship with God. The enemy wants the Church to lose its effectiveness in the world. That won't happen! Looking around today, he might think that his maniacal schemes are working. However, Jesus said, *"Upon this rock I will build My Church; and the gates of hell shall not prevail against it,"* (Matt. 16:18, KJV).

Due to his excessive enthusiasm for destroying the Church, the devil will send his principalities to fight against you, but they will not prevail against you. We are in the "chariot of triumph" and the reins are in Jesus' hands! The Church *wrestles* and the Church *prevails* against principalities. We are called to wrestle for the unsaved, for the sick, and for the down-trodden.

Satan cannot stop God, and so he will try to stop you! He that *touches you touches the apple of His eye* (Zech. 2:8). In other words: Not to worry, God keeps close watch over you as one who is dearest to His heart. He will allow the enemy to do only so much to you, and no more.

No human is capable of fighting demonic spirits in his own strength and so God has provided Christians with spiritual *weapons of mass destruction* to win every wrestling match with evil principalities. Now that you are armed with God's armor, those bad angels aren't so bad after all!

~We Wrestle Against Powers~

Ranking second in Satan's government of evil spirits are *powers*. The word "power" is taken from the Greek word *exousia*. When used in reference to anyone other than God, it speaks of *delegated* power or authority.

Angelic beings are called "powers" (Eph. 3:10). They are the unseen powers in heavenly places. None would have power at all except that it was delegated to them from God. Only God has absolute, unrestricted, unstoppable, and unlimited power! Power belongs to God. God is power!

These lower ranking *powers* are unseen evil forces in the universe; fallen angels who receive orders from their commander-in-chief, Satan. These evil powers have no rules and Satan gives them no restrictions as to who, how, where, or when to attack. His command is, "Just get the job done!" Demonic powers use their delegated authority to perform every kind of evil imaginable.

All satanic *power* is stoppable, restricted and limited by God! This power (exousia) gives demons freedom of action and right to act; nevertheless, Satan and his army of wicked spirits can act only as the Lord permits. Our Father is sovereign; He does whatever He wants, whenever He wants!

It is God's prerogative to exercise His power as He wills. He is the Final Authority on the outcome of any situation you may encounter. The outcome will be what is best for you.

Evil has no power over a child of God. *"And having spoiled principalities and powers, He made a show of them openly, triumphing over them in it,"* (Col. 2:15, KJV). The word *spoiled* literally means stripped. Christ stripped the enemy of his power; he is on the battlefield, naked!

Your adversary the devil, as a roaring lion, is walking up and down in the earth, seeking whom he may devour. Note: *as a roaring lion* (I Pet. 5:8); he is not a lion. Jesus, the Lion of the tribe of Judah, has all power in Heaven and in earth! Jesus disarmed Satan and his powers and made a spectacle of them!

Through Christ, we have the victory over all principalities and powers; nevertheless, we wrestle!

~The Rulers of the Darkness of this World~

The Greek word *kosmokrator* denotes a *ruler of this world* (Satan), the opposite of which is *pantokrator* which refers to

God, the Almighty Ruler. God is the Ruler of the entire world. Darkness is the kingdom that Satan rules.

Darkness is almost always used in a bad sense. Moreover, the different forms of darkness are so closely allied, it can be difficult to set them apart as to which is cause and which is effect (dark, darken, darkly, darkness). Evil powers are so alike that even though there are ranks, it is hard to distinguish one from another. You won't always know whether it is Satan's power or principality that is behind the attack.

These are spirit powers that — under the permissive will of God and in consequence of human sin — exercise satanic, hostile authority over the world. They have no power over the Church of which Jesus is Head (Col. 1:18).

After the fall of man, the world became a kingdom of darkness because of sin. Satan's is a kingdom of darkness. Christ's is a Kingdom of light. These two kingdoms are diametrically opposed to each other.

Satan is the *ruler* of darkness. Keep *him in the dark!*

~Wicked Spirits in High Places~

Satan is a *wicked spirit* that abides in high places; that is, the heavenly realm.

The word "wicked" comes from the Greek word *poneros*, which is used to describe the devil! It is defined as morally bad; sinful; causing harm, trouble, or distress; obnoxious, as a vile odor.

Most people think of spiritual leaders when they read this. They seem to think the Scripture is referring to a pastor or someone in a high office. Remember the words of Paul, *"We wrestle not against flesh and blood,"* (humans). Behind that false prophet, teacher, preacher, sorcerer and so on are evil, wicked spirits at work!

Christians are in hand-to-hand combat with wicked spirits *in heavenly places* (the air that is spread out between the earth and the stars). Satan is the *prince of the power of the air.*

Christ has overthrown them and has exalted us far *above* them. Jesus came *down* (to earth) to lift us *up* (to Heaven). God brought Jesus safely through His conflicts with spiritual wickedness, caused Him to triumph over them, and gave Him to be Head over all things, to the Church.

Christ was raised from the dead and is seated at the right hand of Power (the position authority), *high above* all wicked spirits. Since our position is *in Christ,* we too are above wicked spirits, not beneath!

"But God, who is rich in mercy, for His great love wherewith He loved us, Even when we were dead in sins, hath quickened us together with Christ; (by grace are you saved); and hath raised us up together, and made us sit together in heavenly places in Christ Jesus," (Eph. 2:4-6, KJV).

The Father has set the Son at His right hand, a place of Sovereign Power, and we are seated with Him. Where? Far *above* all principality and power, might, dominion, and every name that is named, not only in this world, but also in that which is to come (Eph. 1:21). Hallelujah!

Since God is For Us, Who Can Be Against Us?

Repetition is a very powerful teaching tool. The Bible often repeats words, phrases, and terms to show their significance and to reinforce their teaching. For these reasons, some parents repeat things to their children over and over again. They want their children to pay attention and not forget what is being said. Do not smoke. Do not drink alcohol. Do not lie. Say no to drugs!

These are some of the things we say to our children over and over again so that when they are tested they will make wise decisions.

The word "against" is used four times in Ephesians 6:12 in reference to satanic powers. We are *not* wrestling *against* humans. Our enemies are unseen demonic spirits. We are wrestling *against,* 1) principalities, 2) powers, 3) the rulers of the darkness of this world, and 4) spiritual wickedness in high places. Most of what comes to harm you is demonic in origin.

Since God is for us, who can be *against* us? The devil is *against* us. Folks can be *against* us, the whole world can be *against* us, but will not prevail *against* us, for we do not wrestle in our own strength. God has provided His great weapons of mass destruction; His unconquerable resources for us to resist the enemy. In the heat of the battle, you can be cool and calm; you will triumph!

Sickness is an adversary. Poverty is an adversary. We wrestle against the adversary clothed in the unrestricted power of Almighty God! Since God is for us, we do not have to fear those who are against us. Whatever comes *against* you, the Lord will stop it! By God's power, we can surmount every obstacle. The weapons of our warfare are powerful and they are effective!

Calvary is where Satan and his powers were defeated. The enemy knows that — regardless of how horrible your situation may be — because of the cross, you win! Choose whose methods you are going to use, God's or the world's methods; spiritual or carnal.

God owns Christ as one employed by Him and, as such, He sent His Son to die for us while we were yet sinners! All of the powers of darkness came *against* the Son of God in a futile effort to obstruct the work the Father sent Him to do. Satan failed miserably in his attempt.

Christ was faithful; He never deviated from His earthly mission. Jesus saith, *"My meat is to do the will of Him that sent Me, and to finish His work,"* (John 4:34, KJV).

We must be determined to keep on doing what God called us to do, even if the devil tries to slam doors shut in our faces! Be willing to suffer disappointments and difficulties that arise as a result of doing God's will. If you remain fully clothed in the armor that God has provided for you, you are guaranteed the victory, come what may! Actually, you are on the very precipice of a new and fresh anointing; a rhythm of miracles and blessings, to the praise and glory of God!

It is God's will to protect and prosper you in every area of your life! In His kindness, God called us to share in His eternal glory. So after you have suffered a little while, He will restore, support, and strengthen you and place you on a firm foundation (I Peter 5:10-11).

Christ came to die for the sins of man. Healing the sick, opening the eyes of the blind, casting out demons, and feeding the multitudes were fringe benefits — miracles that Jesus performed on His way to the cross! His ultimate goal was to die the humiliating death of the cross so that we might have eternal life. That is how much He loves us!

Our victory was secured at the cross. The enemy has no power over us; we have been delivered from the power of Satan unto God. By His resurrection, Christ disarmed Satan and so disarmed his militia. The devil's diabolical army has been reduced to public ridicule and a laughingstock!

When an athlete loses a fight, he always wishes he had trained harder. When the devil gets the best of us, it is not God's fault. It is because we have not trained hard enough.

Lack of training makes it difficult to resist or subdue the devil when he comes against us. Not spending quality time in the Word of God and prayer will weaken you spiritually.

Battles are won or lost in the spirit realm first. Just as the physical man needs to eat natural food for strength; the spirit-man needs to feast upon spiritual food for strength and power. Satan is no match for the Christian who has been dwelling in the presence of Almighty God!

Christ is our Savior, Redeemer, Champion and Overcomer! He is God's only Begotten Son. Since God gave His best, His

Son, for us. Do you really think that He would not give us the lesser (money, food, clothing, housing, healing, employment)?

The devil cannot break us, because he cannot break Almighty God! I'm not saying that we're God. I'm just saying that we are *in Christ* and He is *in us*, and since God is *for us* the whole world can be *against* us, but "greater is He that is in us" than he (Satan) that is in the world!

Since God is for us, nothing that comes against us will prevail: *"And I say also unto thee, that thou art Peter, and upon this rock I will build My Church; and the gates of hell shall not prevail against it,"* (Matt. 16:18, KJV). They will not succeed. All forces that are opposed to Christ and His Church will be vanquished, overthrown, crushed; smashed! Jesus is the Winner-Man!

CHAPTER SIX

THE COMMAND TO STAND

"Wherefore take unto you the whole armor of God, that ye may be able to withstand in the evil day, and having done all, to stand," (Ephesians 6:13, KJV).

The command to stand is preceded by the provision that gives you the ability to stand; the whole armor of God. Warriors use armor for protection. You can feel secure in the armor of protection that God has provided. He would not command you to stand if He had not supplied *the means* for you to stand. You must "take unto you" or put on the complete outfit of God.

Our English word "panoply" is the equivalent of the Greek word *panoplia* which defines all the equipment worn by heavily armed infantry. In each piece of armor there are certain aspects of God's character and attributes. To have on your armor is to put on Christ!

When you are fully clothed in God's panoplia, you will not easily give in to the pressures of life. You will trust God's love and concern for you. Even if you are pressed to the point of despair, rely upon His ability to deliver you. Your heavenly Father is trustworthy.

If God gives you His Word, it will not be otherwise. He is bound by His Word. Meanwhile, the Lord will give you strength to bear that burden until He sees fit to deliver you. God is able to keep you from falling. So take unto you the whole armor of God and stand.

The temptations that you face are no different from the ones experienced by others. No one is picking on you! Everyone has problems; therefore, put on the complete armor that you may be able to stand firm and resist in the day of trouble.

What are you withstanding? You are resisting the urge to quit your Christian race, the desire to throw in the towel of surrender, and the temptation to turn your back on God!

Wherefore, take unto you the whole armor of God. The word *wherefore* serves as a hook or link between what went before and what follows. Paul is saying, *this is why, on account of,* and *for which very reason:* "this is why" you must keep on the whole armor of God; "on account of" these wicked spirits, demons; you must use every weapon God has made available to you.

There are evil spirits that fight against you, "wherefore" (for which very reason), as an absolute requirement, you must skillfully use the complete armor of God to have the ability to withstand them. Nothing needs to be added and no piece should be eliminated from it.

There is an ongoing war between good and evil and the devil is very proficient (skillful) in what he does; *for this very reason,* you must remain clothed in the full armor of God. You will not *be able to stand* or *withstand* in times of trouble if you are naked.

To stand is 1) to have a sense of your own human frailty, and 2) to be confident in God's power and ability to deliver you out of all your troubles. Winning a battle requires discipline as well as purpose. Having on the whole armor of God enables you to stand with surefooted confidence!

All of us, at one time or other, will face situations where we are either going to stand or fall. God is able to keep us from falling. However, in case we fall, He is able to pick us up!

Having God's armor on or not determines whether you get up or stay down.

The armor of God gives you the ability to withstand great opposition and prepares you for everyday conflicts. A stubbed toe, a migraine headache, a past due bill, a bad toothache, car trouble; these seemingly small and insignificant things can ruin your day! It doesn't take a lot to get on your last nerve when you lay your armor down!

Every piece of armor is vital to the Christian's victorious living! You don't have to know when, where or how the enemy will strike. Just stand firm and be strong in the Lord. We are not called to be losers! God is always on the scene, involved in every aspect of our lives, to give us the victory!

God has already designed our battle clothes, but we must put them on. "Take unto you" is a military term that speaks of *readiness* for warfare. Every Christian soldier must be prepared for warfare. He has to *take up* the armor and put it on for himself. Each believer is responsible for his own spiritual condition. Familiarize yourself with your armor. No soldier can fight God's battles unprepared! To preach the Word, one must know the Word.

The phrase, "take unto you" implies that it is possible for you to forget about your armor. The cares and pressures of life may cause us to neglect our spiritual weaponry. Perhaps you have laid it down. Don't leave your Bible on that shelf! Pick it up, open it and begin reading it once more! This process may be repeated over and over again in your lifetime.

The key to remembering our armor is to study the Bible diligently. This will prevent us from repeating the same mistakes over and over again!

~God's State of the Art Weaponry~

Each Roman soldier's armor was designed to fit his physical stature. An excellent illustration of this is found in I Samuel when Israel fought against the Philistine's giant, Goliath. Saul tried to dress David in his personal armor.

> *So Saul clothed David with his armor, and he put a bronze helmet on his head; he also clothed him with a coat of mail. David fastened his sword to his armor and tried to walk, for he had not tested them. And David said to Saul, "I cannot walk with these, for I have not tested them." So David took them off* (I Sam.17:38-39, SFLB).

In the natural realm, if you wear size twelve shoes and try to squeeze your feet into someone else's size eleven shoes, you will not be able to walk in them. You may squeeze your feet into them, but they will hurt like the dickens! The same goes for the rest of your clothing; you must wear the size that fits you! Spiritually speaking, your problem may require you to spend more time in the Word; another person's problem may require that they pray longer.

Only the Lord knows what it will take for you to get your breakthrough; for you to fulfill your purpose. He knows what it takes for *you* to win *your* battle!

Saul did many things wrong: 1) *he* clothed David, 2) *he* clothed David with *his* armor, 3) *he* put the helmet on David's head, and 4) *he* clothed David with a coat of mail. He, *he*, *he* did it!

Saul clothed David in *his* armor and when David tried to walk, he could not. If a soldier is impeded or slowed down in any way on the battlefield, he could lose his life. Imagine David running toward Goliath with his pants falling down around his ankles!

The words *he* and *his* are repeated several times: *his* armor; *he*, clothed. God must clothe us in *His* armor. Put on the whole armor *of God* and you will be able to stand.

God the Creator has custom-made all humans. Like a tailor, He has custom made His armor to fit each believer. Unless we do things God's way, defeat is assured. To be clothed in God's armor is to be empowered with God's power.

With evident determination, David took Saul's armor off and took up the armor that the Lord provided. With five smooth stones and a sling in his hand, he ran toward the battle line to meet Goliath. Using a sling and a stone he brought the Philistine giant down, stood over him, and with Goliath's own sword he cut the giant's head off!

No man-made, state-of-the-art-weapon can overpower God's power! Faith in God's ability to deliver him gave David the victory! In the words of Rick Renner, David was, "Dressed to Kill!"

Wherefore, *this is why* you must put on the whole armor of God and to be able to stand. With God's armor, if I fall I will arise!

David's weapons seemed foolish and laughable to Goliath, but they were mighty through God, who takes foolish things to confound the wise. It was not the sling and the stones that David relied upon; he put his confidence in the Lord.

When threatened by Goliath, David boldly replied, *"You come to me with sword, spear, and javelin, but I come to you in the Name of the Lord Almighty-the God of the armies of Israel, whom you have defied,"* (17:45, LASB). Faith was David's weapon. He fought with the armor God provided and won! Never for a moment did David think that his weapon would fail!

Goliath, who represents the devil, was defeated with the armor that God provided, not man's so-called state-of-the-art weaponry. Man-made weapons cannot enter the realm of the spirit, but the armor of God has the ability to penetrate into the spiritual as well as the material realm!

Do not try to fight your battles on your own; you will fail. Jesus never fails! Only God has the unrestricted, unstoppable, unlimited, supernatural power to bring our giants (fears, difficulties, problems, trials, disappointments, hurts, worries) down!

~Still Standing~

"Therefore, put on every piece of God's armor so you will be able to resist the enemy in the time of evil. Then after the battle you will still be standing firm," (6:13, NLT).

Since we are Christians we should expect ridicule, suffering, rejection, trials, opposition and temptations. For these reasons, we need God's *weapons of mass destruction* in operation at all times. God's weapons are both defensive and offensive.

The Lord empowers you to *stand* and *withstand* the storms of life. Whatever happens, you will be found *standing* firm after the battle, ready for the next encounter. This does not mean that you are looking for trouble, but you are not going to run away from it either!

To "withstand" means to be able to resist; stand firm against; endure, confront, defy, face, hinder, hold out. Your spiritual weaponry gives you the supernatural ability to withstand every foe!

Whenever Christians are armed with God's *weapons of mass destruction,* they have the ability to *resist* temptation; *stand firm against* the adversary; *defy* the devil; *face* every foe; *hinder* and *obstruct* the progress of all opposition and *hold out* to the end.

Put on God's armor and you will have the greatest victories ever! Instead of running away from a problem, you will be able to stand; *confront* and *contradict* anything that does not agree with what God says. The armor of God empowers us with the ability to *defy, face, hold out,* and *resist* the devil in the evil day; that is, in any crisis, at all times!

We will be able to stand under pressure, because the Lord will make our feet like hinds' feet; that is having the ability to stand with surefooted confidence; unlikely to stumble or fall. You will be able to endure every hardship successfully. God does not want His children to lose any battle. He certainly does not want you to be at the devil's mercy. The enemy cannot win unless you forfeit the fight by taking your armor off!

The word "withstand" also comes from the Greek word *anthistemi,* which means "to resist" and is compared to "antihistamine," a drug used to relieve the symptoms of allergies and colds.

The armor of God works like an antihistamine. The first part of antihistamine is "anti," which means *against.* God's armor works *against* the devil's stratagems.

At times it may seem as though your armor is not working for you, but it is. As long as you trust your armor, you trust God. He will make the enemy pay dearly for messing with you! God promises to help you win every battle. He will not only deliver you *out of* the hands of the enemy; He will deliver your enemies *into* your hands and make them your footstool.

The second part of the Greek word for "withstand," *anthistemi,* is *histemi* which means, *to cause to stand.* Your armor will help you *to stand,* no matter how strong the storms of life rage against you. When times are hard your armor will undergird you, lift you up and place you on your feet. Satan will be the one who is down on the ground, looking up at you!

"Rejoice not against me, O mine enemy: when I fall, *I shall arise...*" (Micah 7:8). Even if the Lord allows you to fall, you will get up stronger, wiser, and better!

Be it ever so slight, God takes offense at anything and anyone who tries to hurt His children. He views the attack as coming against Himself; to borrow a phrase from the sermon, "The Prodigal Son" by James Weldon Johnson: Satan, "your arm's too short to box with God."

Antihistamine *puts a block on the* production of histamines, a white crystalline compound that occurs in plant and animal tissue and is believed to cause allergic reactions.

In using the word "withstand," the apostle is saying that the spiritual armor of God is to the believer what an antihistamine is to an allergy or cold.

Antihistamine *blocks* histamines, which cause allergies and colds. Similarly, the armor of God has the supernatural ability to *block* Satan's jabs. His punches will be like a boxer's jab hitting air. You will not *yield* to Satan's temptations!

To withstand in the evil day is not a passive idea, but strongly suggests that you must forcefully stand your ground. The Word of God says, "Put on the whole armor of God" and you will be able to withstand in *the evil day.* The "evil day" is the Christian's every day clashes with the forces of darkness. You have the ability to block every swing that the devil takes at you!

We know the outcome of the war, but individual battles can be lost if you have not done all that is required of you. Be armed when you face the enemy in combat. God's soldiers stand to see the salvation of God with them.

The person that is *still standing* after a face-to-face encounter with the devil is always the one who is clothed in God's armor. Doubting God or His armor means that you are unprepared and it gives Satan advantage. Keep your war clothes on! Be fully equipped and prepared to pursue your purpose.

In the event that you are not *standing firm* after a battle, don't blame yourself and don't blame God. You should be stronger than the storm that you are going through.

The command is: *having done all to stand* (v.13). After you have done everything necessary to win the battle, stand. Yes, you have defeated the devil in the previous battle, but don't let your guard down; he's coming back. Satan is persistent. That is why he is called *diabolos*. He is just waiting for the right time to strike again and again!

Indeed you may be a good Christian, but you still have an enemy to fight! Although you walk in the Spirit, pray continuously and preach to the masses, trouble will come your way. Even though you are a soul winner and you give to the poor and needy, the enemy will assault you. Your defense is to be clothed in your armor.

Jesus said of Himself, "But this *happened* that the Word might be fulfilled which is written in their law, *'They hated Me without a cause,'*" (John 15:25, SFLB). After you have done all that you know to do, stand; remain in a battle stance. Never be chased by the enemy; we do the chasing!

Until Christ comes back for His Church, the enemy will be in an ongoing war with Christians; always waiting for an opportunity to pounce on them like a lion. Good news! God has fixed the fight so that at the end of every battle, the fully armed believer will be found *standing!*

We can safely put our confidence in God. He will never abandon His children; "*Lo, I am with you always,*" (Matt. 28:20) and "*I will never leave you, nor forsake you,*" (Heb. 13:5). No one else can make this promise and keep it but God!

Life consists of hills and valleys, ups and downs, but our warfare will only be accomplished after we *have done all* that we are called by God to do. If you are alive and still on the earth, then you have not done *ALL*. Keep on standing!

The Bible says: "*Whatever your hand finds to do, do it with your might; for there is no work or device or knowledge or wisdom in the grave where you are going,*" (Eccl. 9:10). "*The race is not to the swift, nor the battle to the strong…*" (9:11). "*…he that endures to the end shall be saved,*" (Matt. 10:22). To "withstand" is to patiently endure to the end!

After you have done all that the situation demands, continue to stand firmly in Christ. It could be that God has already answered your prayer, but it's not the answer you were expecting. The devil is a con artist; do not let him con you into thinking that God has deserted you! He can be very con-vincing; do not underestimate him.

God permits Satan's attacks, trials and tests to expose the hypocrisies of man and help us become more like Christ. Presently, we are not quite what He has in mind.

Nothing is impossible with God. When you are facing hardships, it may be an indication that you have taken a stand for Jesus.

When the *dust clears,* you should be found with your head held high, shoulders back; *standing* with your feet firmly planted on the Solid Rock, Christ Jesus!

CHAPTER SEVEN

THE WRITTEN WORD OF GOD

"Stand therefore, having your loins gird about with truth ..." (Eph. 6:14).

Every Christian soldier must be clothed in God's armor, ready to go onto the battleground (world) and fight a good fight! The Lord's battles must be fought the Lord's way!

Scripture declares that "the god of this world has blinded the minds of them which believe not," (II Cor. 4:4). Throughout the ages Satan, the enemy of God, man and the Church, has lied, deluded, cheated, misled, outwitted, duped and blinded man from seeing truth.

Due to his impending doom, Satan has vehemently accelerated his attacks upon this world, and especially upon the Church. The spirit of error that has crept into the Church comes from Satan. For this reason, every soldier of the Lord must have his *loins gird about with truth*. Christians must be rooted and grounded in the Word of God, in Truth. Clothe your mind with Truth!

All Christians should have an intimate knowledge of the Bible. Only truth can set man free from the bondage of sin and Satan. When believers fail to put on the girdle of truth, the enemy will attack the Church with the spirit of error!

Christians must wear the same belt of truth that Christ wore to conquer the enemy. He faced every attack with His loins girded with truth. Jesus Christ knew the truth concerning who He was (the Son of God), and His mission and purpose; to destroy the works of the devil. He was prepared for all of Satan's attacks, because His mind was girded with truth. Christians must face every battle with their loins girded with truth. What you do not know *can* hurt you!

The revelation that the apostle Paul received from the Holy Spirit to describe the spiritual weapons of warfare for the Church is derived from the Roman soldier's military outfit. Each piece of the Roman soldier's military armor describes a distinct attribute that is fulfilled in Christ.

Satan uses lies to create doubt in your mind concerning God's Word. If you doubt God's Word, you doubt God! Satan perverts (adds to, takes away from) God's Word to make you question God's love for you. He wants you to doubt God's promises. Satan desires that we believe his word (lies) rather than God's Word (truth). Cover your mind with truth!

Whenever we disregard the Manual (the Bible) we suffer defeat, because the Word of God is the weapon the enemy fears most! The strength and power needed to be an undefeated spiritual warrior depend upon your knowledge of truth. Truth is power and knowledge of truth is power!

Discipline yourself to study the Bible daily; receive the written Word into your heart, meditate upon it and obey its commands. God's people perish for lack of knowledge.

The Holy Spirit (the Spirit of Truth) leads and guides into all truth. Since it is still God's truth versus Satan's lies, truth must be held on to tightly, as a person wears a girdle. There is no other weapon as powerful as the Word of God, yet men continue to reject God's truth and believe Satan's lies.

Our knowledge of the written Word of God is a *weapon of mass destruction*, a lethal weapon against Satan. It renders the enemy powerless! The more you use it, the more effective you become in hitting your target (the devil)! Through the Holy Spirit, the Agent of the Word, you can experience your personal breakthrough of power every day of your life.

Jesus was able to stand against Satan's tactics because His mind was girded with Truth. He knew that He was the Only Begotten Son of God (truth); He knew that the Father sent Him to die for the sins of the world (truth); Jesus knew that Satan would be defeated at Calvary (truth); and Jesus knew that after His work was finished, He would return to the Father (truth)!

The Bible is the only *visible* armor of God by which the *invisible* Spirit of God works through the believer. If you desire to be filled with the Holy Spirit, you must be *full* of the Word.

Being filled with the Spirit is the direct result of studying and meditating upon the Word of God every day of our lives. When we study the Bible, we are dealing with the Words that the Holy Spirit teaches (John 14:26). The Holy Spirit only teaches that which God the Father gives Him to teach or speak. Don't rely upon what "he" or "she" said; trust what God says!

Regardless of the consequences, we must always seek after Truth. Jesus said to Pilate, "To this end was I born, and for this cause came I into the world, that I should bear witness unto the truth," (John 18:37). Christians must strive to follow Christ's example.

The Bible helps us to know and keeps us in harmony with the mind and will of God for our lives. The will of God is what the Word of God declares. His will is governed by His Word. The more you read and obey the Bible, your knowledge of God increases; you will grow spiritually and you increase in favor with God and man. Your efforts will be richly rewarded.

Never let a crowded schedule keep you from Bible study. Set aside some time each day to read the Word of God. If you desire to be a powerful warrior for the Lord, you must gird your mind with truth. Jesus' mind was girdled with God's *weapon of mass destruction* — the Word!

Being caught up in the day-to-day cares of this world can cause you to neglect your armor. To undervalue spending quality time reading your Bible is a sure way to experience defeat. You cannot make it without the Word. The ability to stand is based upon one's knowledge of the Word of God. Your loins must be girdled with truth; "Thy Word is Truth!"

The devil loves it when we are busy. As long as we are too busy to read the Bible, the devil is happy! He loves it when we are so overwhelmed with the cares of life that we neglect the Word of God. Instead of getting up a half hour earlier or staying up a half hour later in order to search the Scriptures, we succumb to the wiles of the devil.

Satan's strategy is to keep you from the only weapon that God has designed to seal his doom! The Word of God is a lethal weapon that will soon bring Satan's evil reign to an end!

The *centerpiece* and *foundation of the Christian's life* is the Bible. It is the believer's source of provision, protection and strength. The Bible is the most important Book in the world. No other book anywhere, written on any subject, is more important or even worthy to be compared to the Bible. He that loves God loves His Bible. Neglect of it will be to your ruin.

The Bible has been described as the believer's road map to victory! When we are ineffective, defeated and lose our way in life it is usually due to a lack of knowledge of the Word; or else we have allowed the cares of this world to choke the Word of God out of our hearts.

It is unnecessary for Christians to worry. Apply the Word to every situation. No circumstance or crisis is stronger than the Word of God. Word in, worry out! Be constant and vigilant in reading and studying the Bible. The indwelling Holy Spirit will help you to trust the Word of God, a mighty weapon sent down from heaven to earth; from God to man.

Jesus Christ, the Living Word, was obedient to the written Word. Although one can physically handle the Holy Bible, it only works when you read it and obey what is written therein.

Anchor your life upon the Word of God. In the very beginning of his letter to the Ephesians, Paul prays that believers would *know* the hope of God's calling; *know* the riches of God's inheritance and the great power of God witnessed in Christ's resurrection and ascension.

The Bible is filled with blessings God has for His followers. Nothing can alter or reverse His promises or provisions for the Church; however, the way to appropriate these blessings is to *know* the Word. It's not what *he* said, or *she* said, or *they* said; it's what God said! Know the enemy, know yourself, but most importantly, *know* the One in whom you believe. *Know* God!

Lack of knowledge of the Word dims and blurs your vision of Christ. God increases you as His Word increases in you. Defeat is possible when our spiritual vision is obstructed!

How can we know Him and the power of His resurrection if we do not read His Word? Quality always wins over quantity! We should not let one day pass without spending *quality* time reading the Bible. Sometimes it only takes five minutes and one verse of Scripture to make your day!

~The Loin Belt~

The first article of clothing that the Holy Spirit draws the apostle's attention to is the soldier's belt. On the surface, this illustration seems odd when referring to the Word. In complimenting someone on their attire the first thing out of your mouth will hardly be, "I love your belt!" You may comment on the outfit or the shoes, but the belt (though important to the entire ensemble) is not usually the first article of clothing that catches one's attention.

When a Roman soldier was completely outfitted, he was a sight to behold, standing with his head held high, shoulders thrown back and his feet firmly planted on the ground. Spectators gasped at how gorgeous the soldiers looked, but they were never so impressed with his belt.

"Stand therefore, having your loins girt about with truth;" (6:14, KJV) *"Stand therefore, and fasten the belt of truth around your waist,"* (v.14; NLT).

The military belt is also called the girdle. The apostle wrote: *fasten the belt of truth around your waist.* When referring to the belt as "truth," Paul is speaking of sincerity and integrity.

The Roman soldier's belt was made of strong, durable leather and measured about six inches wide. For the Christian to "stand therefore" as the Scripture says, they must utilize each and every piece of their spiritual armor. The belt was no exception; actually, the belt was the underpinning of the soldier's armor and clothes.

Truth (sincerity and integrity) is the underpinning, the foundation of the Christian life.

The soldier's belt may have been the least attractive in appearance, but it was the *central* and most important of all the armor. Without the belt, the soldier's outfit would fall apart. Pulled tightly around the soldier's waist like a girdle, the belt held the entire outfit together. The Roman soldier depended on this support, because it helped to free his hands when fighting.

Central and most important to any believer is the *belt*, the Bible, the written Word of God which holds your life together when everything seems to be falling apart. All that we do as Christians should be based upon the Word of God; it should line up with the written Word, the Bible, sometimes called the Court of Final Appeal.

The Word of God (the belt, Bible) holds everything together (girds); your mind, your life, your family, ministry, and so forth.

Scripture cannot be broken or deprived of its inerrancy! The Bible is the inspired revelation of God. My father Ezekiel (not the prophet) who is now with the Lord; lovingly, respectfully and fittingly called the Holy Bible "the Good Book!" The Bible is indeed the greatest Book.

Bend your head; lean toward the mouth of God; put *your ear to the Words of God's mouth*. Diligently study the Bible. The Word of God is eternal and unfailing.

God is outspoken! His Word is irrevocable and irreversible; it cannot be altered, restricted, restrained, checked, stopped, or changed. No human is smart enough to edit the Bible, to add to it or subtract from its contents.

When the Lord gives you His Word, it cannot be otherwise! It is written in the Bible that the righteous are blessed and no one can reverse it! *"Behold, I have received commandment to bless: and He hath blessed; and I cannot reverse it,"* (Num. 23:20, KJV). Man cannot reverse what God says! Shame on those who don't spend time reading the Holy Bible and abuse this wonderful, God-given privilege!

The loin belt was very significant in that it was: 1) used to protect the lower part of the soldier's body, and 2) it held everything together — the clothing underneath and the soldier's weaponry.

The key to advancement in the Kingdom of God is *spiritual* knowledge and understanding of the Bible. God is Spirit. They that worship Him must worship Him in Spirit and in Truth.

Throughout our lives, we are going to experience difficulties that will require God's help. How will you cope with your problems? How will you make it through those trying times? Only in the Bible will you find a solution to every one of your problems. No one can be an effective witness for the Lord and testify of His goodness without an intimate knowledge of His Word.

God made promises to you that He must keep, for God cannot lie. If He promised it, He will make it good. The Lord takes responsibility for everything He says; it will surely come to pass. Tighten your belt. Immerse yourself in the Bible and He will demonstrate His mighty power to you and through you, for His glory!

The Word of God is like medicine; it works best when taken as prescribed. It's not the doctor's fault if the medication doesn't work as it should if instead of once a day as directed, you have been taking that medicine only once a week! You wonder why that fever won't go down!

Spending time in the Word of God is the most important, and the best thing that we could do. It's not God's fault you lost that battle! You may need to tighten your belt (study). Roman soldiers won battles, because the belt was pulled tightly around the loin area for protection.

Their weapons were the best made, but what good is the weapon if the soldier is not using it? Confident that their reproductive area was well protected, soldiers were able to concentrate on wiping out the enemy army! A good, working knowledge of the Bible gives you confidence.

Satan is the prince of darkness. He wants to keep you in the dark (ignorant). The devil wants you to think that God doesn't care about you. If he succeeds, you may find it difficult to read the Bible. God never turns His back on us; we turn away from Him. He wants to provide for your every need. Do not be ignorant of Satan's devices. Do not be ignorant of the promises of God, either!

When the Roman soldier's belt was fastened tightly around his waist, this was a sign that he was prepared for warfare, or that he was still *on duty*. When his belt was loosely fastened, it meant that he was *off duty*. No Christian soldier is ever *off duty*. Christians should meet each day with their belts tightly fastened, ready to fight the battle when necessary. The girdle of truth should be tightly buckled around the waist at all times.

Just as the belt was the foundation and centerpiece of the Roman soldier's armor, the Bible is the Foundation and Centerpiece of the believer's life. If, for some reason, the believer loosens his belt, he must quickly repent and tighten that belt again!

The Bible is not just for show, to be utilized only on Sunday or for some special occasion. God's Word is the rule and standard of conduct by which Christians live every day of their lives.

The rules have not changed, and God will never lower His standard to make up for our lack of knowledge of His Word.

At the end of verse thirteen, you will find the word *stand* with a period after it: "...and having done all, to *stand*." A period means to stop. It speaks of an interval of time.

Problems may cease for a while. The enemy seems to have gone away. He may stop bothering you, but it's only for a period of time. Brace yourself!

To stand means to maintain an upright position with your armor intact, even after a battle. After you have done all that the situation demanded, continue to stand, ready for the next battle.

Stand therefore, having your loins gird about with truth (v.14). In spiritual warfare there must be a continual dependence upon God's Word, the belt which represents the written Word of God, the Bible. You can stand, withstand, and stand again on the Word.

The Bible is complete. The Word of God is perfect. It needs nothing added to or deleted from it to make it better. No one is smart enough to edit the Bible. What human being is there on earth that has the knowledge, wisdom or capability to do so? God's Word is infallible. The Bible will remain forever, unchanged!

The word "stand" at the end of verse thirteen is followed by a period (stop), implying the end of something. In other words, the Lord has brought you through that situation and you have the victory. There is an interval of time between the end of verse thirteen and the beginning of verse fourteen. There is a "period" of rest. No war lasts forever. You breathe a sigh of relief. The bills are paid; you've been promoted on your job and all is well in the family.

Do not let your guard down. Do not take your armor off! Paul goes on to say that each victory only sets the stage for the next battle. The "stand" at the end of verse thirteen is not the same "Stand" that begins verse fourteen. He is intimating that another battle is coming. No sooner is one battle over than another begins! Be ready for the next problem, the next difficulty, the next trial.

To "have on" teaches us that even when we are not actively fighting, we should remain clothed in our armor; prepared for war at a moment's notice! Who knows what emergency may arise? The enemy is just waiting for the right moment to strike. Do not worry! Trust God.

Like a girdle, keep that belt pulled tightly around your waist. Study the Bible and you will learn that God intends for you to win every battle. Scripture reading will increase your confidence in the Lord your God. He will bring good out of the worst situation.

You may have heard someone say, or you yourself may have said, "As soon as I come out of one situation, another problem arises." With your loins girded with truth, *you will not fall apart* under the weight of your burdens. The *belt* will keep you together when everything seems to be falling apart around you.

Being clothed in God's spiritual armor makes you thick-skinned; you will not fall apart when bullied, mocked, ridiculed, or derided. Regardless of the situation, you will remain rock-steady!

When all hope seems to be gone, cling by faith to the Word of God. Read the Bible. Apply the Word of God to your situation and keep on standing. Believe the Word. God is not bound by anything but His Word. Either you trust the armor that God has provided for you or you do not. The stream is divided and there is no middle ground.

If we suffer defeat, it is always our fault, not God's. He promises, "I will be with you," "I will not fail you" and "I will not forsake you," (Josh.1:5). Wherever you go, whatever you do, whatever you are going through, God is with you to give you good success!

Clothed in God's armor with every struggle, every problem, every attack of the enemy, believe it or not you're getting stronger and stronger! Maybe you do not feel like it, but, *"Nay, in all these things we are more than conquerors through Him that loved us,"* (Rom. 8:37, KJV).

When you need a word to bring you out and keep you going, you can go to your Bible, open it, read it for yourself, and believe it. The Bible is trustworthy! In it you will find everything that you need. Your mind must be prepared; girded for action!

"Wherefore gird up the loins of your mind" before going onto the battlefield! If the loins (mind) fail, the entire body fails. The best way to prepare for victory is to make Bible study a daily priority in your life. The first piece of armor that the Roman soldier put on as he prepared to go into battle was the belt!

What a powerful weapon the belt (the Bible) is to the believer! Do not accept everything you hear others say, regardless of who they are. Search the Scriptures yourself to see if what you are hearing lines up with the written Word of God!

"And the people of Berea were more open-minded than those in Thessalonica, and they listened eagerly to Paul's message. They searched the Scriptures day after day to see if Paul and Silas were teaching the truth. As a result many Jews believed, as did many of the prominent Greek women and men," (Acts 17:11-12, LASB). The truth set them free!

To stand, with your belt pulled tight like a girdle and your loins girded or "girdled" with truth, denotes *readiness for action;* it speaks metaphorically of *readiness for active service.* Knowing the Word of God and living it qualifies one for *active service:* to win others to Christ. If anyone asks you about your Christian hope, be *ready* to explain it in a loving and respectful manner.

The written Word of God is the only weapon whereby the devil can be defeated! He is not afraid of or intimidated by carnal weapons such as profanity, knives, guns, spears, daggers or swords.

The devil is not concerned about your feelings. Your tears do not invoke any sympathy from Him. The only thing that makes him tremble is the Word of God, because it seals his doom!

The Church is in the heat of a battle fighting against a cunning, tenacious and persistent foe. He may strike at any time, and so we must keep our *loins girdled* tightly *with truth.*

During the time of the Jews' Passover, the best rabbis of the land would gather to teach great truths among themselves. The Coming Messiah would be the theme of discussion.

In Luke chapter two, at the age of twelve, Jesus was found (not that He was lost) in one of the temple apartments where the doctors of law held their schools for debates, teaching and hearing the Word of God (v.46). All who heard Jesus were amazed, not at His age, but at the depth of His understanding, His probing questions, and answers. His *loins were girded* with truth.

The apostle Paul studied in the Temple courts under Rabban Gamaliel, a celebrated doctor of the law, who was respected by all the people as one of its foremost teachers. Jewish doctors of law state that at the age of twelve, Jewish boys must begin to fast on the Day of Atonement, and at the age of thirteen he becomes *a son of the commandment.*

While other children were playing, Jesus sat inquiring after knowledge of the Word of God. All Christians must be girded with that which Jesus was girded –Truth! Jesus loved the Word. Shouldn't we love what Jesus loved?

Jesus' *life* and His *lips* reflected the fact that He delighted Himself in the commandments. As to the perfection of His divine nature, there could be no increase at all. As to His human nature, the child grew physically, and His soul grew and increased in wisdom through His knowledge of the Word. Jesus desired to increase in knowledge and to communicate that learning to others. He was *preparing* Himself for *active service* for His Father.

David said, *"Thy Word have I hid in my heart, that I might not sin against Thee,"* (Psalm 119:11, KJV). The word "hid" used here means to *treasure.* It is not the same as our English word "hide," which means to remain out of sight. What good would that do? Who would it benefit to hide God's Word and save it for future use or, even worse, never put it to work?

We must spend the time of waiting for Christ's return caring for His people and doing His work here on earth, both within and without the Church. The statement made by David shows the depth of his love for God's Word.

With the Scriptures *treasured* in your heart, you do not have to be afraid of what the enemy can do to you. Be afraid of having a lack of knowledge!

During the time of trouble, you can draw strength from the Seed of Truth that is *treasured* in your heart. Let the Word of God dominate your life. The one who has the Word accumulated in his or her heart will not sin very easily. Christians whose minds are girded with Truth will not be easily swayed or deceived by Satan's lies. Truth dispels lies as light dispels darkness.

Make the Bible a vital, integral part of your life by reading and meditating upon it daily.

Prayer is vital to ministry and worship is vital to ministry, but ministry cannot be successfully built on praise and worship only. You cannot serve well as a Christian when the Word of God does not have an active, functional role in your life. It takes natural food to grow physically; likewise, it takes spiritual food to grow spiritually.

Make daily Bible study the number one priority in your life, and then you will prosper and have good success. *"Study this book of the Law continually. Meditate on it day and night so you may be sure to obey all that is written in it. Only then will you succeed,"* (Josh. 1:8, LASB).

The belt held everything together, including the soldier's tunic that was worn under the armor. This freed the soldier's hands to wield his sword or throw his dagger. Without the belt the soldier would have a serious problem fighting; not only would his military outfit fall apart, it would be virtually impossible to fight and carry the extremely heavy equipment at the same time.

Roman soldiers utilized all of their weapons in battle. To have to omit even one piece, regardless of its weight, meant the difference between life and death. He might be able to fight for a while without the belt, or the sword, but not for long.

Daily Bible study and meditation are essential for Christian growth and development. It may seem as though you are prospering even though you have neglected your Bible, but sooner or later you will find that you are falling apart; that you are not functioning as well as you thought. You may get by for a while, but not for long! The Word should be in your mouth and in your heart. The Bible will not always be at your immediate disposal.

The Holy Bible — the "Book of Books," a precious gift, and the only *dependable* light in this dark world — was sent down from heaven to earth; from God to man. It is the most powerful Book that has been or ever will be written! How will you escape if you neglect such a great gift?

Think of the blood of Jesus; think of the blood of the all those who died that we might have the Bible in our possession. Thank God for His unspeakable gift!

God doesn't speak to everyone through a burning bush that is not consumed, or in thunder and lightning, but He does speak to everyone through the written Word. Some things are only known to God; nevertheless, the commands of His voice are written down for all to read and obey. To obey God's Word is to obey His voice!

Clothe your mind with truth and you will not be deceived by the devil's lies. Jesus confronted, disarmed, and conquered Satan by quoting Scripture.

Having His mind girded with truth, when the devil approached Christ with a *perverted* version of the Word, He spoke the unadulterated version with power and authority. Jesus had the treasure of the Word in His heart; out of the abundance of the heart the mouth speaks. From the Word stored up in His heart, Jesus spoke three small but powerful words, "It is written!"

The legacy of the Word of God in days of old was passed on by word of mouth. Later, when man began to write, we were given a more permanent and accurate method of passing on the Word of God. We have the Bible, the *written* Word of God.

Satan is very skillful and cunning in trying to make Truth sound like a lie. If you are not grounded and rooted in the Word of God, he will have no difficulty deceiving you! Satan said unto Him, *"If thou be the Son of God, command this stone that it be made bread."* Jesus had not eaten for forty days; He was human and He was hungry, but Jesus answered him, saying, *"It is written, that man shall not live by bread alone, but by every word of God,"* (Luke 4:3-4, KJV).

Christ stood the severest tests and temptation undaunted, undeterred, and unafraid. Satan's aim was to make Christ bypass the cross; however, the wilderness experience where He spent forty days fasting and praying, did the opposite of the devil's intent; it prepared Jesus for His earthly ministry. *"And Jesus returned in the power of the Spirit,"* (Luke 4:14).

Paul admonishes believers to wear the loin belt of truth and never take it off. Jesus is the Way and the Truth. Satan wants you to lose your way; to believe a lie instead of Truth.

The Bible exposes the lies of Satan and men, but the entire message of the Bible is that of Truth. The truth that Christ reveals in the Bible is the way to eternal life and happiness.

The devil took his best shot, but Jesus couldn't be blindsided. He permitted the enemy to say and do all that he could against Him, but did not yield to Satan's temptations.

One of the things that the enemy attacked was Jesus' Sonship. He said, "If thou be the Son of God…" Jesus knew that He was the Son of God, because God said so, *"Thou art My Beloved Son,"* (Luke 3:22). Satan used this trick: "Did God indeed say?" on Eve and it worked, but it did not work on Jesus!

The Word of God reacts like a mighty hammer that breaks rocks in pieces. It pounds home its message. Satan got the message. The devil departed.

If you are experiencing something painful right now, if there is a crisis in your life, trust your spiritual armor; tighten your belt. Put your confidence in what the Bible says: *"Many are the afflictions of the righteous: but the Lord delivereth him out of them all,"* (Ps. 34:19, KJV). Your circumstances are the Lord's opportunities to show you His power to deliver!

Discipline yourself to read the Word. Do not tuck your Bible away on the back shelf and expect to be on fire for the Lord. Hold on to the truth of Christ's teachings, because your life depends on it. In spiritual warfare, we must never forget the reality of Christ's life and His love for us.

Church functions are fine. Prayer meetings, praise and worship are essential to spiritual growth and maturity; but none of these should supersede or take place of the Word of God. Be strong in the Word and you will be strong in the Lord. Never let the Book of Instruction, through neglect, depart out of your heart, your mouth, or your hand!

Roman soldiers maintained proper upkeep of their weapons daily. They were always prepared for war! Likewise, Christians are to pay close attention to their *spiritual* armor. Spend quality time in the Word of God and prayer. No spiritual battle can be won without the Word.

Unfortunately, there are some Christians who dust off their Bibles for Sunday services and do not pick it up again until the following Sunday. Then there are those who leave their Bibles in the car on the dashboard until the next Church service! That way they don't have to be burdened with carrying it. It's too much trouble! So what makes us think we can escape if we neglect and ignore this great gift from God?

Relying upon someone else for a word is no substitute for reading it yourself. Most of us do not have a clear understanding of Scripture, because we do not read the Bible consistently, with a desire to know the Word of God ourselves and to obey what it says.

Folks have a million excuses why they do not read the Bible. They say, "The Bible is hard to understand." "The Bible has too many rules." "I cannot understand the Old Testament. Why do we have to read the Old Testament anyway? We are under a new covenant!" "The Bible was written by man to brainwash you." "The Bible is boring." The excuses go on and on.

We can always find an excuse for something we don't want to do. There is a serious neglect of Bible study. We must take some time out of our busy day to read the Word of God.

The belt represents the canon of Scripture, the sixty-six Books of the Bible. All Scripture is given by inspiration of God; that is, the Bible came from God to man (II Tim. 3:16). He is the Originator and Author of the Book, not man.

The Holy Spirit illuminated God's Word to men's minds to guard against error and to write down God's Word to us. Likewise, the Holy Spirit will guard our minds against error and will open up our understanding. He lifts off the veil and removes that which blocks our view of God's promises and commands.

The *natural* man is blinded to Truth and cannot receive *the things* of the Spirit of God, for they are *spiritually* discerned. This does not mean that he cannot learn any of the facts of the Bible; he just considers what he reads to be foolishness (I Cor. 2:14).

You cannot imagine all that God has in store for you, both in this life and in the hereafter. When you read the Word, however, He opens the eyes of your spirit and brings His promises into view.

Paul's words are not his opinion or his personal view of things. It was the Holy Spirit that moved the apostle to write. Even from prison his words were encouraging and authoritative, because the Holy Spirit was the Source of his teaching. Christians who are mature in the Word are led by the Spirit of God; they have the ability to see the evil one coming from a mile away.

Maybe you haven't been feasting on the Word and your spirit-man is hungry. The spirit must be sustained with its necessary *spiritual* food, the Bread of life, just as the physical body is sustained with natural food. Neither the spirit-man nor the natural man can live without its necessary food.

Search the Scriptures; read the "Book of Blessings" that was sent from our Heavenly Father to sustain the life of every Christian. Job said, *"Neither have I gone back from the commandments of His lips; I have esteemed the words of His mouth more than my necessary food,"* (23:12, KJV).

The Bible has to be a part of our daily *input* or there will be very little *output*. What a privilege and an honor to be able to enjoy the oracles of Almighty God!

The world is filled with books that give rules for being successful and instructions on how to achieve wealth and happiness. They may indeed be best sellers, but the authors never go home with you to explain how to follow the rules. On the other hand, the Author of the Bible does.

Turn the computer off. Don't call anyone for a word today! Put away the self-help manual. Pick up your Bible, open it and begin to read. You will find that belt gradually tightening around your waist and fitting you like a girdle once again!

~The Reproductive Area~

The loin belt is designed to protect the reproductive area. This was the very first piece of armor that the soldier put on as he readied himself for battle. The belt protected the soldier's loins, the area of his reproductive organs (that part of the body between the ribs and pelvis).

The male must make sure that this area is well protected if he wants to be *fruitful and multiply;* reproduce naturally. After the Roman soldier tightened his loin belt, he was ready for battle!

Having your *loins girt about with truth* is to live according to the standard or rule set forth in the Bible. The Word of God is not like a menu where you are given the choice of ordering what you like; chicken, fish, or steak! The entire Bible is a yardstick designed to free you, push you to be all that God created you to be, and to do what God has called you to do –reproduce, *spiritually*!

As the seed of the Word of God is planted in the hearts of men and women all over the world, countless are being reproduced daily! Jesus' death and resurrection brought many sons to glory (reproduction). Today He continues to reproduce by the seed of His Word.

Where there is no Word, there is no seed; therefore, there can be no reproduction. A soldier might become impotent (incapable of producing children) if he were seriously hurt in the reproductive area. To avoid injury, the soldier made very sure that his loins were protected by wearing his belt.

The believer's ability to reproduce spiritually (win souls) is directly tied to his or her knowledge of the Word; the belt. Absence of the Word in your life will cause you to become malnourished, spiritually weak, and impotent; diminished to a state of spiritual *barrenness*.

Where there is seed, there will be a harvest (Gen.8:22). The ability to reproduce is directly linked to the written Word of God. The Word of God should always be actively functioning in your life. The Bible was written to be studied, understood and applied.

God creates and produces by His Word. He *said* and it was done. Matthew (13:3-23) refers to the Word as seed. The word for *seed* is taken from the Greek word *sperma*. The Greek word *sperma* is the equivalent of our English word *sperm*.

Seed must be planted in order to produce a harvest. When a woman is injected with a man's seed, she conceives and produces a child. When we become born-again, God injects His own *divine seed* (the Word), into our spirits (spiritual womb) to produce (conceive) a harvest (souls) for His glory! This makes the Church a *living organism*, not an organization.

When there is a profession without godliness, there is little trouble, because there is little, if any, spiritual *life* or reproduction!

When God, by the Holy Spirit, injects the seed (His Word) into our spirits, it immediately begins to grow and reproduce the character of Jesus in us. Jesus walked in integrity and sincerity; *"The truth is in Jesus,"* (Eph.4:21). The personality and character is in the seed. Like Father (God), like Son (Jesus); like (earthly) father, like son!

Believers are born again of incorruptible seed and must walk according to the Word. This divine seed will not allow you to live as you once lived before you met Christ. The Scripture says, *"Therefore if any man be in Christ, he is a new creature: old things are passed away; behold, all things are become new,"* (II Cor. 5:17, KJV).

The character, life, attributes, and nature of God are in His seed (the Word). The more we read His Word, the more we become like Christ.

Genesis 3:15 is referred to as the first Gospel; the Good News that promised the Coming of the Messiah, the Seed of the woman (virgin birth). "Seed" in this verse points to an individual, Jesus. God recreates man with His Divine Seed. As a matter of fact, everything God produces, He reproduces through seed; His Word.

From the moment God pronounced judgment upon the serpent (Gen. 3:15), Satan and his wicked family began to oppose God and His family. The enemy of God is Satan; the enemy of our soul is Satan. The Deliverer of our soul is Christ. In this, we see that the stream is divided and the war is on! We are enlisted in God's army and He has called Christians to active duty!

The *seed of the serpent* (Satan) would bruise the heel of the *Seed of the woman* (Jesus). The bruising of Christ's *heels* speaks of serious injury. This is contrasted with the bruising of the serpent's *head*, depicting a mortal blow!

Jesus' heels were bruised when they nailed Him to the cross. He suffered the agonizing death of the cross, but that was only a temporary injury. The devil will be cast into the lake of fire and brimstone where he will be forever doomed! There is no salvation for Satan. His ultimate demise is a done deal (Rev. 20:10)!

In the meantime, Satan continues to wreak havoc upon the lives of people. For this reason we must put on the whole armor of God that we may be able to stand against the wiles of the devil. Keep your loins girdled with truth.

The Word of God is the one weapon that Satan fears more than anything! We cannot emphasize this enough! Tighten that belt every day of your natural life. "For though we walk in the flesh, we do not war after the flesh," (II Cor. 10:3). We are human, but we don't fight as humans do.

When they laid Christ's dead body in the grave, the powers of darkness thought they had gained the victory. However, Christ rose from the grave and His Resurrection sealed the devil's fate! Jesus, the Seed of the woman, became *the firstborn* (reproduction) among many brethren. Christ wore the military belt first: *"He will wear righteousness like a belt and truth like an undergarment,"* (Isa. 11:5, NLT). The Scripture was fulfilled.

We are born-again spiritually (that which is born of the flesh is flesh) to reproduce spiritually. Be fruitful and multiply. Through the seed of the written Word, countless are being reproduced! Be sure to protect your reproductive area. Have your loins girdled with Truth. Read your Bible every day, then *go* make disciples (reproduce)!

~Don't Judge the Book by its Cover~

The Tabernacle of Moses was covered with badgers' skins. The tough, weather-beaten skin was dull, unattractive and had no beauty or loveliness. The rough badger's skin which protected the exterior of the tabernacle was all that an onlooker could see.

The beauty of the tabernacle; the golden altar of incense; the golden candlestick; the beautiful, intricately woven linen curtains of blue, purple and scarlet; the golden vessels; the lovely veil, and so forth, were all found on the *inside*.

The Bible may not be attractive to onlookers, but if they would open the Book and read it, they would see the beauty of the Lord that is revealed within its pages. It was when the priests and the high priest entered the tabernacle where the Ark and other furnishings were that they saw the beauty and splendor that was *inside*. *In it* we have eternal life. *In it* there is liberty. *In it* are the many promises of God made to Christians. *In it* we have direct access to our Heavenly Father.

David said, *"One thing have I desired of the Lord, that will I seek after; that I may dwell in the house of the Lord all the days of my life, to behold the beauty of the Lord, and to enquire in His temple,"* (Psalm 27:4, KJV).

Do not judge the Book by its cover! Christ "has no form or comeliness;" and *when you see Him*, there is "no beauty" that we should desire Him. He is despised and rejected, and yet, He is called the Lord's Darling (Psalm 22:20).

Believers must not despise and reject Christ by neglecting the Bible. Pull that belt tight around your waist. What worked for Jesus will work for you. His use of the Word demonstrates the importance of trusting, reverencing and obeying a 2,000-year-old!

CHAPTER EIGHT

THE BELIEVER'S BODY ARMOR

"...And having on the breastplate of righteousness..." (Eph.6:14)

Following the illustration of the belt, the Holy Spirit directs Paul's attention to another powerful piece, the breastplate. The breastplate was the heaviest of all the armor. It covered the soldier from the neck all the way down almost to the knees. Some plates weighed forty pounds or more.

The belt of truth is followed by the breastplate of righteousness. Righteousness describes God's nature. God wears the breastplate of righteousness; *"For He put on righteousness as a breastplate,"* (Isaiah 59:17). We have been made righteous through the blood of Jesus: *"For God made Christ, who never sinned, to be the offering for our sin, so that we could be made right through Christ,"* (II Cor. 5:21, LASB).

To prevent this heavy body armor from pressing down too hard on the shoulders, it was bound with the girdle (belt) around the waist. Righteousness is a powerful spiritual weapon that is produced by the Word of God!

The breastplate was especially designed to protect the soldier's vitals (the chest area where the heart and lungs are located). It was referred to as the "heart protector" for to be struck in the heart (a principle organ), unlike getting hit in the arm or leg, meant certain death!

No Roman soldier would march onto the battlefield without this covering! Confident that his vitals were well protected, the soldier was able to concentrate on carrying out his commander's orders.

The righteousness of Christ is inwrought in us by the Holy Spirit at the point of conversion. The Lamb of God without spot or blemish; Jesus, the *sinless* Redeemer, took all of our sins upon Himself so that we might take on God's righteousness. The moment you became born again, God clothed you with the same breastplate that Christ wore when He walked the earth.

Jesus resisted every temptation of Satan (the wiles of the devil). To be a Christian is *to be* like Christ and *to do* what Christ likes! The righteous Christ *loves* righteous living.

What is righteousness? Doing what is right by God and man. The breastplate of *righteousness* is the practical, righteous character, works, and everyday living of Christians. This plate of armor represents the believer's integrity, his daily walk and godly conduct.

There was a back piece; however, the breastplate was primarily to protect the front. Satan is a backstabber; nevertheless, in observing the Roman soldier's military outfit, Paul's attention doesn't seem to be drawn to a back piece.

Maybe there is no focus on the back, because a soldier would never turn his back on the enemy (a cowardly act)! The true test of a soldier is how he conducts himself on the battlefield! Will he run when the battle begins, or will he stand firm, confront the enemy and fight?

For a soldier to be hit in the back implies that the soldier was running *away from,* instead of bravely resisting and boldly confronting, his opponent. David did not run away from Goliath. The Bible says that "he hasted and ran toward" the army to meet the Philistine.

God's armor of protection was designed so that you *will be able to withstand* the enemy. You will be empowered to *face* any adversity. God's got your back! Never run away from the enemy.

Never run away from a problem. When you come in contact with evil forces, do not run or wave the white flag of surrender! Do not fear what man or the devil can do to you. Trust your armor of protection! Stand still and see the salvation of the Lord, for the enemy you see today, you will see them no more forever (Ex. 14:13).

Paul urges the believer to wear righteousness as a Roman soldier would wear his breastplate, and for the same reasons. Our vitals must be protected; as a man thinks in his *heart*, so is he. No one wants to die of a wounded heart. The part of us that God is most interested in is the heart; the seat of our affections.

When a man or woman is married to a spouse, but does not have his or her heart, the situation can be miserable for both. Jacob was married to Leah, but Rachel had his heart. All three — Jacob, Leah and Rachel — coped with the situation, but they were miserable. When Jacob finally married Rachel he was happy, because he was with the one who had his heart (Gen. 29:15-18, 21, 30).

With the breastplate of righteousness covering your heart, the enemy doesn't stand a chance! Satan the accuser is seeking to find something to accuse you of to God. The Bible tells us to be blameless. This does not mean that we will not be blamed for things of which we are not guilty.

The enemy brings circumstances into our lives during the course of a day to make our lives a contradiction and our walk unworthy. For example, your boss may ask you to lie to a client. He may ask you to tell the client that he is not in the office (a little white lie). Again, a lie doesn't care who tells it! Tighten that belt; your integrity (truth) is at stake.

As a Christian, to lie would make your life a contradiction, because the Bible says, "God hates a lying tongue," (Prov. 6:16).

The breastplate is bound with the belt. Righteousness is directly tied to the Word. To say one thing and do another makes your walk unworthy!

The breastplate was made of hard, durable leather. This piece of armor was constructed in such a manner that it would not fall apart in battle. No believer wearing God's armor will ever fall apart in spiritual warfare. God's armor will make you strong, durable and sin-resistant! When you hide the Word in your heart, you will not sin (habitually).

Another important feature of the breastplate is that it was made of highly polished *brass* metal. The more the soldier wore the plate, the more the small, scale-like pieces of brass metal rubbed together and the *shinier* the armor became. The breastplate was a beautiful sight to behold, but it was not for show or to be on display; its purpose was to protect the soldier's life!

When the soldier was marching to war, the afternoon sun would hit the shiny brass pieces on the breastplate. The glare from the sun was so bright that it blinded the enemy! With his vision obstructed, the enemy could not see to fight. This gave the Roman soldier the opportunity to run up to his opponent and kill him, receiving no harm to himself! Oh, the wisdom of God!

Christ came into a dark world of sin. The time that Christ was in the world, He was the Light of the world. When Christians put on Christ, they put on His body armor. "Ye are the light of the world," (Matt. 5:14). Living in this dark world, we should shine brightly for Jesus.

Righteous living is the best way to influence others; to win them for Christ. Unrighteous living brings a reproach upon the Name of the Lord and the Church. Our conduct (good or bad) affects others. Have you ever visited a relative or friend where several people were gathered and when you arrived, folks began to leave? A transformed life speaks volumes. Your character threatens their ungodly way of living.

Righteousness is manifested in the way we live, not necessarily in what we say or do. Others may not see your acts of righteousness, but God does, and the Lord will reward you as *He* sees, not as man sees. Everything that you do will either bring glory or disgrace to the Name of your God.

The manner in which you conduct yourself when you are caught off-guard, or when you think that no one is watching, reveals the real you. To keep that extra money that the clerk gave you by mistake is not the righteous thing to do. You know that is not a blessing. At the end of the day, that person will have to remedy the loss. Guard your heart (vitals). No unrighteous act is small.

You can live a godly life in the power of the Holy Spirit by keeping Biblical principles always in front of you. The one who spends time in the Word of God will not easily stray from the paths of righteousness. "Righteousness shall be the belt of His loins," (Isa.11:5). The new nature is one of right living; "he that doeth righteousness is righteous," (I John 3:7).

The righteousness that God desires is more than turning from sin and attending Church services on a regular basis. Having on the breastplate refers to a show of love for God and concern for others. Help those who are weak and pray for them. Righteousness can be seen by what we do, not merely by what we say. Actions speak louder than words; so *speak up*!

Paul was determined to preach the Gospel; to win others to Christ whatever the cost. His body armor was righteousness, the conduct and behavior of the ministry (II Cor. 6:3-10, LASB).

- *"We try to live in such a way that no one will be hindered from finding the Lord by the way we act, and so no one can find fault with our ministry,"* (v.3).
- *"In everything we do we try to show that we are true ministers of God. We patiently endure troubles and hardships and calamities of every kind,"* (v.4).
- *"We have been beaten, been put in jail, faced angry mobs, worked to exhaustion, endured sleepless nights, and gone without food,"* (v.5).

- *"We have proved ourselves by our purity, our under-standing, our patience, our kindness, our sincere love, and the power of the Holy Spirit,"* (v.6).
- *"We have faithfully preached the truth. God's power has been working in us. We have righteousness as our weapon, both to attack and to defend ourselves,"* (v.7).
- *"We serve God whether people honor us or despise us, whether they slander us or praise us. We are honest, but they call us imposters,"* (v.8).
- *"We are well known, but we are treated as unknown. We live close to death, but here we are, still alive. We have been beaten within an inch of our lives,"* (v.9).
- *"Our hearts ache but we always have joy. We are poor, but we give spiritual riches to others. We own nothing, and yet we have everything,"* (v. 10).

When your level of confidence rises like this, you will have a new attitude! Being clothed in the *breastplate of righteousness* enables you to live in such a way that no one is hindered from finding the Lord. The world will know that you have been restored to a right-standing before God by the way you *act* or *react* to the problems in your life.

Notice please, that the Word of God does not say *put on*, but *having on* the breastplate. To "put on" something means that it was off at some point. The word *having* implies ownership. Own it! Never take your breastplate off! Satan strikes at the heart, the vitals and the seat of our emotions, all the time. It is the good character of the righteous to keep the truths of God in their hearts, and ever before them.

You cannot expect to win others to Christ if they do not respect you. Live righteously. *"The Lord rewarded me according to my righteousness; according to the cleanness of my hands hath He recompensed me,"* (Psl.18:20). Righteousness is essential to godly, victorious living!

CHAPTER NINE

THE GOSPEL OF PEACE

"And your feet shod with the preparation of the gospel of peace," (Ephesians 6:15).

From the beginning, God planned for man to enjoy peace on earth. Through disobedience, peace with God was shattered. With His blood, Jesus purchased back our peace. He has made it possible for us to have peace with God and with each other.

"Yet it was our weaknesses He carried; it was our sorrows that weighed Him down. And we thought His troubles were a punishment from God for His own sins! But He was wounded and crushed for our sins. He was beaten that we might have peace," (Isa. 53:4-5, LASB)!

Peace comes from the Gospel; a message of peace. During a time when it seems that all you hear is bad news, it is a blessing to share a message of peace; the Gospel of Jesus Christ! We need peace! Not the shallow, temporary peace that the world gives, but everlasting peace that comes from knowing the Savior, Jesus Christ.

The apostle Paul's mind was clothed with God's peace, even in the face of his own death. He was not fearful, frantic or hopeless. Paul knew that his purpose was fulfilled; his work was finished. To Timothy, his son in the Gospel, he said, *"I am now ready to be offered, and the time of my departure is at hand,"* (II Timothy 4:6, KJV).

The devil could not steal Paul's peace! He kept his shoes buckled on tight. His feet were always shod with the preparation of the Gospel of peace in the same manner that in preparation, Roman soldiers bound the military shoes (weapons for warfare) tightly on their feet before going to battle.

Roman soldiers' shoes were made of a mixture of metal (usually brass) and leather. The top and bottom of the shoes were *shod*, or bound together with several strips of strong, durable leather. These were no ordinary shoes. They were made to withstand prolonged wear and tear. Roman soldiers hardly ever needed new shoes!

The Gospel is forever! Nothing can be added to it to make it better or more durable. *"Heaven and earth will disappear, but My words will remain forever,"* (Matt: 24:35, LASB).

The Greek word for "shod" is the same as the word for "bind," *hupodeo,* which means to *bind underneath*. This word is used to describe a person binding their sandals tightly on their feet to go somewhere. This Gospel is meant to *go* somewhere; to all nations, to the world!

Hupodeo speaks of *a sole bound under the foot* like a shoe that is bound tightly to your feet; wherever you *go,* the Word will go with you. How beautiful are *the feet* of the ones who bring Good News (Rom.10:15).

Under the soles of these military shoes were *extremely dangerous nails* (cleats or *spikes*) that were up to three inches long! As the soldier walked or ran, the long spikes would dig deep into the ground; this helped him to run faster and farther without stumbling or falling.

The spikes steadied the soldier's footing and helped him to *stand firmly* in place when in hand-to-hand combat. Spikes also made the soldiers' military shoes lethal. Roman soldiers used their shoes to stomp, crush and even mortally wound the enemy. These shoes were designed, not just for walking, but to kill! They were killer shoes; God's *weapon of mass destruction*.

Having the long spikes underneath his shoes, a soldier could actually rip a man apart underfoot. Sometimes he would kick the opponent in his shin to break his ankle. With a broken ankle, the opponent was unable to stand. While down on the ground, nursing his ankle, the Roman soldier would lift his foot over the fallen soldier and stomp the man to death! Those shoes were deadly!

"Kill or don't come home" were the soldier's orders; therefore, whatever found its way under the soldier's foot was in serious trouble! Like the Roman soldier's killer shoes, the weapon of peace *destroys* a feeling of anxiety. Peace puts worry in reverse and rips anxiety to pieces! The Gospel brings peace even during the most troublesome times.

The Holy Spirit likens the *Gospel of peace* to the Roman soldier's lethal shoes, because peace is a powerful *weapon* in spiritual warfare.

As the soldier used his shoes to stomp the enemy to the ground and kick him to death, believers are to use the Gospel of peace to stomp the devil down and to kick his butt! Having your mind clothed with God's peace, you are protected from all of Satan's attacks! The Bible says we are to "seek peace, and ensue it," (I Peter 3:11). Search for peace and work to maintain it.

The more time that you spend in the Word of God, the more you will experience the peace of God operating in your life! A heart that is safeguarded by the peace of God puts the enemy where he belongs –under our feet!

Folks are hurting and we have the answer! To put your shoes on implies that you are going somewhere for a purpose. The Great Commission is to go and tell others about Christ, the Prince of Peace. Jesus Christ is the Way, the Truth and the Life. Jesus is the Answer!

A fully armed soldier was fearless! With the lethal shoes bound tightly on his feet, he was able to quickly advance deep into enemy territory. Christians should always be ready to promote the Kingdom of God. Go and tell others, "We have Good News for you!"

A Time of Preparation

Heaven is a *prepared* place for a *prepared* people. Jesus Himself said, "I go to *prepare* a place for you." There must be quality time spent in Bible study before one can effectively minister the Word of God to others. In the military, before the soldier is sent to war, the very first thing he experiences is basic training. He must go through a period of preparation.

The Lord will never send a Christian soldier onto the battlefield unprepared. It takes time to learn the tools of your trade. There are invisible enemies of darkness that have waged war against the Church since the beginning. The victory that God wants the Church to experience requires that we receive His spiritual strategy for warfare. Our main defense is the Bible.

As we go about our daily activities, Satan and his imps are feverishly at work devising ways to assault the people of God. Let us make sure that we *bind our shoes on tightly*, and are *prepared* to *withstand* any foe. Be *ready* to fight the unexpected and when problems arise unexpectedly, you won't find yourself in panic mode.

Our English word "preparation" (6:15) is the same as the Greek word *hetoimasia*, which means *readiness*, *preparation*, and *firm footing*.

Having your "feet shod with the *preparation* of the Gospel of peace" speaks of a *readiness* to spring into action; *a readiness* to proclaim the message of peace. Nothing gives true and lasting peace except the Gospel; it is the firm footing and solid foundation upon which we stand. The world is our battleground; it needs to hear Good News. Folks may not come to us; however, with our shoes tightly strapped on our feet, we must go to them.

Preparation is essential to effective witnessing. Satan wants to catch you off guard. One of the most meaningful plans of action that Jesus used to whip Satan was that He was prepared. The Holy Spirit led Jesus in the wilderness, where He spent forty days locked in with God, fasting, praying, and resisting the devil!

Jesus' wilderness experience prepared Him for His earthly ministry. The Bible says, "And Jesus returned in the power of the Spirit into Galilee," (Luke 4:14). Jesus returned after forty days, "full of the Holy Ghost" and with power!

As believers press on, they must be *prepared* for *every good work*. Never be caught off-guard. Make sure that you spend quality time in spiritual preparation. When you trust and obey God, your sandal straps will not be broken. You will run and not be weary; walk and not faint. Now go: boldly proclaim the message of peace to tear down strongholds in the lives of others.

Soldiers of Jesus Christ are prepared *before* they go into any battle. Unfortunately, too many Christians are *getting* ready when they should *be* ready. Some only want to hear about material wealth and prosperity. Spiritual warfare is not a popular subject. The idea of warfare disturbs people; however, Scripture tells us that the "gates of hell" (forces opposed to Christ and His Kingdom) are working together against the Church. They will not prevail!

The enemy sets his traps and snares to hinder us from making progress in spreading the Gospel. For this reason, it is essential to keep your shoes on. The long spikes underneath will prevent you from falling. As Christians travel along the way, the enemy slyly lays traps and snares to cause unprepared believers to stumble. If you fall, it means that your straps need to be tightened. God is able to *keep you from falling* (Jude 24).

~Peace with God~

The Godhead enjoyed an intimate relationship and it was the Creator's desire for man to enjoy that same kind of relationship with Him forever. Before the fall there was no violence, no pain, no distress, no death and no guilt. Man enjoyed perfect peace, unity, harmony and fellowship with God. When man sinned, all of this changed!

Through man's disobedience, out went peace, life, unity, and harmony; in came murders, lies, poverty, hatred, violence and death. Sin caused broken fellowship with the Lord. God was not caught off-guard, however. He always planned to restore peace and to bring heaven and earth back together in perfect harmony through the Prince of Peace, the Lord Jesus Christ!

Jesus bought back our peace with God! He took upon Himself our sins; endured shame; was scorned, bruised and nailed to the cross. He carried our sicknesses and bore our pain. He was mocked, ridiculed, and suffered violence that we might have peace with God!

An unbeliever cannot experience the peace *of* God until he has made peace *with* God. Only through the blood of Jesus can man and God be reconciled.

"For it pleased the Father that in Him should all fullness dwell; And, having made peace through the blood of His cross, by Him to reconcile all things unto Himself; by Him, I say, whether they be things in earth, or things in Heaven," (Col. 1:19-20, KJV).

Having been justified by faith, we have peace *with* God through our Lord and Savior, Jesus Christ! Peace with God is restored immediately upon conversion!

Paul did not always have peace *with* God. He found peace *with* God when he was converted while on his persecution campaign against Christians. Many of Paul's letters begin with "grace and peace be unto you." He uses the word "peace" to mean "blessings and prosperity in every area of one's life."

~The Peace of God~

There are two kinds of *peace* spoken of in Scripture. First, we have peace *with* God, obtained *at* conversion, based on Christ's sacrifice of Himself on the cross. Peace with God becomes your birthright. Secondly, we have the peace *of* God, experienced *after* conversion. Christ desires that we walk in God's peace every day of our lives.

The enemy wants to disrupt your peace by bringing up past failures and mistakes! Your sins are under the blood of Jesus. Let the peace of God rule your heart. Having your feet shod with the Gospel of peace, you can stand strong and unmovable.

Jesus Christ is the remedy for both; the peace *of* God and peace *with* God. Many Christians have peace *with* God, but unfortunately, due to their negligence of Bible study and prayer; the upkeep of their spiritual armor, they do not experience a continuous flow of the peace *of* God operating in their lives.

It *is* absolutely possible for Christians to walk in the prevailing, conquering peace *of* God every day. Folks worry about so many things over which they have no control. The cares and problems of life should not cause us to become emotionally upset.

The moment you take your eyes off the Lord, stress and worry will take the place of peace. You will start feeling as if you've gone through the wringer! Endurance in suffering is evidence that you are experiencing the peace of God. Most of the time you will find that the more severe the storm, the more glorious the outcome, and it was worth the wait!

Relax, God promised that He will never forsake or leave you alone with your problems. Rest, the Gospel brings peace that comforts. Do not lose heart over things that you cannot change. Remain steadfast and confident in God who is able to deliver you, even in matters of life or death. The Gospel is the power of God (Romans 1:16)!

Christ suffered for us and He is our example. Problems are opportunities for us to know more about God and learn to appreciate His presence with us in time of trouble!

Oh, what peace we often forfeit; oh, what needless pain we bear;

all because we do not carry everything to God in prayer.

"The Lord will give strength unto His people; the Lord will bless His people with peace," (Ps. 29:11, KJV). He is able to deliver us out of all our troubles!

Peace is a powerful weapon that blocks worry, anxiety, fear, doubt and anything else that would interrupt our rest. These negative emotions will reverse your peace of mind. Study the Bible and you will easily recognize Satan's style and tactics.

Paul was in a Roman prison when he penned this epistle. He wasn't sitting at home in his easy chair; however, in reading this letter to the Ephesians you would never think that the author was in any type of dilemma. Readers will have to constantly remind themselves that Paul was by no means living in the lap of luxury! Nevertheless, his is a letter of contentment, hope, and encouragement to the saints. The spirit of the apostle's warfare letter is one of peacefulness, not distress.

Paul wasn't the least bit anxious concerning his situation. As a matter of fact, the apostle wrote that he had learned, through adversity, to be content in whatsoever state he was in (Phil. 4:11).

Paul told others not to worry when he had so many reasons to be worried himself. Not only was the apostle in prison, the Holy Spirit also revealed to him the horrible manner in which he would die. He would be beheaded for the sake of the Gospel, and yet he continued to be at peace.

Anyone who walks the path of righteousness can expect troubles and difficulties in life. With your *feet shod with the Gospel of peace,* trials won't be able to impede your progress in God. In spite of the problems, continue to walk the straight and narrow path of duty and godliness.

Christ's death and resurrection *destroyed* the works of the devil; sin, sickness, death, hell and the grave! The peace of God renders them harmless. None of these things will have ill effect on the one who confidently walks in the peace *of* God.

Trials come to help you grow closer to the Prince of Peace. Do you trust the Lord to bring you through, or are you burdened down with worry? The answer to this question will help you ascertain whether or not you are experiencing the peace *of* God in your life! "Worry is misuse of the imagination," (Dan Zadra).

Christians often become frustrated and defeated because their needs, desires and expectations are not immediately met. The mind that is safeguarded by the peace *of* God is free from worry.

The Bible says, *"Be careful for nothing; but in everything by prayer and supplication with thanksgiving let your request be made known unto God,"* (Phil. 4:6, KJV). The word *careful* used here means "anxious." Do not be *anxious* about anything! To be anxious is to be *uneasy* or to *worry*. This is in direct contrast to peace; therefore, to be anxious overrides your peace.

Our English word *worry* comes from an old Anglo-Saxon word that means *to strangle*. The cares of life, worry and anxiety will strangle the peace *of* God right out of your heart.

The term "be careful" or "be anxious" also means *to be torn apart.* When something is *torn apart* it *goes in all different directions.* For your mind to be *torn apart,* it means that you can't think straight; your mind is in turmoil and is headed in all different directions.

Worry tears your thought process apart and causes you to make bad decisions. Have you ever tried to fix a problem, thinking it was the best thing to do at the time, but it made the situation worse? Later, you thought, "Why did I do that?" Worry caused you to panic! You did not trust God to come to your rescue! The peace of God is able to prevent you from becoming emotionally distraught. It will keep your mind whole and sound until that problem is solved.

God knows what is best for you. Your deliverance is going to cause more than a ripple effect. At the time of your deliverance, there will be a tidal wave of blessings!

"And the peace of God, which passeth all understanding, shall keep your hearts and minds through Christ Jesus," (Phil. 4:7, KJV). There may be times when going through a serious crisis, you should be worried, but you're not! Some things are just "so God" that you cannot understand or explain them.

Imagine never worrying about your family, your bills, your ministry, or your job ever again! It is possible. Cast your cares upon the Lord. This does not mean you will not be concerned about anything. It means that you trust the God of your situation.

Lasting peace comes from knowing that God is in control of everything, even when it appears that He is not! Your attitude determines the outcome of your circumstances. Problems will do one of two things: 1) make you better, or 2) make you bitter. Better or bitter; it's your choice.

True peace comes from trusting and obeying God, not positive thinking. Paul looked at his life from God's point of view. He was in prison, but he viewed himself as a prisoner of the Lord Jesus Christ. While his own life was in danger, he was telling the Church how to have peace. The devil cannot take anything from you — your peace, your joy, or your dreams — unless you surrender them to him.

When we view our lives from God's standpoint, there will be no need to worry. The Gospel of Jesus Christ gives our lives support, strength, and stability, as well as peace!

God does not want His children to worry about anything — *let not your heart be troubled*. Above all, He does not want you to be at the mercy of Satan. The enemy loves conflict. He hates peace.

The devil wants you to think that God is not caring enough to come to your rescue. Shake every negative thought right out of your mind. Trust your armor. Every glorious promise that God has made to His children will come to pass.

The Gospel *of* Peace gives a firm footing. All other ground — your title, family, your possessions, and so forth — is sinking sand. On Christ the Solid Rock; the Prince of Peace, I stand!

Keeping your mind stayed on Christ, our Peace, will give you perpetual, perfect peace. The peace *of* God will grow and mature in your heart as you trust Him one day at a time, one situation at a time. It guards your emotions and keeps you from cracking under pressure. If you find yourself stumbling or falling, quickly bind those shoes tightly on your feet and continue to run the race!

Many of us often don't realize how difficult a situation really is until after the Lord has delivered us. One day we may look back and wonder, "How did I make it through *that* without losing my mind?" It is God! He kept your heart and mind in perfect peace.

In the beginning, Adam thought like God thought. In his fallen state, man can no longer think like God. Study and obey God's Word and He will change your way of thinking. With the peace of God reigning in your heart, you will always experience a sense of calm.

The devil cannot disturb your peace; if he cannot disturb your peace, he cannot disturb you. Do not wait until you are physically dead to *rest in peace*. In Christ, you can have spiritual rest and peace right here and now while you are physically alive.

Keeping your feet shod with the Gospel *of* peace is vital to victorious living! If the enemy cannot steal your peace one way, he will try another. God has planned for you to be fully equipped with His armor of protection. This is the only sure way to prevent the devil from being successful in his attacks against you. Your shoes are as important to victorious living as your breastplate.

Like the Roman soldier's shoes, the Gospel of peace will crush the devil underfoot and rip him apart. One swift kick in the devil's shins will put him down!

Now that your shoes are tightly bound on your feet, *go* and share the Good News, the Gospel of peace, with others! *"How beautiful on the mountains are the feet of the messenger who brings good news, the good news of peace..."* (Isa. 52:7, NLT)!

~Peace in the Midst of the Storm~

When the disciples tried to cross the Sea of Galilee, a terrible storm arose that threatened their lives. Jesus, the Prince of Peace, was in the boat with them, asleep at the back of the boat. Very high waves began to break into the boat and nearly filled it with water. Emotionally distraught, and afraid, the disciples woke Jesus up, shouting for His help!

To add insult to injury, after all Jesus had done for them, after all the miracles they had seen Him perform, they asked, "Don't you even care that we are going to drown?"

Satan has some of us asking Jesus that very same question today. He wants you to think that Jesus doesn't care about you. Gird up the loins of your mind with truth and he will not be able to convince you of such a terrible lie! Jesus gave His life for you. That proves that He *does* care!

After the disciples cried out to Jesus in fear, He woke up and rebuked the wind and said to the waves, "Peace, be still!" Suddenly, the wind ceased and there was a great calm (Mark 4:35-39).

Don't waste your storm. Storms are sent to bring you to a place where you cry out to God. In the midst of your storm, when nothing else works you can depend upon the Prince of Peace.

You may think that Jesus did not panic, because He was God, but the reason why Jesus did not panic was that He trusted God's Word. Jesus already knew that He would not die by drowning. The Messiah had to die on the cross. He had to go to Calvary and die outside Jerusalem. All that the prophets spoke concerning the Messiah had to be fulfilled!

The disciples were fearful, anxious, and frantic. These emotions are the exact opposite of peace. The believer need not be mentally distressed about anything. You should be stronger than the storm that you are going through.

Jesus had performed so many miracles in the presence of the disciples, and yet they still did not trust Him to deliver them. They said among themselves, "Who is this man, that even the wind and the waves obey Him?" (Mark 4:41). Jesus' disciples still didn't get it! They did not yet know who He was! Some of us still don't get who Jesus *really* is!

The God who controls the forces of nature was in the boat with them! Through this sudden storm, Jesus was giving His disciples an unexpected examination. He was testing them. They failed the test miserably. Believe in your heart that the Lord is going to deliver you out of all your trials. He is not going to prevent them from occurring, but He will bring you out of them.

Even though you do not know how your situation is going to work out in the end, you do know that you have the victory because of who you are, and because of Whose you are.

Think about the storms in your life; the bills, sickness, the job. We often encounter fierce storms in our lives where we feel that God won't help us. We know that He can, but we do not believe that He will. At times like these, we must cover our hearts and minds with the Gospel of peace.

That problem is designed to draw you closer to your Heavenly Father. Until He delivers you, the Lord will give you peace. With Jesus in the boat, you can laugh at the storm.

The devil sends raging storms to interrupt your peace. A troubled mind will only weaken you and make you unfit for battle. Put up your defenses against things that would bring defeat. Christians should never be uncertain about God's promises, for their fulfillment is sure. The same God who said to the waves, "Peace, be still," and calmed the storm will come to your rescue.

Satan will tempt you with false ways of achieving peace. One of his lies is, "If you had more money, you would have peace." Talk to some rich folks. He wants you to think that if you were married (or single), you would have peace. Only the Gospel of Jesus Christ gives real, lasting peace! Secondary things (other than God) can only give you *temporary* peace.

"Thou wilt keep him in perfect peace, whose mind is stayed on Thee: because he trusteth in Thee. Trust ye in the Lord for ever: for in the Lord Jehovah is everlasting strength," (Isa. 26:3-4, KJV). The phrase "perfect peace" literally means "peace, peace;" that is, *full of well-being*; happiness and health. Trust the Lord and you will have *shalom, shalom*, "peace, peace" – perfect peace!

To have perfect peace, the Gospel must always be within reach; in your mouth and in your heart. When you let the peace of God rule your heart and mind, the enemy doesn't stand a chance! Just like Christ in the boat, we too can be in peace for we serve God, who never slumbers or sleeps.

Sometimes, Christians get so involved with the day-to-day cares of life that the Word of God becomes secondary; it is put on the back burner. This will cause your mind to be in a constant state of turmoil. Eventually, you may become overwhelmed with the circumstances that you are facing, and the peace of God that you once experienced will be broken. Never allow yourself to be so busy doing everything else that you neglect your spiritual armor.

Be ready to speak a word of peace in season to those who are weary, even while you are in the midst of a storm yourself! As you go forth telling others about Jesus Christ, the Prince of Peace, you will experience peace yourself. Do not let your troubles hinder you from sharing the Good News. Remain undaunted and undeterred by what you may be experiencing.

God's peace is available to everyone through His Son. *"Peace I leave with you, My peace I give unto you: not as the world gives,"* (John. 14:27, KJV). Worldly things give you a false sense of peace that comes only when things are going well.

Having *your feet shod with the preparation of the Gospel of peace* is to live in peace and to seek for ways to help others experience that peace. In the midst of your storm (problems, persecution, sickness, trials), let the peace of God govern your heart. Then be ready to tell others about the Prince of Peace. The enemy does not want you to share this message with anyone. He will try to convince you that society is too depraved to be saved; that what you are doing is insignificant.

The world is our battleground. The powerful message of peace needs to be heard by everyone.

Be ready to proclaim the message of salvation through repentance to others, today!

"Now the Lord of peace Himself give you peace always by all means. The Lord be with you all," (II Thess. 3:16, KJV).

~The Greaves: Leg Armor~

Every piece of God's armor must be used collectively to resist the enemy; for endurance, and for strength and stability to stand strong in the heat of every battle. Peace is a powerful weapon that gives Christians a firm footing when they battle against the enemy of their soul, Satan.

Besides the belt, another powerful piece of armor that may be treated as insignificant is the greave. The greave was a beautiful, tube-shaped covering for the leg. It began at the top of the knee, extended all the way down the leg and rested on the top of the foot. Each soldier's greave was specifically formed to fit around the calf of *his* legs.

When the shoes and the greaves met, they looked like army boots (one piece) that was made of bronze or brass metal. The greave was not an afterthought; it was a very important piece of the soldier's armor of protection. With the soldier's legs protected by greaves, the enemy could kick as long and as hard as he liked and it wouldn't even make a dent in his leg armor!

No weapon is meaningless in warfare. The breastplate that covered the heart was important, but so was the greave. Soldiers wore the brass greaves to protect their lower legs. If a soldier got kicked in his shin and he fell down to the ground (a vulnerable position), that broken leg could cause him to lose his head! He could easily be decapitated.

Another reason why wearing the greaves was so important is that soldiers were not at liberty to choose their battleground. The commanding officer often sent them into dangerous tracts of land that was covered with thorn bushes or razor-sharp rocks that could cut the legs to pieces! With his legs protected, the soldier could proceed through dangerous terrains without getting a scratch!

It was not Jesus' idea to go into the wilderness (a thorny place) where He was tempted of the devil for forty days (Mark 1:12-13). He was led there by the Holy Spirit. The Father sent His Son into the wilderness so that He would be able to identify fully with human beings. Going through the temptation, Jesus demonstrated that *having on the whole armor of God*, we too can prevail.

At the Father's direction, there are times when the Holy Spirit will lead us into uncomfortable, problematic situations to prepare us for ministry. There were no thorns before the fall. Thorns (pain, sickness, sorrow, poverty, hatred, death) entered the world as a result of sin and sin made the world a wilderness place. Jesus' wilderness experiences prepared Him for ministry; to bring Light into a dark place; to save His people from *their* sins.

God, our Chief Commanding Officer, does not always send us on pleasant assignments. Take the message of salvation wherever He sends you; whether it is in a drug infested area to rescue one soul from the enemy's grip, or to witness to someone who has never heard that God loves them. Put your shoes on;

be ready to go! Everyone has to hear the Good News before Christ comes.

The Gospel requires universal proclamation, "But *how can they call on Him to save them unless they believe in Him? And how can they believe in Him if they have never heard about Him? And how can they hear about Him unless someone tells them? And how will anyone go and tell them without being sent? That is why the Scriptures say, 'How beautiful are the feet of messengers who bring good news,"* (Rom. 10:14-15, LASB)!

Dare to go where no one else will and tell them how Jesus penetrated Satan's territory, overcame him and, through His blood, bought back our peace!

When the fully clothed Roman soldiers were marching, wearing their military killer shoes, no one got in their way. They kept on walking, face forward, not looking to the left or to the right. No one got in the way of this army, because they would be crushed underfoot!

What a revelation! When the peace of God reigns in your heart, you will advance — sometimes slowly but surely, sometimes quickly and abruptly — through the most difficult situations. Let nothing stop your progress. Fearlessly face the enemy. If he gets in your way, like a marching army, keep right on walking. Crush the enemy underfoot! Stomp the devil down! Break his spinal cord. Set your face like a flint; don't look to the left or to the right. Keep on advancing, even under rocky conditions!

Satan's temptations (thorns) are designed to hurt, to cause you pain and suffering. God allows "thorns" (difficulties) in our lives to teach us how to function in His peace! Don't be afraid of what the enemy can do. God is in control. Satan does not want folks to experience peace *with* God, nor the peace *of* God. When others seem to be falling apart around you, Christ wants you have peace, not turmoil, ruling your heart! To worry or not is your choice!

As you go declaring the Word of the Lord, you may get drenched by the rain, or scorched by the sun; the weather is not always favorable. Just beneath the surface of everyday living is a fierce spiritual struggle between light and darkness. Our main defense is having our feet shod with the Gospel of peace. Just keep right on marching! If he gets in your way, stomp the devil down with your lethal military shoes!

Undaunted by his surroundings, Paul never wavered in his assignment. The apostle never asked the saints to pray for his release from prison. He considered it an honor to suffer for the sake of the Gospel. He did ask them to pray, however, that he would speak the Gospel of peace boldly, as he ought to speak!

When you personally experience God's mighty hand at work during times of trouble, you will have a better perception of His goodness, mercy and loving-kindness. Those who have not this experience think that you are crazy if you do not faint under your suffering. They may wonder why you aren't on suicide watch!

One of my favorite Scriptures is: *"It is good for me that I have been afflicted; that I might learn Thy statutes,"* (Ps. 119:71, KJV). During the severest storms of my life (the home going of my parents and siblings, sickness and so on) the Spirit of God has taught me to cling to the Word.

Soldiers that guarded Paul must have been amazed by his calm demeanor. That he could rejoice, knowing that he was going to be killed, had them baffled! Subsequently, many of them believed his Word and received Christ as Lord and Savior. We are living epistles; someone is reading you. They want to see how you react to your problems.

Satan wants to silence you. He does not want you to tell the world about the Prince of Peace. Jesus reigning in the hearts of men creates both peace *with* God and the peace *of* God.

Peace is a powerful weapon! God has planned for all men everywhere to have His peace, but just as the Roman soldier had to pick up his military shoes and put them on before marching onto the battlefield, we must reach out by faith and receive the peace that Jesus Christ freely offers: *"May the Lord of peace Himself always give you His peace no matter what happens. The Lord be with you all,"* (II Thess. 3:16, LASB).

CHAPTER TEN

THE SHIELD OF FAITH

"Above all, taking the shield of faith, wherewith ye shall be able to quench all the fiery darts of the wicked," (Eph. 6:16).

J esus is the Author and Finisher of our faith. There is much teaching, preaching and talking about faith, but there is not much of it being put into action. Faith in God's Word is a powerful weapon. Without faith, it is impossible to please God. Faith not only moves mountains; faith moves God.

Each piece of the Roman soldier's military outfit describes a *spiritual weapon* that God Himself has provided for the Church. The manmade armor, the shield, is the equivalent of our spiritual armor, faith; *"He is my shield, the power that saves me,"* (II Samuel 22:3, NLT).

From the Holy Spirit, Paul received the revelation of the whole armor of God (God's *weapons of mass destruction*) for the Church. He began by addressing the Roman soldier's belt (Truth), his breastplate (Righteousness), his shoes (Peace), and now his shield (Faith).

The order in which Paul addresses the Roman soldier's outfit is the order in which the revelation came to him by the Holy Spirit. He was inspired to write as the Holy Spirit directed.

Christ Himself conquered the enemy wearing the belt of Truth. Faith comes by hearing the Word. When the soldier was not using his shield, he rested it on a clip that was attached to the belt. Similarly, our faith rests upon the Scripture. Faith that prevails is generated by the Word.

Faith makes all, or everything, possible. It brings *all things* into the realm of possibilities. Not even the sky is the limit when faith is in action! The Scripture says that God is able to do more than we can ask or think! Meditate on that for a moment, please.

To write "above all," Paul was describing the shield's *position,* not its importance. In order for your faith to grow and mature, it must be fed the Word. The amount of time you spend studying the Bible determines the absence or presence of strong faith.

Faith comes alive when we apply Scripture. All of the Roman soldier's armor rested on his belt when not in use. Each piece of armor is important, but is based upon God's Word! Yes, by faith we can do all things through Christ who strengthens us, but we can only do what the Word of God says we can do!

The phrase "above all" is translated "out in front of all" or "covering all," which speaks of *position.* At times, the Roman soldier held the shield *out in front of* his body to safeguard himself from the enemy's arrows. At other times, the large shield was held *above* his head like an umbrella to *cover all* of him. The shield was large enough and wide enough to cover everything: the soldier, his clothes and his armor.

God has given the Church the shield of faith as part of the whole armor of God that we use when the enemy's fiery darts of fear, turmoil, worry, and unbelief assault us. Doubt is the enemy of faith. Get rid of the doubt, keep the faith! With the shield in its rightful position, *out in front of* or *covering everything*, you will have the victory!

Faith covers everything; in all things taking the shield of faith with which you will be able to quench all the fiery darts (flaming arrows) of the evil one.

Roman soldiers used two kinds of shields: 1) the *aspis,* which is a small, round, beautifully decorated shield, used for show in parades or public ceremonies, and 2) the *thureos,* a large, oblong or square shield. The *thureos* was large enough to protect every part of the soldier.

Little faith is likened to the *aspis* shield, which would not serve the soldier well on the battlefield. It was entirely too small. When you are at the end of your rope, a little faith will not suffice. The *aspis* shield was primarily for show. A soldier at war isn't trying to look cute.

The *thureos* (Greek) shield was the one utilized in battle. This was not an ornamental piece like the *aspis.* Since the shield is used as a figure of speech to represent faith, the *thureos* shield comes closest to describing the kind of faith Christians are to live by.

As the Roman soldier takes up" his *thureos* shield in battle, the believer is to take up faith in all things. The results of faith are limitless!

The *thureos* shield usually measured two and a half feet by four feet, which was *large enough, wide enough* and *long enough* to completely cover and protect the soldier when it was held in the *out in front of* position where it belonged.

Genuine faith should be *out in front of* all of your thoughts and actions; it should precede every decision you make. When your faith is where it belongs, *out in front of everything,* it will *cover all* of the circumstances of your life.

Faith not only brings everything into the realm of possibilities; it will break through every natural limitation. With God all things are possible to them that believe! The demonstration of the power of God in your life depends upon your obedience to the Word of God and faith. The exploits of a godly man or woman of faith are unlimited!

Jesus defeated the devil by faith, performed miracles by faith, *never wavered* in His faith. Not once did Jesus doubt His Father's Word. He confronted Satan and took authority over him using His shield of faith. The Son came to earth to do the will of the Father, by faith.

The moment God makes a promise to you, Satan shows you the exact opposite of that promise to make you doubt God. As soon as the Lord promises to heal you, the devil does something to make the symptoms seem worse than ever. At that precise moment when you need it most, the Holy Spirit will bring a Scripture verse to your remembrance. Your faith comes alive and you begin to believe God all over again!

Another common strategy of Satan is to attack your finances. The Lord may have told you that this year you are going to be debt free. What happens? An emergency arises which causes you to accumulate more debt! Worry and unbelief start creeping into your thoughts. With your mind covered with Truth, you will withstand all of the strategies of the devil and shake off the spirit of doubt. Your faith will be re-activated and confidence in God will be stronger than ever!

Trust the Lord wholeheartedly! The enemy will try to deceive you with, "Did God indeed say?" Your circumstances almost always contradict what God says. It may be the last second of the last day of the year, but if God said it, it is already done! Every other doubt is insignificant when compared to a believer doubting God; that is sacrilegious!

There will always be a need in your life. The Lord will see to it, that the need may be supplied (Phil. 4:19). Faith is being *fully persuaded* of victory *before* the battle is won! It does not matter how strong a person is, he or she is weaker than God and needs His help!

It is safe to have to trust God. To rely upon the creation rather than the Creator is to be irreverent. There is nothing wrong with putting *some* faith in others, but not to the extent of trusting them more than God. Man is limited, unreliable and not always trustworthy. Surely you have discovered by now that, at times, folks can be fickle, unreliable and selfish.

Having on your *shield of faith* is to have faith in God! The Sovereign God promises to reward faith, a powerful weapon that brings Him *into* the situation. God, in turn, uses the problem for His glory and honor by causing you to triumph in it! There is no situation that the devil can keep you in wherein you believe God and He will not bring you out!

In describing the shield of faith, Paul's emphasis is on *living* by faith, not *saving* faith. Now that you have been *saved* by faith, *live* victoriously every day of your life by faith! Salvation faith comes at conversion. The just shall *live* by his faith!

Active faith does not take no for an answer. Either we believe in the God who can do anything but fail, or we do not. To believe that Christ was born of a virgin, cast out devils, died for our sins and rose from the grave on the third day as He said He would, and not believe that He can heal your body, save your family, or get you out of debt is hypocrisy! "O, ye of little faith!"

You do not need more faith. "Lord, give me more faith!" God has given you all the faith that you are going to get. Faith becomes fat and grows as you feast upon the Word of God.

Sometimes our faith becomes weak due to lack of daily Bible study. Faith comes by hearing, and so does doubt and unbelief. Do not allow the enemy to talk you out of your blessing!

God is still the God of miracles, signs and wonders. Be patient under suffering. Take your eyes off your problem and fasten them on Jesus. Faith does not look at the problem; it looks to God, who is able to solve the problem! As the *thureos* shield was wide enough to completely cover the soldier, each believer has been given enough faith to *cover* every situation in their lives.

God has given you all the brain you are going to get, all the muscle you're going to get, and He has given you all the faith that you are going to get. You do not need a thousand tongues! Use the tongue, the brain and the faith that you have. Busy faith, be it ever so small, overcomes the greatest difficulties!

Sometimes we think that someone is so successful, because God has given them more than He has given us; more knowledge, wisdom, anointing, and so forth. Not so! God has equipped you with all that you need to fulfill your own destiny and purpose, not someone else's.

"But all these worketh that one and the selfsame Spirit, dividing to every man severally as He will," (I Cor.12: 11). Take the measure of faith you have been given and use it for God's glory.

The Roman soldier's *thureos* shield was covered with thick, durable leather, made from several layers of animal hide. These thick layers of leather were firmly laid on top of a foundation made of wood. Six layers of animal skin were tanned, then woven together so tightly that the shield became as *strong as steel!*

Proper upkeep prevented the shield from cracking; this determined its effectiveness. No enemy arrow could penetrate it and hit the soldier's vitals. Left unattended, a soldier's shield could become brittle and crack. Problems cannot make you *crack under pressure* when your faith has been properly maintained, soaked in the water of the Word and rubbed with oil; anointed.

When the Roman soldiers interlocked shield to shield it formed a long, steel-like wall. Standing side-by-side and shoulder-to-shoulder, in battle formation with their shields firmly locked together and held *out in front of them all*, the army boldly marched toward the opposing army to attack, confident of victory!

As the unit marched onto the battlefield, the only thing that the enemy army saw was one huge, long, steel wall quickly advancing upon them!

The Church is strongest when there is a spirit of oneness among believers. Where there is unity, there is strength! Even with his shield properly maintained, no Roman soldier would dare fight alone on the battlefield. One fully equipped soldier cannot defeat an army of soldiers. Alone, he could easily be defeated. With his shield locked together with his fellow soldier's shield, they became an invincible army!

If the people of God would come together as a unit, the enemy wouldn't stand a chance! Miracles would take place more than ever before! One can chase a thousand, but two can put ten thousand to flight (Deut. 32:30). A lone sheep could become lamb chops for the devil!

Locked together as a unit, believers become army strong; like a steel wall that the enemy cannot penetrate. Wielding the weapon of faith, there is no limit to the amount of damage the Church can do to Satan's dark kingdom.

Faith reacts like a shield; it blocks that which aims to sidetrack you from the plan and purpose of God. When the people of God unite, they become like a moving, steel wall, entering the enemy's camp to take back what he has stolen from us. If he stole your peace, take it back! If he stole your joy, take it back! Armed with God's mighty weapon of faith, we are marching on to victory.

Do not allow an arrow of fear, unbelief, negativism, gossip or doubt penetrate your mind and find a lodging place there. Let us work together as a unit and build each other up, not tear one another down! Division, doubt and unbelief are opposing forces to the weapon of faith.

The wiles of the devil are meant to weaken your faith and make you spiritually bankrupt! Let us take our believing faith and use it as a key to unlock the door to our miracle, breakthrough and deliverance. Faith that comes by the Word of God gives us the ability to overcome the world!

~Soaked in Water~

The shield was covered with strong, durable leather that required daily maintenance to prevent it from becoming stiff and brittle. Even when Roman soldiers were not at war, they continued the regular upkeep of their armor. This meant that the equipment would be ready for use at all times.

You may not be experiencing any difficulties right now, but that does not mean trouble is not on the way or that the enemy is finished with you. Having on your spiritual armor means never taking it off! Faith is an action word! Faith comes! How does faith come? By hearing the Word!

To quench the fiery darts of the wicked, you must soak your shield in water. Strong faith comes by hearing the Word of God. The water of the Word has power to extinguish all the fiery darts of the wicked one. Maintain your shield of faith daily. Search the Scriptures daily. Take up your shield of faith and saturate it with *"the washing of water by the Word,"* (Eph. 5:26).

As weapons of war, arrows were instruments of power and action. During Paul's day, the military used different types of arrows: 1) regular arrows, 2) arrows with the tips dipped with flammable materials such as tar, and 3) arrows made of cane with an explosive hidden inside.

1. Regular arrows usually caused little or no damage at all.
2. Arrows with the tips dipped in tar and set on fire were called "fiery darts" or *flaming arrows*. The arrowhead would be ignited and shot through the air at the opposing army; however, the *fiery dart* would be extinguished immediately upon impact by the water-soaked shield! If a soldier did not soak his shield in water, it could be fatal.

A flaming arrow had the potential to be deadly. A flaming arrow could set fire to a dry wooden shield, clothes, cloth tents, and even the soldiers themselves! The water-soaked shield would put the fire out and the enemy's fiery darts would be ineffective! A Roman soldier would be fully protected as long as he kept his water-soaked shield in its *out in front of all* position.

Terms such as "take," "take unto you" and "taking" mean that you must receive or accept the weapons of warfare by faith. As you continue to receive the Word of God into your heart, your faith will be strong; *"...faith comes by hearing, and hearing by the Word of God,"* (Rom. 10:17). Try and imagine what would happen if a soldier was so lazy that he neglected to soak his shield in water and a flaming arrow hit the dry, brittle, cracked leather. He could lose his life!

Faith makes you invincible! You will not crack under pressure if your shield is well saturated with water. If you find yourself listening to the devil's lies, there may be a crack in your shield. You may not be spending enough quality time in the Word. How does faith come? Faith comes from hearing the Good News about Jesus!

Without faith, you cannot *see* (spiritual things). Some things may appear to be harmless, but they can be deadly traps set by the devil. When the enemy shoots his *fiery darts* of temptation, selfish ambition and fear, we can put our shield in its *out in front of all* position and quench them all.

Never fear the worst. Believe God, by faith, for the best. Faith is a fight. Fight the good fight of faith. In order to run your Christian race effectively, you must run with faith and patience.

Grecian athletes did not look behind, neither did they look at their opponents when they were in a race. Do not look behind at your failures, and do not look at your current circumstances. It will only impede your race and become a weight that will slow you down.

"Above all, taking the shield of faith, wherewith ye shall be able to quench all the fiery darts of the wicked," (v.16). Your shield of faith must remain in its out-in-front-of-all position. Faith must not change with the wind or with the way you feel due to your circumstances. Remain steadfast and unmovable in your faith no matter what, come what may!

The word wherewith is defined as *with* or *by means of which.* In other words, the "fiery darts" or flaming arrows of the enemy are extinguished *with* or *by means of* the water-soaked shield.

Water puts out fire! Faith that is produced by the Word of God is like a shield that blocks the flaming arrows of the devil.

During a battle, the shield separated the Roman soldier from his opponent. Likewise, Christians must place faith between them and doubt. Doubt becomes your adversary when it is directed towards God. Doubt anyone else, but not God. It is one of the main causes for defeat.

The shield of faith will extinguish the spirit of doubt! My dear mother used to sing, "You can't make me *doubt* Him. I know too much about Him. You can't make me doubt Him, in my heart!"

Flaming arrows could not penetrate the fireproof shield of the ancient Roman soldier; neither can the *fiery darts* of the devil (depression, poverty, sickness) penetrate the believer's thoughts and emotions when his or her faith is *saturated with the water* of Word. God has given you power over *all* the power of the enemy and nothing shall by any means hurt you.

How you respond in difficult times will be the test of your faith. Obstacles are sometimes placed in your way to test you. So have faith, do not lose heart or hope. God Himself is going to come between you and that fiery dart to protect you. When you murmur against God, it grieves the Holy Spirit and Satan gets the glory. The Lord will put no more on us than we can bear. To do so would only *quench you*!

God's aim is not to break us, but to make us; not to quench us, but to drench us! Trust that God knows what He is doing in your life. He always considers our frame; nevertheless, He does allow trials and temptations. They cause us to depend on Him; otherwise we may become self-reliant.

Take the shield of faith so that you may be *able* to quench all the fiery darts of the wicked. The word "able" comes from the Greek word *dunamis* which describes a "powerful explosive strength" or "power." God is the Source of the *explosive strength* and *power* that gives you the ability to overcome adversities. There is no power that is more *explosive* than God's power!

God created Satan; therefore, he is no match for the Creator! Since he is no match for God, he is no match for the Christian who, during the worst time of his life, still has faith in God. To have unwavering faith in God is to have unwavering faith in His armor.

The Lord knows what makes the devil tick! Only God can beat the devil at his game. Being clothed in God's *weapons of mass destruction* makes you invulnerable and unconquerable!

The devil is actively pursuing Christians; doing all that is within his limited power to turn them away from God. Faith actually *creates* challenges and conflicts in your life. The weapon of faith must be tried, tested and proved. How else will you know whether it works or not? *"Beloved, think it not strange concerning the fiery trial which is to try you, as though some strange thing happened unto you,"* (I Peter 4:12, KJV).

Regardless of the trials you are facing right now, have faith in God's promises. Be convinced that God's Word works in your favor, even when it does not seem to be working. Do not walk by sight or common sense; walk by faith in the Living God!

The devil should never win a battle against a Christian, since God's armor never fails. We lose a battle when we have disobeyed His Word in some area of our lives. Find out where you went wrong and repent; turn around. He is faithful and just to forgive you and to cleanse you from all unrighteousness.

Jesus did not win a partial victory over the enemy; He didn't partially redeem us from the curse of the law. The Bible states that Jesus *completely* overcame principalities and powers. In Jesus' death, He openly and publicly defeated the kingdom of darkness for all to see. He stripped Satan naked and, being repulsed by him, *pushed* the devil *away* from Him. Christ did His part on our behalf until He was able to say, "It is finished!"

We must do our part and follow Christ's example in order to obtain victory over satanic powers; to quench *all the fiery darts* of the wicked one. *"For whatever is born of God overcomes the world. And this is the victory that has overcome the world –our faith,"* (I John 5:4, SFLB).

When Christ was laid in the grave it seemed like all hope was gone, even to those closest to Him. Nevertheless, on the third day Jesus miraculously rose from the grave and all power was given to Him in heaven and in earth! In His resurrection Jesus triumphed over the enemy, causing us to triumph.

The Holy Spirit gives you the ability to go on with your work likewise, until you have finished your course. The fight between you and Satan has already been fixed by Christ-*in your favor.* Even when you have been wounded by the enemy because of the cracks in your shield through neglect of daily maintenance (reading the Bible, prayer, and meditation), you can repent, take up your shield of faith once more and continue the fight of faith for what you believe.

Weapons made by humans are easily disarmed by God. The flaming arrows that Satan shoots at the believer (sickness, doubt, fear, depression and so forth) are no match for the weapons of our warfare: the Word of God, the Name of Jesus, love, righteousness, hope, faith, and prayer!

If you are troubled by your circumstances to the point of giving up, you may have neglected the daily upkeep of your shield. The Roman soldier soaked his leather covered shield in water daily, whether he was at war or not! His equipment was kept in top-notch condition. You must soak the shield of faith in the water of God's Word every day of your life!

Trust in God becomes strong by feasting on the Word daily. This takes discipline. It doesn't happen overnight. We must get into the habit of seeking the Lord for ourselves every day. Strong faith removes barriers of unbelief and prevents Satan from attacking our emotions with his lies, garbage and trash!

Christians do not live by what they see, but by every Word that proceeds out of the mouth of the Lord. We walk by faith, not by sight: *"For we live by believing and not by seeing,"* (II Cor. 5:7).

We cannot *see* Jesus, but He lives in our hearts by faith. We cannot *see* God, but we believe that He exists by faith. We believe in redemption by a God that we cannot *see*. We love a God that we cannot *see*. We pray to a God that we cannot *see*. By faith, we believe all of God's promises even before we *see* them come to pass!

Every human being has been given a measure of faith. However, when you become born-again you no longer walk in human faith. As Christians, our faith has been elevated (moved up) *from faith* (human) *to faith* (faith of Christ; Romans 1:17). Human faith changes according to the circumstances. When things are going well, human faith goes up! When things are bad, human faith goes down! The righteous live by faith, whether times are good or bad.

God is a shield to those who put their trust in Him (Prov. 30:5). In like manner that the Roman soldier's shield protected his vitals, when you put your trust in *everything* that the Word of God says, your faith becomes like a steel wall of protection for you; so strong that the enemy cannot penetrate it! Though God may be invisible to us, we are not so to Him: *"He that formed the eye, shall He not see?"* (Ps. 94:9).

Faith does not look at the things that are *seen*, but the things that are *not seen*. Don't let the devil blur your *spiritual* vision.

Hearing the Word of God increases your faith. The more you soak your shield in water (read the Bible, trust and obey its commands), the more your faith will stretch and grow. With your water-soaked shield in its *out in front of all* position, you will be able *to quench all of the fiery darts* of the wicked one.

~Anointed with Oil~

God's armor never loses power or effectiveness. It is due to our frame (human), that our armor (Divine) requires daily maintenance (Bible study, prayer, faith and works). In addition to soaking his shield in water every day, the Roman soldier also rubbed a heavy ointment into the leather to make it flexible. This procedure also kept the shield from cracking.

To quench all the fiery darts of the enemy, your faith must be anointed by the Word. Oil and water may not mix in the natural; however, in the spirit realm, the Word of the Lord (water) and the anointing of the Holy Spirit (oil) mix very well! The anointing comes from God. As the soldier rubbed the heavy ointment (oil) into the leather, God Himself will rub His oil *in* you through His Word, by His Spirit.

Over a period of time leather will dry out, become hard and brittle and will eventually crack. To prevent the leather from cracking, the soldier would soak his shield in water every day. After the moisture from the water made it pliable, the soldier rubbed oil into the leather. The now flexible leather would easily absorb the heavy ointment! First the water, then the ointment; first the Word then the anointing!

If the shield was not taken through this process daily, it would eventually crack or break and be of no use to the soldier on the battlefield.

Jesus was prepared for His earthly ministry: 1) He was sent by God, 2) He knew the Word, and 3) He was anointed by the Holy Spirit to destroy the works of devil.

Without the washing of the Word and the anointing of the Holy Spirit, you can build up a wall of resistance and unbelief (become brittle, crack) which can prevent you from receiving the flow of the Holy Spirit's power to work in and through your life!

The Lord wants to rub you with fresh oil daily. The just shall live by faith, daily. The Word of God and the anointing of the Holy Spirit will change our hearts into soft, pliable vessels and make us fit for the Master's use. Absence of the Word or the anointing can cause your heart to become hardened. A hardened heart will hinder you from receiving new ways of thinking that Christ brings. A pliable heart is a teachable heart.

Every day, His mercies are new. Christians need to be soaked in water (read the Word) and rubbed with fresh oil (anointed by God) every day of their natural lives. The child of God who walks in anointed faith will not be caught off guard by the enemy's tactics. Take up your well-oiled shield of faith daily and you will not crack, but surely walk in victory! Anointed faith believes that with God, all things are possible!

Oil denotes divine enablement. No believer can function effectively without the anointing oil of the Holy Spirit. When something is oily in the natural, it is very hard to get a good grip on it. That object will slide right out of your hands. Likewise in the spirit realm, if you are anointed (greasy), the enemy cannot get a firm hold on you. Every time that he tries to hold you down, you will slide right out of his grip and get right back up.

One of the Greek words for "anoint" or "anointing" is *enchrio,* which means "to rub in" (oil); to "besmear." The Greek word *epichrio* is used to denote, "to rub on."

To anoint has to do with "rubbing" or "smearing" oil *on* or *in* someone else. God rubs His oil *on* and *in* Christians; therefore, the Source of the anointing is God. God is the Anointer, not the anointing. According to Acts 10:38, God anointed Jesus of Nazareth with the Holy Ghost and with power; that same anointing is *on* and *in* every truly born-again believer!

As we grow and mature in the Lord, our troubles do not necessarily decrease. As you increase, your problems may also increase. God allows the tempter to come along and tempt you, because your response to trouble will reveal to you how much your faith in Him has or has not grown. Problems that you could not handle a year, a month or even a week ago should be treated as a *light affliction* to you by now.

Every believer has the God-given privilege of facing his or her battles using *the same shield of faith that Jesus used to defeat Satan*. If you find yourself worrying about your problems rather than trusting God, your shield may need to be anointed.

Perhaps you have been neglecting the daily maintenance of your armor; if so repent, pick up your Bible and saturate your mind with the water of the Word. After that, ask God to rub that heavy ointment *on you* and *in you* so that your faith becomes alive and active once again!

In the same manner that the Roman soldier rubbed the heavy oil into his shield every day of his natural military life — rain or shine, sleet or snow, tired or not, sick or well — we too must receive a fresh anointing from God daily. Each day has its own evils. The anointing that you received yesterday was sufficient for yesterday's battles. The fight is fixed, but it is not finished.

Don't be afraid of "the arrow that flies by day," (Ps. 91:5). Having on the complete armor of God is to have twenty-four hour protection! The "arrow that flies by day" speaks of some unexpected danger!

As previously mentioned, during New Testament times there were three types of arrows used by the military:

1) The first was a regular arrow used in normal combat, similar to arrows that are shot from bows today.
2) The second type was called a flaming arrow because the head was dipped in tar and set on fire.
3) The third type of arrow had the combustible material hidden on the inside! It was used against fortified encampments.

Paul refers to the third arrow as a "fiery dart" or "flaming missile" (6:16). This was the deadliest of them all. These flaming arrows, unlike the ones with the tip dipped in tar and set ablaze, had its explosives hidden on the inside! Talk about the devil in disguise!

This third type of arrow was made from a long, slender piece of cane which was cut at one end, held in an upright position and then the combustible material was poured into the cane, filled up to the brim and sealed on the inside. This clever disguise made the arrow extremely dangerous, because it resembled the less harmless one used for normal combat.

When the enemy soldier shot this deadly missile, his opponent could not see the explosive that was concealed on the inside. Upon impact, this arrow that carried the fire would burst into flames and explode like a bomb!

An unprepared soldier would be in trouble if his shield was cracked; the enemy's fiery dart could stick in his shield, explode and blow him to smithereens! However, with his well-maintained shield in its *out in front of all* position, and lifted up over all as a covering, the fiery darts would immediately be quenched!

This is the picture of the Holy Spirit's revelation to Paul when he wrote: *"Above all, taking the shield of faith, wherewith ye shall be able to be able to quench all the fiery darts of the wicked,"* (v.16). With God's armor, you can reject every evil thought and temptation aimed at you by the devil. Not all satanic attacks are apparent!

One of the serpent's characteristics is subtlety. Satan always has a hidden agenda; nevertheless, Christians should be able to recognize the way he is operating and put a stop to him! Most likely, the enemy's operations in your life right now are barely perceptible. Whatever the obstructions, you can overcome them using the powerful spiritual weapons at your disposal! To try and deal with the devil in the natural realm, in your own strength, will turn out to be a natural disaster!

God is our shield and buckler. The shield is the symbol of authority and protection. Do not dwell on your problems, failures, or your own inabilities. Trust God! Take the shield of faith and you will be able to quench all of the enemy's fires! For the Christian's faith to be strong and ready to face any foe, it must be soaked in water (the Word) and rubbed with oil (anointing). If you read the Bible daily and obey what it says, God will rub His fresh oil in you!

~Putting Faith to Work~

When you are Spirit-filled, Spirit-led, and Spirit-controlled, all that you are is anointed. As faith *covers all*, the anointing *covers all*. Being a Christian does not mean that we will escape all of the evils of this sinful world; however, we must not become dull to the conditions of the world in which we live. Our faith must not lie dormant. Using our weapon of faith, we can push back the enemy, turn the battle around, and actually change the course of nations!

Do not give the devil a foothold by neglecting your spiritual armor. Living by faith requires you to do something. Faith is active, not passive. Anointed faith must be put to work.

How do we put our faith to work? Working your faith means that, although you truly believe God is going to grant you that prayer request, even though you know that it is yours and you see it in your mind's eye, just keep on believing until that thing you asked the Lord for is manifested in the natural! As long as you continue to work, that faith it will stretch and grow.

Faith demands action. Scripture declares that faith without works is dead. Active faith is what stirs up the old oil. The more active you are for the Kingdom of God, the more anointed your shield of faith will become. Faith is what God is looking for, not failure.

Christ stands at the center of the Bible's teaching concerning faith. God desires the Church to function, by faith, in the same anointing that was upon His Son. One cannot truly define faith. We know that faith is not mind over matter, using your common sense, or the absence of fear. The apostle describes faith this way: *"Faith is the confidence that what we hope for will actually happen; it gives us assurance about things we cannot see,"* (Heb. 11:1, NLT). Assurance rests upon believing the promises of God.

Wielding your shield is putting faith to work. As you take up the shield of faith and carry it into battle, you will *go about doing good* as Christ did. How wonderful it would be if you could face all of your problems, circumstances and troubles full of faith! Well, you can, because God has already given us the victory!

Luke 17:6 is Jesus' response to the disciples' request for more faith (v. 5). Do not focus on the *size* of your faith. It is the *quality* of faith that matters. Even a little bit of anointed faith in God is capable of moving mountains. Active faith based upon God's Word has the ability to bring *all things* out of the sphere of impossibility into the realm of possibility. Put your mustard seed faith to work and it will grow to become strong faith.

The God-kind of faith uproots sycamine trees, kills giants with a sling and a stone, quells storms, and heals the sick! No giant, no obstacle, no stumbling-block, no-thing has the ability to stand before a trusting and confiding faith in the Lord Jesus Christ.

Weak faith will not give you victory over cancer, poverty, depression and discouragement. Faith must be strong! The problem that you may be facing right now requires strong, anointed faith *in action*. The giants of faith spoken of in the Bible were ordinary people made strong through faith! God has provided the same powerful weapon of faith to the Church today!

Totally depending on God is putting your faith to work. Doubt and unbelief will cause your faith to become inactive. The evidence of your faith might not be *seen* at first, but when the just live by faith, they will eventually *see* major results.

As time goes on, your little faith that is watered by the Word of God will take root and, like a tree planted by the rivers of water, will bring forth fruit in its season.

The Roman soldier's shield required daily maintenance or it would be of no use to him in battle. For the Christian soldier to develop a healthy habit of feasting upon the Word of God, it requires discipline. This habit does not develop overnight, and it doesn't happen accidentally.

The Word of God is the Bread of Life. Faith increases as you feast upon the Word. When your knowledge and understanding of the Person and Work of the Lord Jesus Christ (the Object of your faith) increases, your faith will increase. Believe that the power of God works *through* you and *for* you, by faith, and nothing shall be impossible *to* you!

Faith works best in hard cases. Our life in Christ is a life of faith. Whether you are climbing mountains, walking through valleys or weathering storms, rest; remain steadfast and unmovable from your faith. Problems are all the same to the powerful weapon of faith.

Going through rough places teaches you how to *speak those things that are not as though they are*. Trouble will cause you to release your faith in God and the impossible becomes possible!

The anointing will take you to a place where difficulties are to manifest His power to the world through you; to demonstrate that His power is like Himself: limitless.

Jesus sits at the right hand of *power;* the right hand of *God* (Mark 14:62). Power is His Name. Your weapon of faith puts Power to work. Since failure does not bring glory to His Name, failure is not an option. If you are suffering a lack attack right now, it is your own fault. In Christ there is no lack!

Tell that mountain, "Get out of my way!" Whatever the hardship, trust God, He does not make promises He will not keep; for then He would cease to be who He is! Don't let the enemy talk you into taking a shortcut instead of waiting on the Lord to deliver you. Go through the process!

If you try to work that problem out for yourself, the actions you take may be contrary to God's will which, in the long run, will do more harm than good. Put your faith to work now; tomorrow is not promised.

This is the victory that overcomes the world, our faith. Greater is He that is in us than he that is in the world. Through Christ you can experience greatness in every area of your life.

The greater the conflict, the greater the opportunity there is for the Great I AM to perform His mighty acts on your behalf!

Victories are not decided here on earth, they are decided in the Judgment Courts of Heaven, for *the battle is not ours* (II Chron. 20:15), but the Lord's. He decides the types of encounters that we face during our lifetime and He alone determines the outcome. The end result is that we win!

Out of obedience to the Word, the faith that we have in us will grow stronger and stronger. We have all the brain, muscle fiber, and all the faith we are going to possess. Exercise the brain, spiritual muscles and faith that you have. Whenever the devil comes against you with his bag of tricks, flex your steel-like faith muscles and he will flee!

God is looking for folks who will say, "The enemy is bread for us. Let us go forward by faith and possess the land!" This kind of confidence does not take *no* for an answer. It does not understand the "n" or the "o." Faith doesn't see obstacles when it is in its *out in front of all* position; it seizes opportunities! God's supernatural power is put into operation as you put your trust in Him.

If you look to God as the Source of all your supply, even in the midst of a crisis, your faith will not be shaken. Do not look to the natural, look to the supernatural. To doubt your faith armor is to doubt God. Behind every problem, there is a purpose.

Walk by faith, not by sight. Faith believes that He is. You cannot *see* God; therefore, without faith it is impossible to believe that He is. *He is* with you on the job, *He is* with you in the sick room, *He is* with you in the court room, in the car, in the kitchen, *He is* with you in trouble, and *He is* a rewarder of those who diligently seek Him (Heb. 11:6)!

Carnal weapons cannot penetrate into the realm of the spirit. They are not capable of locating and dealing with the unseen forces that are at the root of your problems. Spiritual weapons can go wherever God sends them and succeed in doing what He wants.

Equipped with the knowledge of who you are and Whose you are, *work the works* of God by faith. Whether your situation improves or not, continue to trust Him. Do not overburden yourself with the cares of this life. Try leaning on the everlasting arms of the Lord. Work your faith and your faith will work for you! Resist the spirit of complaining and reject anything that causes you to feel like a loser! Trust God to supply all you need, as well as the insufficiency of others.

Obey the Word and the shield of faith will operate in your life. You will not be influenced by what you see; disobedience brings defeat! Whenever trials come, you will have a firm footing like a soldier! Live the victorious life. In the realm of faith, all things are possible!

Set your faith in motion. Believers cannot live a victorious life without busy faith. Oh, they may experience a triumph every now and then, but not consistently. Since Jesus is Champion and we are clothed in the same armor that He wore, we can assume our rightful position of authority and dominion in earth and take back all that the enemy has stolen from us!

Faith is one of God's productive, progressive, and powerful *weapons of mass destruction*! With faith in its rightful "out in front of all" position, you can live and have a good finish to your life!

Paul endured many things at the hands of evil men; he was beaten, wrongly put in jail; faced death again and again until he was beheaded. Nevertheless, his life had a great finish!

Paul never removed his shield of faith from the "out in front of" position. He wrote, *"I have fought a good fight, I have finished my course. I have kept the faith,"* (II Tim. 4:7, KJV).

CHAPTER ELEVEN

THE HELMET OF SALVATION

"And take the helmet of salvation..."
(Ephesians 6: 17).

There is yet another powerful spiritual armor that Paul mentions — the helmet. God is spoken of as arming Himself for the defense of man; fully armed, going forth to defend His people. *"For He put on a helmet of salvation upon His head,"* (Isa. 59:17). Having a helmet of salvation on His head teaches us that salvation is "the crowning act" of God.

Through disobedience, the first Adam sinned and sin brought death into the world. God was not caught off-guard. He had already made provision for man's redemption. Salvation, like a helmet worn on the head, was already in God's mind. Saving mankind was His plan and purpose.

Man is restored by the death, burial and resurrection of the Last Adam. As the God-man, Jesus Christ was fully armed when He came to earth wearing the helmet of salvation. The salvation of man, his fellowship and communion with God, was the mindset of Christ.

Jesus came into a dark world as the Light of the world to save man from his sin through the shedding of His own blood, to *destroy all the works* of the devil. Our salvation does not rest

185

upon our feelings; it rests upon the finished work of Christ. It is a gift that God freely gives by His grace.

We do not work for salvation, nor can we earn it by good behavior. If you spent a thousand years in Hell, it could not purchase your salvation! Receiving the Lord Jesus Christ into your heart is the beginning of salvation and eternal life with Christ.

We must "take" the helmet of salvation. The word *take* used here is translated, "to receive."

Through Adam, all have sinned and have need of a Savior. We cannot save ourselves. Our Heavenly Father offers the Gift of salvation that one must either *receive* or reject.

When Adam and Eve sinned through disobedience, their eyes were opened. They realized their nakedness and immediately felt a strong sense of guilt. Ashamed of their nakedness, Adam and Eve hid from God. They sewed fig leaves together and made aprons "to cover" themselves (Gen. 3:7), only to discover that you cannot hide from God. Their nakedness was exposed.

Man has always tried to do things his way. *"For by grace are ye saved through faith, and that not of yourselves: it is the gift of God,"* (Eph. 2:8, KJV). Salvation through faith in God alone *covers all* of our sins. *"Unto Adam also and to his wife did the LORD God make coats of skins, and clothed them,"* (Genesis 3:21, KJV). Once more, faith covers all!

The coats were God's provision for reconciling man back to Himself. Man could not bridge the gap that sin had caused. God restored the fellowship by covering their nakedness with coats made of skins; suggesting that an animal had been slain and blood had been shed.

The wages of sin is death; physical and spiritual. This points to Christ, the Lamb of God that was slain (His blood was shed) from the foundation of the world (Rev. 13:8). The question is: "What can wash away my sins?" The answer is: "Nothing but the blood of Jesus!"

Life is in the blood. Man sinned and a Man with sinless blood had to die to pay the price for our sins. The wages of sin is death. It was not an animal that sinned. Under the old covenant the sacrifice of animal blood was only temporary until the Perfect Sacrifice (Christ Jesus) came to earth, was wrapped in human flesh and died for the sins of the entire world.

Animals had to be sacrificed over and over again; but Christ died once, for all! *"Neither is there salvation in any other: for there is none other name under heaven given among men, whereby we must be saved,"* (Acts 4:12, KJV). Salvation is the unmerited, unearned favor of God. Spend 900 years burning in Hell and that could not save you, because salvation is not by works. It is the gracious gift of God!

Adam and Eve tried to cover their sins by sewing fig leaves together. They made aprons that were too narrow to totally cover themselves. God, on the other hand, made them coats of skins that were large enough, long enough, and wide enough to *cover all*. God gave them a covering that was fit for them. In and of himself, man will always come up short.

We have *received the helmet of salvation*, not to live a trouble-free life, but to serve Christ and build up His Church. The helmet of salvation is a powerful weapon in our struggles against the enemy and the world. Those who are appointed for salvation will find that to be their protection.

The Holy Spirit painted a beautiful picture by likening salvation to a soldier's helmet. First of all, the helmet was handed to the soldier by an armor-bearer. It was his responsibility to reach out and receive it. Likewise, God stretches out His hand and freely offers us salvation. In turn, we must reach out and freely receive the gift of salvation from Him.

God is a Gentleman. He will not force Himself upon anyone. Likewise, Christians should not try to shove salvation down someone's throat. Lovingly offer them the free gift of God and leave the results to the Holy Spirit.

Some people are so burdened with guilt by their past that they feel God could never forgive them or love them. Before Christ came into Paul's life, he scoffed at Christianity. However, the Lord loved Paul, forgave him of his sins, and used him for His honor.

Now consider your own life before you received salvation! No matter how shameful your life may have been, God loved you, forgave you and is using you mightily for His glory!

Man by nature (Adam) is guilty in the eyes of God and under penalty of death (eternal). For this reason, He has provided the way of escape through His Son, Jesus Christ, who came to put away sin by the sacrifice of Himself (Heb. 9:26). Christ tasted death; that is, He died in the place of every human being. His death is the basic requirement for *every blessing* that we enjoy.

Since salvation is the greatest gift offered to man by God, it is every one's responsibility to receive the helmet of salvation for themselves.

Just as the soldier's helmet was worn in battle to protect his head, the helmet of salvation is worn to protect our thoughts from contamination and condemnation. To have on the *helmet of salvation* is to keep His Word in mind; to think saved thoughts. Those who retain God in their minds think like He thinks!

Before the fall, God created man in His image and likeness. Therefore, when Adam was created, he thought like God thinks. After the fall, man's mind became corrupted. In his sinful state, man cannot think like God. He must put on the helmet. He must be born-again (from above) and renewed in the mind by the Holy Spirit!

The mind is like a swinging door; sometimes it opens and lets the light in, at other times it slams shut to prevent light from coming in. Since sin is first conceived in the heart and mind, our minds should always be open to the Word of God. The helmet keeps you alert and clearheaded!

Seeing that the *eye gate* and *ear gate* are located in the head, these are avenues through which the enemy tries to gain access to the mind. Satan enters our thoughts through the things we *see* and *hear*. The helmet of salvation is designed by God to keep the enemy out! It is not possible for Satan to set up strongholds upon the mind of the one whose helmet is fixed tightly on his head.

A soldier did not always wear his helmet when he was not on the battlefield, but since Christians are always involved in spiritual warfare, we must never take our helmet off!

The believer who has on the helmet of salvation will not be easily duped. He thinks thoughts that are *true* (the devil is a liar), *honest* (the devil is dishonest), *just* (he is corrupt and deceitful), *pure* (he is polluted), *lovely* (the devil is repulsive and repugnant), and things that are of *good* report (his is an evil report).

The helmet represents salvation that has been accomplished by Christ through His suffering, death, burial and resurrection. Christ answered the sin question once and for all. This salvation will come to completion (consummate) when Christ returns. Satan would love to have you believe that Jesus is not coming back or that He is not coming back soon.

Be ready when the Lord comes!

For you know quite well that the day of the Lord's return will come unexpectedly, like a thief in the night. When people are saying, "Everything is peaceful and secure," then disaster will fall on them as suddenly as a pregnant woman's labor pains begin. And there will be no escape. But you aren't in the dark about these things, dear brothers and sisters, and you won't be surprised when the day of the Lord comes like a thief (I Thess. 5:2-4, NLT).

To receive the Second Coming of Christ as more than a doctrine just for the future will have a strong impact on how we live. Christ is coming back again. Knowing this, let us live in such a way that our lives will be acceptable and pleasing to Him. If Christ were to return today, right now, how would He find you living?

Although Jesus said we would not know the day or hour of the Second Coming (Matt. 24:36), He promised we would know the season. Therefore, we must live each day ready to welcome Jesus with open hearts and arms! The mind that is stayed on

Jesus and His imminent Coming will be found saying, "Even so, come, Lord Jesus," (Rev. 22:20).

The Greek word for "helmet" is a compound of the words *peri* (around) and *kephale* (a head). When these two words are put together, the new word, *perikephalaia*, is formed to describe something that is *tightly fixed around the head in order to protect it.*

With *the helmet tightly fixed around your head to protect it*, whenever thoughts and desires come to your mind that are contrary to the Word of God, be they ever so subtle, you will recognize that they are coming from the enemy of your soul and will immediately reject them! They will not find a lodging place in your heart.

In the natural, the Roman soldier's helmet was *tightly fixed around his head to protect it from the enemy's arrow, sword or dagger.* Placing the helmet on tightly also prevented it from falling off the soldier's head. Spiritually speaking, the helmet of salvation is to be *tightly fixed around your head in order to protect it* from ungodly suggestions.

The helmet, like all the other armor, must be worn at all times. Do not put your salvation on a shelf! Demons are unclean spirits. They will attack your unprotected mind with thoughts that will make you question your salvation! Warfare begins in the mind. If you think that you've lost the battle before you even walk onto the battlefield, then you have already lost.

If you are unsure concerning whether you are saved or not, you may not have your helmet on tightly enough. If you think you're saved one day, and are not so sure the next, your helmet needs to be tightened. Start spending personal quality time in the Word of God, daily.

Once again, all the other armor rests upon the belt, the Word; it creates a spiritual hedge around our minds. The Word is the only armor that builds this spiritual hedge of protection for our thoughts. Without it, Satan will set up strongholds around your mind. Furthermore, when a Christian meditates on the Word of God, he will become aware of the many blessings that are included in his salvation.

The Greek word for "stronghold" is *ochuroma* which describes a *fortress*. God builds His wall for protection; Satan builds a wall for destruction.

By definition, a fortress (*ochuroma*) is set up to keep outsiders from getting in. For example, Jericho was constructed like a fortress. The city was surrounded by great walls to keep Israel from getting in. Later, the word *fortress* came to mean "prison." A prison is designed to keep insiders (prisoners) from getting out!

Whether he uses a fortress or a prison, Satan wants to set up a stronghold around your mind. If you allow him to gain access to your mind by neglecting your spiritual armor, he will *lock you in* a state of oppression, depression and despair. The enemy will steal your confidence, your peace and your joy in the Lord! He cannot accomplish this with the helmet of salvation worn tightly around your head.

Like a fortress, Satan wants to shut the knowledge, blessings and promises of God *out* of your thoughts. He wants to keep light, love, and all that pertains to godliness, *out*. As long as you neglect Bible study (shut the Word out), Satan's strongholds will remain. Like a prison, Satan wants to lock the spirit of despair, fear, doubt, negativity and hopelessness *in*.

The attitude of evil has not changed. Nevertheless, if you have been storing up the Word of God in your heart, the devil will not be able to seduce or deceive you. Use the authority of the Word to counterattack the devil's schemes. Do not allow him to set up strongholds around your mind. He will enter an opening and imprison you. Quality time spent in the Bible will tighten your helmet.

Only the Word of God is powerful enough to pull down the strongholds of the devil. Once these strongholds (hidden sins) are brought down by the power of God's Word, do not allow the enemy to build them up again. The Lord is our Fortress. He will build a fence all around you. He will keep out that which needs to be kept out (evil), and will keep in that which needs to be kept in (goodness, righteousness, peace, prosperity, and health).

Wear the helmet at all times! A double-minded man is unstable in all his ways. You've got to know-that-you-know that you are born again. Your salvation must be more than a theory, an assumption or guess. Hold fast the profession of *your* faith without wavering (Heb. 10:23)!

Satan wants to inject his lies into your thoughts and if he succeeds, like an opponent with a battle-axe, he will chop your head off! He will chop off all of the promises and blessings that your salvation contains. He will chop them right out of your mind! Even when you mess up, you can be confident of your salvation and continue to enjoy every day with Jesus.

Another striking feature of the helmet was its appearance. Helmets were painted with rich, vivid colors. They were dazzlingly beautiful and elaborately adorned. Many were embellished with skillful workmanship of fruits, vegetables and animals engraved upon them. Some had long feathers or plumes protruding out of the top, which made the soldier look much taller than he actually was. One could not help but notice the soldier's helmet!

Like a Roman soldier's beautiful helmet, salvation is not dull. Salvation is beautiful! Living for Jesus is not dull and boring. When you have on the helmet and are living in the awesome reality of all that your salvation involves, you won't have to walk around with a huge Bible under your arm to attract attention; you will be noticed!

Deliverance from sin is the best thing that could ever happen to anyone. It is altogether lovely, dazzlingly beautiful and flamboyant in a great way. When you are born-again, you cease to be mediocre. God gave His Best (His Son) *to* us! Christ gave His best (His life) *for* us!

Salvation brings with it all kinds of blessings, but the greatest blessing of all is eternal life. The helmet refers to the mind that is governed by God. Closely inspect what you put in your mind through social media — television, videos, magazines, conversation, the internet, and so forth. Fill your thoughts with the Word of God, which has the power to transform you into a new person by the renewing of your mind. The Word will change your way of thinking!

Know what the Bible says concerning your salvation! That knowledge becomes a helmet of protection for your entire life.

Perhaps you do not have a personal relationship with the Lord Jesus Christ. If not, you do not have the helmet of salvation on for protection. You may receive salvation right now. Let God break the power that Satan has over your life by saying this short, yet powerful prayer.

"Lord Jesus, I confess that I am a sinner. Forgive me. I believe that You died for my sins and that You rose from the dead. Come in to my heart. Save me, for I cannot save myself."

The Bible says that, *"if you confess with your mouth the Lord Jesus and believe in your heart that God has raised Him from the dead, you will be saved. For with the heart one believes unto righteousness, and with the mouth confession is made unto salvation,"* (Rom. 10:9-10).

If you prayed the prayer of faith with sincerity of heart, you have just taken unto you (received) the helmet of salvation and are in right-standing with God. This means immediate forgiveness of sins, justification (just-as-if-you-had-not-sinned), and sanctification. *Congratulations!*

Salvation entitles you to all of the blessings given to men through the Holy Spirit, but you must continue to believe this truth and stand firmly on it. Keep your helmet *tightly fixed around your head to protect it from the enemy's dagger* and you will not drift away from the assurance that you became a new creation the precise moment you heard and received the Good News!

The helmet represents the mind that is Holy Spirit renewed and controlled. The Roman soldier maintained his weaponry every day of his military life. Salvation is not the end of the process. After you have given your life to Christ, ask the Lord to send you to a Bible believing Church where the Gospel of Jesus Christ is being preached and taught.

God has fitted the helmet of salvation tightly around your head; keep it that way. Jesus is coming back soon for His Bride, the Church. Do not let the enemy convince you otherwise. All who do not believe in the Rapture may stay here and enjoy the Tribulation Period!

Let us live each day as though Jesus may return at any moment. Who knows? He may come back for His Church today! *"Night is the time when people sleep and drinkers get drunk. But let us who live in the light be clearheaded, protected by the armor of faith and love, and wearing as our helmet the confidence of our salvation,"* (I Thess. 5:7-8, NLT). God bless you.

CHAPTER TWELVE

THE RHEMA WORD OF GOD

"And take...the sword of the Spirit; which is the Word of God," (Ephesians 6:17).

Another powerful spiritual weapon of our warfare is the Sword of the Spirit which represents a special, spoken Word of God: Rhema.

~The Gladius Sword~

The Roman soldier had several types of swords at his disposal. One was the gladius sword, which measured from twenty to twenty-four inches long. It was extremely heavy, broad-shouldered and had a very long blade that was *sharpened only on one side*. Because of its weight, the gladius was difficult to carry; therefore it was mostly used in an up-close battle. Though very cumbersome, the gladius was not useless.

There is not one person in Christ who is not vital to His war. Young converts should join mature believers in spreading the Gospel message. One may not be knowledgeable enough at conversion to spontaneously quote Scripture, but they may be spiritually prepared in other areas (hand out tracts, pray, give testimony). There is not one Christian in the household of faith that is useless.

The real problem with the gladius sword is that *the blade was dull on one side*. This means that, if the opposition was accidentally hit with the blunt side of the sword, he would probably only sustain a bad bruise. Wielding the gladius could backfire, because it had the potential to cause serious injury to the soldier if he accidentally hit himself with the sharp side of the sword!

Unlike the *gladius* sword, the Word of God is never meant to hurt anyone except the enemy.

The dull side of the gladius sword also represents the Christian who is not familiar with, or does not have a close intimate relationship with, the Bible. As the gladius was dull on one side, it is quite possible for believers to become dull of hearing, dull in their prayer life, and dull in their devotions with God. When you are dull of hearing what the Spirit has to say, you will not see many miracles, nor do many exploits for the Lord.

The dull side of the gladius sword represents the one who neglects Bible study. He needs to be sharpened. A sharp tool cuts best. *"Give ear, O My people, to My law: incline your ears to the words of My mouth,"* (Ps. 78:1, KJV). The human side may become dull due to the lack of Bible study but, like the sharp side of the gladius sword, God's side is always sharp, cutting, and effective!

In Matthew chapter seventeen, we have the story of a man whose son had epilepsy. He brought his son to Jesus' disciples, expecting them to heal him. Unfortunately, the man went away hurt and disappointed, because the disciples could not cure his son. When Jesus was made aware of the man's predicament, He said, *"Bring him to Me,"* and the son was healed immediately!

Jesus' side was sharp! The disciples' side was dull. They failed because of their dullness, which was caused by their lack of faith in the Word of God.

Another sword that the Roman soldiers used was shorter and narrower than the gladius. It was approximately seventeen inches long and about two and a half inches wide. This sword was very popular throughout the Roman Empire because, unlike the heavy gladius sword, this particular one was much lighter and easier to carry and swing.

The problem with this sword, however, was that a swinging motion *did not guarantee* a kill! The Word of God never fails or comes up short. It *always* accomplishes what He sends it out to do. *"So shall My word be that goeth forth out of My mouth: it shall not return unto Me void, but it shall accomplish that which I please,"* (Isaiah 55:11, KJV).

Another sword used mainly by the cavalry was made long and slender, in contrast to the more durable swords that were carried by the infantry or foot soldiers. No one in the military wanted to go into combat with this long, slender sword, because it bent too easily. The Sword of the Spirit, which is the Word of God, will *never bend* to man's way of thinking!

~The Machaira Sword~

Unlike the gladius which was sharp on one side and dull on the other side, the machaira was a two-edged, cut-and-thrust sword that was razor-sharp on both sides! The Roman soldier attached this sword to his belt on the left side when not in use, for easy access!

This was the deadliest of all the swords! It had the ability to inflict a wound far worse than any of the other swords. Armed with this sword, the Roman army had the ability to make its way into the enemy's camp, subdue them, and bring the opposing army under their control.

The machaira was used to stab the enemy in the heart and in his belly. Likewise, the Word of God has the supernatural ability to probe the conscience and subdue the impulses to sin.

Holding the machaira tightly with both hands, the soldier would violently thrust the sharp blade up to its hilt into the enemy's belly — not merely to wound the enemy, but to kill him — inflicting as much pain as possible!

With the sharp, two-edged sword plunged deep inside of the enemy's belly, the soldier twisted the blade back and forth, shredding the opponent's entrails (guts). After that, he quickly snatched the weapon out! As the sword exited, his opponent's shredded intestines spilled out onto the ground. No one survived that kind of assault! Death was certain. This was truly a lethal *weapon of mass destruction*. Its sole purpose was to kill!

The two-edged sword of the Word kills and makes alive! It kills only what needs to be killed; whatever the enemy has planted inside of you will come out quickly *at the entrance* of God's Word! Hatred, bitterness, envy, malice, discouragement, doubt, fear, and such cannot remain in the heart where God's Word abides.

~The Rhema Word of God~

"And take...the sword that the Spirit wields, which is the Word of God," (6:17, Amplified).

The Sword of the Spirit, which is the Word of God (Eph. 6:17), is called "Rhema" (Greek), which means, "to speak out" or "to speak a word;" a special spoken Word based upon the written Word. Rhema (spoken Word) is married to the Bible (written Word).

Rhema is a *special* Word, phrase or verse of Scripture that the Holy Spirit imparts *clearly* to your heart. It is a precise, revelatory impression upon the mind that the Spirit of God makes known to an individual. You will not need an interpreter. Before receiving a spoken word from anyone, be very sure that it lines up with the written Word. God only keeps promises that He makes!

Rhema is an on-point Word from the Lord for a particular situation. It is never ambiguous, loose or slipshod! The Spirit of God will make it plain and on point.

Rhema comes from the Lord out of a regular storing up of the *written* Word into your heart. Scripture memorization is very important. For the two-edged sword to come *out of your mouth,* the Word must be *in* your heart!

David said, "Thy Word have I hid in my heart." To "hide the Word in your heart" does not mean to bury the Scripture somewhere in the back of your mind. It means to treasure the Word in your heart. Then out of the abundance of the heart, the mouth speaks good things!

Whatever your need, God has a word for you. Let's say you are facing a financial problem; that Rhema may come from Philippians, *"But my God shall supply all your need according to His riches in glory by Christ Jesus,"* (4:19, KJV). There is always a seed (word) to meet your need!

Input determines your output. If you do not put in, you will not be able to put out! Words that come out of your mouth determine the course of your life! The more you put out for God, the more God will put in you.

Abbott-Smith wrote: "It is the articulated expression of a thought." One must articulate, speak a Rhema, clearly and distinctly. Before one can articulate a Rhema, the Word of God must abide richly in your heart (Col. 3:16) and take up residence there.

Rhema comes to renew your strength, not necessarily to deliver you out of that situation. More often than not, that *special spoken* word comes to help you make it *through* a trial until the Lord delivers you! Nothing stays the same; you and your situation will change, for the better!

The Bible says, *"Death and life are in the power of the tongue,"* (Prov. 18:21) and *"Call those things that are not as though they already exist,"* (Rom. 4:17)! We must take responsibility for what we say and, since your mouth is the facilitator of the Word, start wielding your Sword of the Spirit! Speak life into that situation today!

~The Rhema Word of God is Quick and Powerful~

"For the Word of God is quick, and powerful, and sharper than any two-edged sword, piercing even to the dividing asunder of soul and spirit, and of the joints and marrow, and is a discerner of the thoughts and intents of the heart," (Heb. 4:12, KJV).

The written Word does not become a Rhema Word until it comes out of your mouth. When you speak the Word of God to any dead situation, it has the potential to be quickened, or come alive! Don't bury that dead thing; resurrect it by the power of the living Word!

The blood that is circulating throughout the pages of the Bible, from Genesis to Revelation, gives it *quickening* power. Without blood, the Bible would be just like any other book and of no more value. Because of the blood of Jesus, the Sword of the Spirit is a Living Word and a *life giving* Word. The Church is a living organism, not an organization!

When the *written* Word is *spoken*, it influences the results of every situation. Since the Word is empowered by the blood of Jesus, when spoken into dead situations that business, that marriage, those children, that ministry, your dreams and aspirations, must come alive and grow! No good thing ever dies; it lies dormant until the living Word is spoken to it!

God responds to His Word. For this reason you must pick up your Bible, read it and allow the Holy Spirit to declare, "The Word of the Lord says..." to you or through you!

When reading the Scripture, believers may experience a special word from the Word in which a particular passage appears to be relevant to an individual situation in a fresh, new way. This is called a *quickening* of the Word!

The Word of God is not a dead letter. It is a living Word that *quickens* those who are spiritually dead and gives them life; not just life, but eternal life! The Sword of the Spirit is more powerful than any two-edged sword, which is designed to kill only. The Sword of the Spirit in the heart wounds and heals; kills and makes alive!

Everything is capable of dying — believers die physically, sinners die physically and spiritually — but the Word of God never dies! Every Word is jam-packed full of life-giving power!

~Two-Mouthed~

The Roman soldier's machaira sword required the use of his hands (physical) in order to exert its power. The Sword of the Spirit, the Rhema word from God, has its own power (spiritual) and needs no assistance in accomplishing its goal! The Roman soldier wielded a manmade sword.

The Sword that the Holy Spirit wields is the all-powerful Word of God! You don't have to use your hands to make the Word work for you — use your mouth to decree a thing!

Roman soldiers had to thrust the deadly machaira sword into his opponent, but the softest and most gently *spoken Rhema* has power to break the bones of (defeat) the enemy. You can speak to that mountain and tell it to get out of your way! Speak to the devil and tell him he is defeated!

Gethsemane and Golgotha were the battlegrounds for the conflict between Good and evil. Light and darkness would collide. This would be the fiercest of all battles to be fought –ever! Jesus fought the greatest battle ever and won. The key to Jesus' success was that "out of His mouth" went a "two-edged sword," (Rev. 1:16). He defeated the devil by *saying*, "It is written!"

The machaira sword was the most effective and deadliest of all the swords that the soldier had at his disposal. The problem was, the more the Roman soldier used this sword, the duller it became.

Unlike the manmade sword, the more you use your spiritual weapon (the *Sword of the Spirit*), the *sharper* and *more cutting* it gets! God's Word can never be overworked; it never gets dull!

It always succeeds in doing what God sends it out to do. The more you use it, the more you speak it, the sharper you will get!

When soldiers used this sword they had one thing in mind; to cause the opponent excruciating pain before death. The two-edged Sword that proceeded out of the mouth of Jesus was sharp, but He never spoke the Word of God to destroy or to condemn people beyond redemption.

The Father commissioned the Son to destroy the works of the devil (I John 3:8), not people!

Everywhere Jesus came in contact with the works of the enemy, He took authority over him by *speaking* the Word. No magic portion was used, He simply said, "It is written!" Darkness was dispelled, because the entrance of His Words gives light.

The Greek word *distomos* literally means, "two-mouthed." *Distomos* is a compound of the words *dis*, meaning "two" and *stoma*, which means "mouth."

According to this definition, the phrase *two-edged* means *two-mouthed*. Likening the Word of God to a two-edged sword is saying that it has two mouths: 1) God's mouth and 2) your mouth.

In the beginning, when God spoke, the Word was one-mouthed. Man was not yet created.

When the prophets (who are sometimes referred to as the mouthpiece of God) began to *speak*, the Word of God became two-mouthed. God spoke and the prophets spoke; for this reason the prophet's mouth has become the facilitator of the Word! Every time you *speak* the written Word of God it becomes two-mouthed (two-edged); sharp on God's side and sharp on your side.

The Lord makes the preacher's mouth like a sharp sword, but one that does not cause death to the Church. A servant must never use the Word of God to injure the people of God. Many folks are already hurting. The last thing they need is to go to the House of God and be injured even more. The Word of God must be proclaimed to comfort, to build and to edify; not to destroy (except that which is harmful to the individual — sin).

Rhema will foil every attack of the enemy. Never go into a battle thinking that you might lose! Wield your sword, use the Word of God *skillfully,* and it will be *effective!*

Each time Satan used a perverted version of God's Word to tempt Jesus in Judea's wilderness, he failed miserably, because *"Out of His mouth goeth a sharp sword."* Jesus quoted more Scripture than anyone. He was not deceived by Satan's distortion of Scripture. The sword that came out of Jesus' mouth was two-edged; sharp on the Father's side and sharp on the Son's side!

That Bible *in your hand and in your heart* is a powerful weapon. However, when it comes out of your mouth, it becomes a two-edged sword; sharp on God's side and sharp on your side. God rules the world by His written Word (the Bible) and His spoken Word (Rhema)!

~The Rhema Word of God Pierces~

God's Word is: *"Sharper than the sharpest two-edged sword, cutting between soul and spirit, between joints and marrow. It exposes our innermost thoughts and desires."*

The apostle Paul was referring to the Greek term *Rhema* when he spoke of the Word of God as being "sharper than any two-edged sword."

The Greek word for "pierce" is *diikneomai* which means, "to go through," "coming through," "penetrate," and is used regarding the power of the Word of God (Hebrews 4:12).

A Rhema Word is described as a two-edged sword that cuts through the flesh, down into the very deepest thoughts and intents of the heart. The weapons of our warfare are mighty through God!

The phrase changes from natural (joints and marrow) to spiritual (soul and spirit). God's Word has the power to cut through (pierce) the flesh and penetrate, even to the depths of the soul and spirit, so as to divide them without leaving any visible scars! No surgeon's scalpel, be it ever so sharp, can penetrate through flesh without leaving a mark.

The Word of God has the supernatural ability to cut through the lust of the flesh, the lust of the eyes, and the pride of life (1John 2:16).

"Nothing in all creation can hide from Him. Everything is naked and exposed before His eyes. This is the God to whom we must explain all that we have done," (Heb. 4:13, LASB).

Hidden thoughts and evil desires, be it ever so concealed, are exposed by the Word. They can be buried so deep that even you may not realize that they exist. The Word distinguishes between spiritual and carnal (flesh and spirit) so as to divide, reveal and remove them. God never has to say, "Oops! I made a mistake!"

Manmade weapons cannot locate the unseen forces that are at the root of your problems. Man's *weapons of mass destruction* destroy without distinction; good and evil. Nuclear bombs, nerve gas, biological and chemical weapons are used to kill masses and bring serious harm. They destroy everything they come in contact with: humans, mountains, manmade structures such as buildings (World Trade Center) and so on.

Give the Word of God an authoritative place in your heart and like a razor-sharp, two-edged machaira sword, it will pierce through and cut out sin, rebellion, anger, malice, bitterness and anything else that pertains to the old nature. When God takes away something, He replaces it with something better; a better life and better promises!

~Discerns the Thought and Intents of the Heart~

The Sword of the Spirit, which is the Word of God, is a *"discerner of the thoughts and intents of the heart."* The Greek word that describes "discern" is *kritikos*, which literally means "critical of; discriminating and passing judgment on the thoughts and feelings."

Nothing in all of creation can hide from God, be it ever so minute. He knows everything about everything. He knows our past, present and future. *"For there is not a word in my tongue, but, lo, O Lord, Thou knowest it altogether,"* (Ps.139:4). God said to Israel, *"I know the things that come into your mind, every one of them,"* (Ezek. 11:5).

Humans, however brilliant, do not know everything and may wrongly *pass judgment*. The sword of the Spirit differentiates between *thoughts* and *intents* of the flesh, as well as those that are of the spirit, then judges each accordingly and correctly. Man may falsely accuse and unlawfully punish someone, but God will never punish a person for something that he did not do.

We cannot truly judge what is in our own hearts, let alone someone else's. Nevertheless, God can detect the most secret thoughts. Do not try to hide what you are thinking from Him. Speak your mind freely to the Lord; after all, He already knows what you are thinking. God is able to sort out what you say and feel from what you really mean!

Nothing can be hidden from the all-seeing eyes of God. The sword that the Holy Spirit wields is able to detect and to separate good from evil as one sifts through a sieve used for straining.

Just because a person weeps after hearing a Rhema from the Lord or weeps at the Lord's Table, does not mean that his heart is pure. Those emotions may be expressions of the flesh, not necessarily of the Spirit; but do not judge. The Word of God will discern and pass judgment.

The sword of the Spirit is a critic that probes into the deepest and innermost (marrow) parts of our being and discerns what is of the Spirit and that which is of the flesh. Therefore, as believers, we must not role-play with worldly people.

Ask God to search your heart for anything that is displeasing to Him. He will reveal hidden sins so that you repent and, through His forgiveness, get rid of them. Ask God to do exploratory surgery on your heart and cleanse you from all unrighteousness. "Let us go on to perfection," (Heb. 6:1).

~The Power of the Word Works Through You~

The Sword of the Spirit (the Word of God) becomes a two-edged sword when you *speak* it. The more knowledgeable you are of the Scripture, the easier it will be for you to boldly and confidently *wield it* as Jesus did. Our mouths should be full of the Word of God, which is the Bread of Life. When the godly speak, many are fed and encouraged!

Rhema is an invincible sword! Many of us are content with giving the devil a *black eye* when he needs to be confronted and resisted! When the spoken Word enters the atmosphere, it puts the enemy back down under our feet (posture of defeat), where he belongs. The Word needs to go out of your mouth into the air so the *prince of the power of the air* may hear it and flee.

Wield your sword wisely and efficiently. Do not focus upon your inadequacy. Allow the Holy Spirit to thrust that sword right into the heart of the matter! He will speak a divine revelation from the Lord to that unique situation through you, and all of Heaven will back up that Word.

Rhema does not have to be lengthy or so deep that it becomes confusing. It can be ever so short, like a dagger piercing the heart and just as effective. It may be one word, a verse of Scripture, or a reminder of a promise God made. When the Spirit of God brings about the illumination of that Rhema to your mind, you will not have wonder if it was God, man or the devil speaking to you.

Your mouth is your deliverance or your demise; *death and life are in the power of the tongue* (Prov. 18:21). Input determines output! Like Jesus Christ our Victor, wield your sword and stab the enemy with, "It is written!" Hide the Word in your heart (sheath), the place from which the sword (Word) is drawn. For out of *the abundance of the heart* the mouth speaks!

CHAPTER THIRTEEN

FACE-TO-FACE WITH GOD

———————•———————

"Praying always with all prayer and supplica-
tion in the Spirit, and watching thereunto with
all perseverance and supplication for all saints,"
(Ephesians 6:18).

N ever allow yourself to be so busy *doing* that you become
too exhausted to pray. Never, ever become too anything
— too distressed, discouraged, tired or too lazy — to pray! No
prayer, no power! Little prayer, little power! Being caught up in
the day-to-day cares of the world can cause you to neglect this
powerful weapon. Prayer gives you spiritual energy.

The Bible does not say to preach without ceasing, or sing
without ceasing; however, it does say to pray without ceasing!

The Word of God, the belt, is the foundation piece for all the
other pieces of armor. God speaks to us through His Word; we
speak to God through prayer! We pray according to the Word!

Prayer brings blessings all the way down from heaven to
earth; from God to man. It is always beneficial whether we
are experiencing some great trial or not, because it keeps us in
touch with God. As we pray to God, the focus of our attention
shifts from ourselves to Him.

Paul clearly mentions six pieces of armor 1), the *belt*, 2)
breastplate, 3) *shoes*, 4) *shield*, 5) *helmet*, and 6) the *sword*.

There is no natural weapon mentioned to represent prayer. However, the colon at the end of verse seventeen shows that he is not finished with his series. The colon introduces the final part of the series found in verse eighteen. The apostle concludes his teaching on the whole armor of God with the powerful weapon of prayer.

He does not mention the lance or spear; nevertheless, the spear was also a weapon used by the military. The spear had a long shaft with a sharp, pointed metal head, used for throwing at a distance. The ministry of prayer can be likened to a spear. Prayer has a long reach; you do not have to be in the presence of the object of your prayer.

What is prayer? Prayer can be defined in many ways. It is talking to God about anything and everything, things that you cannot share with anyone else.

Prayer is communing with God, both publicly and privately. Jesus was never too busy healing the sick and casting out demons to pray. Prayer was His link to the Father. Christ's public ministry opened in prayer. His ministry also closed in prayer. As He was dying on the cross, the first of Jesus' seven sayings was a prayer for the souls of His murderers: *"Father, forgive them; for they know not what they do,"* (Luke 23:34).

Thank God, Jesus prayed! What a powerful example of the importance of prayer!

We may think that finding time to pray isn't easy but, like Christ, we must make every effort to break away from others and our busy schedules to commune with the Lord. This may mean getting up a little bit earlier or staying up a little bit later than usual. It will be beneficial to you and others. Jesus took time to pray and so must we.

Prayer is worship and adoration, asking and receiving, making your requests known unto God in faith. The moment a child of God says, "Father," His ears perk up!

There are not a number of ways to the throne of grace; there is only one way. The only direct approach to God is through

Christ; the Mediator between God and man. Some folks think they can by-pass the middle Man and go directly to God for themselves, but Jesus says, *"I am the way, the truth, and the life: no man cometh to the Father, but by Me,"* (John 14:6).

The New Testament was translated from the Greek language; therefore, some words make a greater impact on us when we understand what they mean in the original language.

Dr. Arthur W. Pink wrote that the ancient Greeks boasted of being able to say much in little- "to give a sea of matter in a drop of language" was regarded as the perfection of oratory.

For example, the one Greek word *proseuche* is used in this verse for prayer (Eph. 6:18). It is a compound of the two words *pros* and *euche*. The definition of these two words will give us a clearer picture and a deeper understanding of the privileges that we have through prayer.

There is a sea of information found in using this one word. The first part of the word *pros-euche* is *pros*, a preposition that means *face-to-face*. By this definition then, prayer can be defined as, "coming *face-to-face* with God." The original word *proseuche* tells us that prayer brings us *face- to-face* and *mouth-to-mouth* with God!

God is Spirit. We cannot see God as He actually is, for no man can see God and live (Ex.33:20, John 1:18). Nevertheless, spiritually speaking, prayer brings us up-close-and-personal and into the very presence of Almighty God!

The second half of *proseuche* is the word *euche* which denotes a *vow*. In your prayer you may voluntarily make a *vow* to God in order to receive the outcome you desire. When you pray, *"Lord if You heal my body"* or *"If You get me out of this, I will serve You for the rest of my life!"* That is a prayer in which you are making a *vow* to receive something from the Lord. Do not make a vow in prayer to the Lord that you do not intend to keep!

God has planned for you to be fully equipped, strong and energetic in battle! Prayer imparts that strength and vitality to rough the enemy up. Want to worry less? Then pray more!

Prayer increases our *spiritual and physical* energy levels. Lack of prayer and Bible study can deplete you of all your energy and develop into hopelessness.

Some folks will eat sweets, drink coffee, take a pill or drink a 5-hour energy shake to give them strength. After ingestion they may experience a sudden burst of energy, but it's only temporary. This quick increase of energy is usually followed by a severe letdown, leaving them feeling physically and emotionally drained.

On the other hand, God provides lasting energy through prayer without the sugar or caffeine crash! He refreshes the soul realm which consists of our desires, feelings, and emotions.

Prayer gives you enough energy to break the devil's spinal cord! The moment Satan's fiery darts of worry, fear, doubt, and depression come over you, get rid of them. These are not steppingstones; they are roadblocks to your blessings. They will sap you of your energy. A soldier needs stamina to fight a battle.

As long as you pray, you will continue to be invigorated. This we must do continually; prayer is not a one-time, every-now-and-then event. The Bible tells us to pray without ceasing.

Prayer gives us the opportunity to tell the Lord all that we are really thinking and feeling, good and bad. Get rid of the fig leaves. Transparency will be rewarded by a greater awareness and appreciation for God. He already knows everything, but wants to hear it from you.

~The Seventh Weapon~

Let us refer to prayer as the seventh weapon. Seven is the number of completion. The ministry of prayer completes God's panoply of spiritual weaponry. Prayer is not the most important spiritual armor; it is included in God's whole armor.

To the Jew, the number six had a very sinister meaning. Six was for the Jews what the number thirteen is to superstitious people today. Six is the number attached to the creation of man. It is the number that falls short of seven (completion), and failed. Through sin, man has fallen short, *"All have sinned and come short of the glory of God,"* (Rom.3:23). Six does not represent God, because God never falls short.

The number six is mentioned frequently in the Bible. It is no coincidence that the serpent is the sixth character mentioned; it shows the evils of Satan. *"Wisdom is needed here. Let the one with understanding solve the meaning of the number of the beast, for it is the number of a man. His number is 666,"* (Rev. 13:18, NLT). By using the number six three times (6-6-6), it shows the extreme wickedness of Satan! He is evil beyond redemption, but God has His number!

The number six shows the weakness of man. Man cannot defeat Satan *in his own strength.* He must have on the whole armor of God. Our ability to successfully do battle against the forces of evil comes through the weapon of prayer.

Seven was the most sacred number to the Hebrews. Seven is God's number. In completion of his discourse on the whole armor of God, the apostle concludes with the seventh piece, the weapon of prayer (6:18). Seven is the number of completion. Every attribute of God can be seen in these seven pieces or armor. Perfect! Nothing more is needed.

God's provision for the believer's victory is complete; finished (seven-ed). No one can improve upon what God has already done. Our spiritual arsenal is complete!

From the *sword of the Spirit* (which represents the Rhema Word of God), without breaking his trend of thought the apostle goes on to say, *"Praying always with all prayer and supplication in the Spirit, and watching thereunto with all perseverance and supplication for all saints,"* (6:18).

Prayer and the Word are powerful weapons that are married to each other. To Christians, they are spiritual weapons of warfare to bring victory! To evil principalities, powers, demonic forces and the rulers of the darkness of this world, they are spiritual *weapons of mass destruction!*

Paul is often found asking for prayer for himself. Immediately after he says, "praying always," (v.18) he says, "and pray for me too," (v.19). He referred to prayer with a sense of urgency, not as an afterthought. The Church of the Lord Jesus Christ is to be a praying Church; praying for all men everywhere. Prayer waters a revival. It was Paul's prayerful attitude that kept him in the midst of revival, even in prison.

You cannot maintain your victorious position without prayer! Victories are won, first of all, in the prayer closet. Only in a close spiritual relationship with God, developed through prayer, will you receive true power to withstand problems, difficulties, and the attacks of the enemy.

~All Kinds of Prayer~

The spear was made of iron, with a long shaft and sharply pointed head. This weapon was used for throwing. There were different kinds of spears that varied in sizes, length and shapes. Roman soldiers used all kinds of spears: long and short spears, wide and narrow spears; jagged and pointed spears. Each type had its unique importance and effectiveness.

The various types of spears represent the different types of prayer that are available to Christians; long and short prayers, public and private prayers, audible and silent prayers. Like the various types of spears, each type of prayer has its individual uniqueness and effectiveness. However, all are required to put the kingdom of darkness in full retreat mode!

Paul instructed the Ephesian Christians to pray always with "all kinds" of prayer. The Word of God commands us to pray! To "put on the whole armor of God" is not an option. These are real weapons of warfare that Christ has put into the hands of believers.

The *pilum* is said to be the type of spear used by the Roman soldier to stab Jesus in His side, in the lower fifth rib. The *pilum* was about six or seven feet long, made with a spear-head of solid iron which caused it to be very heavy. Roman soldiers used the *pilum* spear when an opposing army tried to invade their campsite.

The enemy army would often try to attack a Roman army's campsite, thinking to catch them by surprise. Seeing the enemy coming from afar, the soldier would reach for his long *pilum* spear and hurl it through the air from a distance in the direction of the enemy.

By hurling the spear at his opponent, the Roman soldier would stop the enemy before he even came near the camp. This was a tactical military maneuver that gave the Roman soldiers the advantage of killing the enemy from afar. As a result, no one in the Roman camp was hurt or killed. All of the casualties were on the enemy side!

Quite unexpectedly, Satan will strike when you least expect it. Believers who have on the whole armor of God will not be caught with their sail down, so to speak. When trouble comes, they will pick up the spear of prayer, hurl that weapon into the air and aim it right at Satan, the *prince of the power of the air.* This will prevent you from becoming one of Satan's casualties!

Spears were designed to inflict excruciating pain upon the opposition and ultimately kill them. The devil is the adversary. Our prayers should cause his kingdom much damage. Pray deadly prayers! Even the shortest prayer can be powerful enough to deliver a death-blow to the devil!

Whether the prayer is long or short, all are important and can be effective. The long spear was used for throwing to stop the enemy at a distance; the shorter thrusting spear was used close-up, to stab the enemy in his heart or cut his head off! No prayer that is uttered in faith is ever useless. When going through difficult times, you may pray a long prayer or you may utter a short prayer. Just be sure to serve the Lord in your prayers.

Pharisees often prayed long prayers, but in pride they served themselves. Prayers and devotions, whether long or short, should always honor God. Genuine utterances that come from a pure heart are never useless and are never discarded. They may have been uttered years ago, yesterday, or today; God never forgets our prayers. He cherishes them all.

No situation is too small or insignificant to pray about. You are important to God and He is concerned about how you are getting along.

~Praying Always~

The Church must give itself to unceasing prayer. *Praying always* does not mean that you are always on your knees. You do not have to be in a certain place or position. Just pour your heart out to the Lord — audibly or silently — whether you are kneeling, standing, or walking.

He that *planted the ear, shall He not hear? He that formed the eye, shall He not see?* God is not deaf, neither is He blind; He sees what you are going through and He hears your cries!

You may ask, "How can I pray all the time?" Well, how can you breathe all the time? No one sits and wonders whether they should breathe or not. They just breathe. If you do not breathe, you will die physically. Prayer is just like that. If you do not pray, you will die spiritually!

No Christian can survive spiritually without prayer. How can you fight a battle without energy? A soldier needed energy to carry his armor, to carry the heavy shield, and to throw the heavy *pilum* spear. Prayer energizes and gives you strength and endurance to fight your battles!

Paul was a prayer warrior at heart! His ministry was successful, because he gave himself over to much prayer. By word and example, he taught the Church to pray without ceasing. Scripture gives much prominence to the mighty weapon of prayer!

To explain "praying always," Paul uses the Greek phrase *en panti kairo*:

1) *en* translated *at*
2) *panti* translated *each* and *every*
3) *kairo* for *times* or *seasons*

Pray *each* and *every* day, and do pray *every chance you get*. Using this phrase is how Paul pressed this vital matter upon the hearts of the people. It implies opportunity and urgency. In it all, pray on each and every occasion (seasons) without ceasing.

Christians should strive to be in a praying frame of mind at all times. Do not wait until you're ill or in a financially depleted position to pray. If you continue to pray *every chance you get*, before long, prayer will become a wonderful habit for you!

As we approach the throne of grace, let us ask the Father to impregnate us with a praying spirit. Start praying for others, since we are all targets of Satan. When you are going to the store you should be in an attitude of prayer; to the doctor's office, to the mall, to visit family members, even going to a prayer meeting, you should pray (Acts 16:16-26)!

Satan is right there in the midst of your prayer meeting, trying to cause confusion in the body of Christ, the Church. If he is crazy enough to push his way into the presence of God to accuse the brethren, he certainly isn't afraid to crash your prayer party!

Manly — that's what prayer is! It is a gift and a privilege that is given by God to man. Man is the *only* animal that can *naturally* look up. Prayer is looking *up* -to God!

Sadly, some men live like beasts. They never look up or lift their faces up to God. So many pitfalls in our lives could be avoided if we would only pray. Spiritual warfare is not something that believers talk about to frighten someone; this is what we do!

Christ was lifted up on the cross and died for our sins. He is the solution for the whole world to be saved, and yet folks are still dying today because they will not look up by faith and live. Prayer is a manly thing; however, man still refuses to look up to Jesus in prayer.

Christ was found often in prayer. Even now, He is sitting at the right hand of God, making intercession for the Church (Rom. 8:34). Since Jesus is praying, shouldn't we pray also? There is nothing wrong with others praying for you, but the Lord wants to hear directly from you!

Through Christ, we have total and free access to the throne of God: *"Let us therefore come boldly unto the throne of grace that we may obtain mercy, and find grace to help in time of need,"* (Heb. 4:16). Make your request known to God yourself, in the Name of Jesus!

~Never Give Up On God~

Without the weapon of prayer, you are not completely dressed for spiritual warfare! Prayer is our conduit to God. Satan wants to clog this pipeline and stop the flow of God's power to you. His tactics will only work on those who are lacking in their prayer life.

The Lord is aware that long spiritual battles can leave you feeling whipped, even to the point of throwing in the towel. He has the power to change your situation in the blinking of an eye, but that does not always suit His purpose, which is to bring you to spiritual maturity.

The Lord chooses to help us gradually, teaching one lesson at a time. He speaks through our circumstances. Unfortunately, we often fail to hear that He is simply saying, "Trust Me!" If you feel beaten down by the cares of life, don't turn away from God. He never slams the door of compassion on His children. What might seem slow to you is perfect timing from God's perspective. He is an on time God; yes, He is!

Take up that spear and pray *through* until you get your break-*through*! God can remove every obstacle; He can remove or by-pass Satan's roadblocks. He will remove any obstruction to bring His Word to pass. God did not lie to you. If He said it, He will do it!

David prayed: *"I am exhausted from crying for help; my throat is parched. My eyes are swollen with weeping, waiting for my God to help me,"* (Ps. 69:3). David cried out to the Lord until he was physically spent, but continued to wait for God to deliver him.

Trust the wise judgment of God. In times of crisis, after you have prayed, your energy level will rise and you will be able to soar on like an eagle. That means you have rolled that burden over onto the Lord and you are no longer carrying it. You have a choice: fly like a buzzard (low), or soar like an eagle (high)! Your prayer life will determine which bird you resemble most.

No matter how devastating your circumstances are, pray. *Pray always*, pray *every chance you get*, and pray on *all occasions;* even when things are going well, pray. Is there a better time to pray than when you are in trouble? Yes — when you are not in trouble. Prayer has a great influence on God, not necessarily on the results.

Give yourself continually to prayer and you will never give up on God. Before Christ ascended back to the Father, He told His disciples to keep in touch by prayer.

This powerful armor is essential to bringing blessings down from heaven to earth. It changes situations, nations and families. The world can be changed through prayer.

~Grasshopper Mentality~

Every common day-to-day problem; every attack of the enemy on your life is due to the war between Good and evil. God is aware of everything pertaining to this war. *"The Lord is a man of war: the Lord is His name,"* (Ex. 15:3). Pray, give that situation to Jesus and watch Him work it out for you. Out of a bad situation, God is going to make something good happen for you!

How can you defeat the enemy if you go into the battle feeling like you are a loser? Some folks go through the motion of praying, but they do not really and truly believe that God is going to answer them. With this kind of attitude, they are already defeated. They make their problems larger than the God they serve. Powerless, "namby-pamby" prayers are produced by unbelief. Get rid of that *grasshopper* mentality and believe God! You have His Word. He promised you!

Individuals with a *grasshopper* mentality have a negative mindset. They can easily be defeated by the slightest difficulty. The battle is already lost in their minds, even before it begins! Every problem is magnified *as a giant!* They do not believe that God can deliver them. Folks with the *grasshopper mentality* "big up" their problems when they should *big up* God, who is able to solve the problems. In their hearts, they are already defeated. God is bigger and stronger than any giant.

In Numbers 13:33, the people of God saw themselves as grasshoppers and they said that the enemy also saw them as grasshoppers. The Bible does not say at all that the giants, the sons of Anak, saw them as grasshoppers. We must see ourselves as giants, not grasshoppers. To see yourself as a grasshopper is like being afraid of your own shadow! See yourself as God sees you; as sons and daughters, overcomers, blessed, victorious!

Fear and unbelief caused the entire generation to lose out on their inheritance except for two men, Joshua and Caleb. These were men of faith who said, "They are bread for us," (14:9). With God's help, we will eat them up like bread! Joshua and Caleb had faith in God, who deals with giants as if they are grasshoppers. It's all the same to Him!

That grasshopper mentality — that "I'm already defeated" attitude — will drain you of your energy spiritually, emotionally and physically. How can you thrust the spear or lance without energy? Prayer generates spiritual energy so that you can run the race and fight a good fight.

Roman soldiers needed strength to carry their heavy armor; to pull the sword out of its sheath; to thrust the spear into the air at a great distance, wound the enemy, run up to him, thrust the dagger into the adversary's heart, then cut his head off! All of these activities took a lot of strength and fortitude, but they were physically and mentally equipped to meet the challenge!

As you commune with God in prayer, no matter how tired or spent you are, your strength will be renewed! It is our own fault when we succumb to trials.

Jesus has fixed the fight in our favor. If you lose a battle, don't get mad at God. He could very easily ask, "Didn't I tell you to *pray always* and *every chance you get?*" "Didn't I tell you to *ask anything* in My Name and I would do it?" "Didn't I tell you to put on the whole armor of God?"

We have not because we pray not! Be persistent in praying. Get rid of that grasshopper mentality and believe God for the victory! Know the Word of God and pray according to His Word. When your heavenly Father hears you pray His Word, He hears Himself; He hears you when He hears His Word. This means that He Himself has spoken and He will make it good!

When He promises, "I will never leave you or forsake you," He means just that. No one else can say those words and is able to keep them, but God!

During those times of asking God, "Why me?" we find that He is not known so much for explaining Himself to us. It is enough for us to know that He *allows* things to happen in our lives that will test our testimony; they are never sent to be destructive.

Victory over that seemingly impossible situation is yours through prayer! Ask God to cultivate in you the spirit of Joshua and Caleb; men of faith. You have not, because you believe not!

Do you want to view yourself as a giant or a grasshopper? Having a prayerful mindset *or* attitude at all times will get rid of that grasshopper mentality. You will be able to say as Caleb and Joshua said, *"With God's help we will eat the enemy up like bread!"* Have faith in the God who deals with giants as if they are grasshoppers! It's all the same to Him!

~Pray Always with all Kinds of Prayer~

The spears that the Roman soldiers utilized were of different sizes and shapes. Similarly, there are different categories of prayer: the prayer of *thanksgiving*, *petitions*, *intercession* and the prayer of *supplication*. There are also the prayers of rest, suffering, healing and radical prayer, to name a few. These categories of prayer cover things that are both natural and spiritual.

A spear is only effective when the soldier picks it up and hurls it at his opponent. Prayer is only effective when we pray. It is not enough to know how to pray; we must pray. Take that spear and aim it right at the enemy's wicked heart. Real praying never misses its mark! It always hits its target. With the enemy down on the ground where he belongs, run up to him and with your *weapon of mass destruction* (prayer) cut the serpent's head off!

Regular care and maintenance of his equipment was each soldier's responsibility. Likewise, it is each believer's individual responsibility to spend quality time in prayer. Set yourself to seek the Lord in prayer. Do not become rusty with the things of this world through neglect of prayer.

Not one piece of our spiritual armor should be preferred to the exclusion of another. Some folks enjoy studying the Word of God, but they do not spend much time in prayer. Do not do one and leave the other undone. To read the Bible and spend little or no time in prayer is to be unarmed. Prayer is vital to the believer's victory in warfare.

When we pray, we acknowledge our dependence on God and bring Him into the battle. The Holy Spirit works through the Word of God *and* prayer. Some of us see prayer as a last resort to be tried when all else fails. This approach is backward. If you pray, when trouble comes, you will not faint. Praying always is staying in continual communion with God.

You can pray while kneeling, standing, walking, driving, cleaning, and yes, even while you are sleeping! Have you ever prayed so hard in a dream it woke you up, and you were still praying? What a beautiful experience! The next day you feel a tremendous surge of God's power and anointing! Prayer ushers you into the Holy of Holies where the shekinah glory resides!

The Church needs gifts and administrations, but these are ineffective without prayer. God has provided the weapon of prayer to bring a spiritually balanced diet to the Church. Unfortunately, prayer is the most ignored and neglected piece of armor that God has provided for the Body of Christ. A prayer-*less* Church is a power-*less* Church. The *less* you pray, the *less* power you will have operating; and the *"less"* miracles you will see performed in your life.

Christians cannot maintain a victorious position apart from a life of prayer! God desires raw, uninhibited, exuberantly uncon-strained prayer from Christians *at all times (en panti kairo)*.

Plans should never be made, not even for vacationing, without consulting the Lord first. Ask Him what He thinks! The Lord wants to be included in everything that you do. Some of us don't even invite Him to accompany us (even though He is everywhere), and when we get into trouble we expect Him to bail us out!

Pray *always*. Come *face-to-face, eyeball-to-eyeball,* and *mouth-to-mouth* with God *every chance you get*. Since God is Spirit, no man has seen Him in His essence at any time. To come face-to-face with God means that prayer brings us immediately into the presence of Almighty God.

Roman soldiers had the freedom to use various types of spears. There were long spears, short spears, narrow spears, wide spears, sharp spears and jagged spears; in a similar way, there are short prayers, long prayers, audible prayers and silent prayers.

One situation may only require a short prayer. Another situation may require all-night praying. Some situations are so difficult, so severe, that a short prayer just won't do! They may require strong crying and praying *all night*. The Spirit will lead you when the need arises. Simply pray until you get your breakthrough or until you feel finished!

Prayer warriors do not punch a time card. Some of us do not need to know *how* to pray, we only need *to* pray. Lord, teach us *to* pray! The more you pray, the better you will be at praying.

Praying always *"with all prayer"* is taken from the Greek phrase *dia pases proseuches,* which literally means praying "with all kinds of prayer."

Paul said, *"First of all, then, I admonish and urge that petitions, prayers, intercessions, and thanksgivings be offered on behalf of all men,"* (I Tim. 2:1). In this verse, the apostle mentions various categories of prayer. In Ephesians 6:18, the prayer of supplication is also mentioned.

Categories of Prayer:
1. Thanksgiving
2. Petition
3. Supplication
4. Intercession

Roman soldiers used the long spear to stop the enemy at a distance. He utilized a short spear up close to cut the enemy's head off! He used the weapon that was appropriate for the situation. All of the various kinds of spears were effective when utilized, no matter what the size, shape or length. In like manner, God has provided different types of prayer — the prayer of thanksgiving, intercession, petition, and the prayer of supplication, to name a few — for the believer's use.

"Come boldly to the throne of grace and bring every need to God in prayer" is an invitation that is extended to all Christians. Every unkindness, suffering, unhappiness and trouble that has come upon this world is due to man's disobedience; to disobey God's command to pray is sin. Do not neglect this blood-bought, Heavenly privilege!

The Church must not adopt a nonchalant attitude towards prayer. All who are led by the Holy Spirit to receive burdens and faithfully take them to the Lord in prayer are the true priests of today. Instead of complaining about them, prayer warriors take burdens to the Lord.

Watch and pray! Be alert! Pray with *every kind of prayer* that is at your disposal.

The Prayer of Thanksgiving

Rather than complain, turn to God in faith and rejoice in your sufferings. In everything "give thanks," (I Thess. 5:18). Prayer and thanksgiving go together. When we bring our problems to the Lord, there should be thanksgiving along with the asking. Give thanks to the Lord when you *feel* like it and when you *do not feel* like it.

Thank the Lord in advance for answering your prayer, because He will respond in a manner that will align your wants and desires with His divine purpose for your life. During tough times, if you are not in an attitude of prayer you may find yourself with a complaining spirit instead of a thankful heart. No one can be miserable while really giving the Lord thanks!

The remedy for a complaining heart is to *look back over your shoulder* and begin thanking the Lord for all He has done for you. Then thank Him for the love, protection, strength, peace, and all the other things that we take so much for granted; like breathing God's air. Above all, thank God for sending His only begotten Son to die for you. With Him, God freely gives us all things!

Our thanksgiving should not fluctuate with our situation, whether we are in a crisis or not. Do not wait until your situation improves to thank Him. Anyone can give thanks when all is well.

Undaunted by the conditions of his surroundings, Paul wrote, *"In everything give thanks: for this is the will of God in Christ Jesus concerning you,"* (I Thess. 5:18). He knew that being locked up in a Roman prison was in God's plan and purpose for his life. It was in prison, not on a beach somewhere sipping piña coladas, that he learned to give thanks unto the Lord!

"Thank you" is a short, two-word phrase that means so much and yet we use it so little. When someone does something for you, be it ever so small, say "Thank you." Let them know that you appreciate what they have done. An attitude of gratitude must be cultivated.

God is always doing something good for you, whether you realize it or not. This is why it is so important to *continually* give Him thanks. Last year, you were laid off. Here it is, a year later, and you own your own business! God did that! God was blessing you and you could not see it.

Thank God for seen and unseen blessings!

We complain about the silliest things. The prayer of thanksgiving will immediately usher you into the presence of Almighty God; murmuring and complaining will not. They will bar the door to your blessing!

God has sacrificed His only Begotten Son and *with Him* has freely given us all things. Jesus gave His life for us. What can be better or greater than that? Let His praise *continually* be in your mouth. Selah. Let us please pause right here for a moment and tell the Lord, "Thank You."

Has lamenting helped your situation? Does it help if you cry and throw a pity party? Do you feel better now after that tantrum? Can you breathe a sigh of relief now that you have blamed the entire world for your problems? Can a person pick olives from a fig tree or draw fresh water from a salty pool? Can thanksgiving come from a discontented heart? A thankful heart cancels out grumbling and bellyaching and gives glory to God for what He has done for us!

The Old Testament world is saturated with the prayer of thanksgiving. David appointed Levites to lead the people in worship before the Ark and gave them a specific charge: "To invoke His blessings, to give thanks, and to praise the Lord, the God of Israel," (I Chron. 16:4, NLT).

Jesus was the utmost grateful Person! Believers must not pattern themselves after the world or an ungrateful society. We serve a loving, generous God. It is not enough to give Him thanks one day out of the year, on the fourth Thursday of November. There is so much to be thankful for every day of our lives! We cannot say "thank you" enough to our parents, our family, friends, even strangers and more than anyone else, to God!

Thanksgiving is an expression of joy God-ward. As believers abound in *thanksgiving,* it brings glory to God the Father. Christ has reconciled us to God and has redeemed us from the curse of the law; therefore, we owe Him thanks, no matter what our situation is like. Paul said, "I will glory in my infirmities," (II Cor. 12:9).

Paul went on to say, "I take pleasure in infirmities," (12:10). Our purpose is to glorify the Lord and to give Him the praise that He deserves, no matter what we are experiencing.

To quote from the Westminster Shorter Catechism of Faith, "Man's chief end is to glorify God and enjoy Him forever." The prayer of thanksgiving is a powerful weapon for spiritual warfare!

If there is an onslaught of attacks upon you by the enemy, the blessing that's coming your way must be enormous! The difficulties that you are experiencing may be an indication that you are *following hard* after God. All of the heartaches and pain that we suffer in this life are nothing compared to the glory which shall be revealed in us (Rom. 8:18)!

An ungrateful heart will keep you from entering God's rest. Be persistent and alert in prayer *with* thanksgiving. The Bible says, *"Continue in prayer, and watch in the same with thanksgiving,"* (Col.4:2). The word "with" causes an unbreakable bond between prayer and thanksgiving; "with" also fastens *asking* securely to *receiving* and forms a kinship between them.

The Bible says if we ask, we shall receive; conversely, to receive one must ask. If you believe you have received that which you asked for, then the Giver should be thanked!

Paul wrote this letter to the Ephesians during one of the most dreadful times of his entire life; yet, there is not even a hint of it in his message. There is no evidence of his complaining in it at all. Christians who are busy giving God thanks don't have time to dwell on their problems.

Why would our heavenly Father withhold any material or temporal blessings from us? Isn't the life more valuable than the dollar, the job, the house, or the car? When you think of the goodness of Jesus and all that He has done for you, how can you not be thankful?

Everything looks cloudy and gray to an unappreciative person. A thankful heart will brighten up your day! Thanksgiving is the antidote for complaining. Whatever the subject of your prayer, it should never exclude thanksgiving! It is God-honoring, God-exalting, and God-glorifying work!

The Prayer of Petition

Another *kind of prayer* and a very common one is the prayer of petition; it denotes asking, an entreaty, a request. A prayer of petition is asking God for something you need or desire; to make your request known unto God. This does not mean you're asking for stuff (money, a car, house, flat-screen TV); you are praying for souls to be set free, healing, peace, deliverance, unity, and so forth.

If we seek first the Kingdom of God above everything else and live righteously, He will give us everything we need (Matt. 6:33). While you are making your requests known to the Lord, let the asking be infused with thanking.

"And if we know that He hears us, whatsoever we ask, we know that we have the petitions that we desired of Him," (I John 5:15).

The Prayer of Supplication

Supplication is the "action of asking for something earnestly; to ask with fervor, determination, diligence and persistence." The Greek word *deesis* is used in Ephesians 6:18 for the prayer of supplication. The prayer of supplication expresses an intense sense of *need. Deesis* speaks of an urgent request addressed to God.

Since the New Testament was translated from the Greek language to English, going back to the original language will give us a better and clearer understanding of what the writer is saying. The essence or meaning doesn't change, it just heightens our knowledge of what is being taught.

Paul is using the Greek word *deesis* for the English word *supplication,* which expresses a cry for help; a sense of need, and a sense of *there is no way out.* Supplication refers to prayers making an urgent cry to God for help in a particular situation. This is when you have absolutely no one and nowhere else to turn; you have no backup plan. Your request needs immediate attention. The situation seems hopeless and you feel helpless!

Supplication is no microwave, quick, fast, and in-a-hurry prayer. The long, heavy *pilum* spear is needed in this case! When you pray the prayer of supplication, you are crying out to God from the depths of your soul! Jesus, *"Who in the days of His flesh, when He had offered up prayers and supplications with strong crying and tears unto Him that was able to save him from death, and was heard in that He feared,"* (Heb. 5:7, KJV).

Here we find Jesus deep in *deesis, supplicating* prayer; deep in agony and anguish, crying out to the Father. There is a great need. The Son is about to take upon Himself the sin of mankind. Jesus was preparing Himself for the walk to Calvary's Cross.

The Son would necessarily be separated from the Father for a short while!

The prayer of Jesus in Gethsemane was that the Father's will be done. Jesus was on His knees praying until sweat *like* drops of blood fell down to the ground (Luke 22:44)! Believers should be able to supplicate with the same degree of intensity that Christ prayed, even when we are not in crisis mode!

In Bible lands, during the day it was very hot, but at night it was very cold. It was nighttime, but Jesus was sweating! He was battling the kingdom of darkness for mankind "with vehement cries and tears" (supplication) to Him who was able to save Him from death.

Sweat gives us a glimpse of His humanity, since the curse upon man was that he would "sweat" (Gen. 3:19). Sweat represents God's judgment upon man because of sin. Jesus never sinned; He was sweating for us! *"For He hath made Him to be sin for us, who knew no sin; that we might be made the righteousness of God in Him,"* (II Cor. 5:21, KJV).

Man did not sweat before the fall. It was not God's intent for man to sweat. *"In the sweat of your face you shall eat bread,"* (Gen. 3:19). Sweat came in after man sinned through disobedience, but Jesus totally and voluntarily submitted Himself to the Father. He naturally flinched from the cup of suffering, but offered up prayers with *strong crying and tears* until He sweat!

This was a fierce spiritual battle between Jesus and the powers of darkness. After asking His Father to remove the cup of suffering three times, the Lamb of God relinquished His will to the will of the Father: "Nevertheless, not My will, but Thine, be done," (Luke 22:42).

Jesus overcame Satan and the powers of darkness, because He utilized the powerful weapon of prayer. "For we wrestle not against flesh and blood;" Jesus wrestled Satan fully clothed in the armor of God. The Son of God *emptied* Himself of His own will and surrendered to the will of the Father!

When we *empty* ourselves of all that is bothering us, God *fills* us with His power. First, the prayer of supplication drains (empties) you, then it strengthens and energizes you. When God takes something out, He puts something better in!

Notice the combination of elements that make up the prayer of supplication, *strong crying* and *tears*. Supplication is warfare praying! God loves us and He will hear and answer our cries for help! Look to God, the Source for acquiring all that you need (*deesis*).

The Prayer of Intercession

One of the Greek words for "intercession" is *enteuxis*. It primarily denotes a conversation, or petition. It is a technical term for approaching a King *on behalf of others*. For example, in the book of Esther, the queen approached the king *on behalf of her people*, the Jews, when their lives were threatened by wicked Haman. The king had the power to deliver the Jews or not! As a result of Esther's request, the Jews were delivered and their enemy, the wicked Haman, was punished!

God is no ordinary king! He is the King of Kings. As we approach the throne of God, we should never lose sight of the fact that He is our Heavenly Father, and He is also King. God is not our homeboy, and we should not try to reduce Him to such.

Our relationship to God should be one of respect and honor. Jesus always addressed Him as, "Father." In intercessory prayer, you do not approach the King for yourself! Intercessors are "gap" people. They stand in the gap for others.

Another Greek word for "intercession" is *entunchano* which means to *meet with in order to converse; to plead with a person* (God), *for others*. Intercessors *meet with God* to plead with Him on behalf of someone else.

This Greek word primarily means to *fall in with*, that is, to feel someone else's infirmity; to *fall into* that horrible situation with that person (don't stay there) and pull them up, through prayer.

229

Go to the Throne of Grace, approach the King of Kings, and pray for someone else's healing, family, ministry and so on. Let us not pray selfishly. Sometime during the day, take a moment to whisper a prayer; intercede for someone other than yourself!

~In the Power of the Holy Spirit~

"Praying always with all prayer and supplication in the Spirit," (Eph. 6:18).

Praying "in the Spirit" is mentioned three times in Scripture (I Cor. 14:15; Eph. 6:18; Jude 20). The Greek word for the phrase "pray in" has many different meanings. It means, "by means of," "with the help of," "in the sphere of" and "in connection to." In other words, Paul is saying: Pray *by means of* the Holy Spirit. Pray *with the help of* the Holy Spirit. Pray *in the sphere of* the Holy Spirit, and pray *in connection to* the Holy Spirit.

Our wills are meshed into the will of God by the Holy Spirit. To pray always with all prayer and supplication *in the Spirit* means that the Holy Spirit assists us in prayer. He is our Helper! Pray *in the power of* the Spirit. Christians are joined by the Holy Spirit in prayer.

Not to the exclusion of the gift, but to say that Paul is referring specifically to praying in tongues in this verse would mean that all other prayers are excluded, since he does say "pray *at all times* with *all kinds of prayer*" -in the Spirit! How can we "pray at all times with all kinds of prayer" for the saints if no one, including the one who is praying, understands what is being said?

"For if I pray in an unknown tongue, my spirit prayeth, but my understanding is unfruitful. What is it then? I will pray with the spirit, and I will pray with the understanding also," (I Cor. 14:14-15). When a person prays in tongues he does not know what he is saying, since it is spoken in a language he does not know. Further, no one else can understand what is being said

unless there is an interpreter. The Scripture says if there is no interpreter, he must keep silent. How can we say "Amen" to an utterance that we do not understand?

Praying *in the Spirit* is to pray according to the leading of the Holy Spirit. He is our Helper; He helps us pray in agreement to the will of God. We must rely upon Him to help us pray, because by our very nature we do not know *how* to pray as we ought. The Spirit prays the kind of prayer that God always hears and answers.

Prayer is like breathing. The Holy Spirit breathes life into our prayer as God breathed life into Adam. If you cannot breathe naturally, you will die physically. If you do not pray, you will die spiritually. Pray at all times, on every occasion, and every chance you get, with all kinds of prayers in the power of the Holy Spirit!

The Lord's Model Prayer is a powerful example of how to wield your weapon for walking in victory established upon God's kingdom, power, and glory. God determines the outcome of every situation; the outcome is –we win! It cannot be otherwise! Amen.

CHAPTER FOURTEEN

THE CONCLUSION OF THE MATTER

B e strong in the Lord and in His mighty power. Put on the whole armor of God, that you may be victorious in every area of your Christian life. This is the conclusion of the matter. God has made absolutely no other provision for your safety and protection.

Eons ago, a great struggle between good and evil was set in motion. This relentless war between the Kingdom of God and the kingdom of Satan still rages on today.

Keep in mind that all that you need for victory is found in the whole armor of God! He is an enemy to your enemies (Satan, man, poverty, sickness)! Through Christ, God has *put our feet* (we are victorious) *on the necks of* (conquered) our adversaries!

The final exhortation from Paul is, insofar as life and its challenges are concerned, "Be strong in the Lord, and in His mighty power." Whatever you are going through, stand strong in the grace that is in Christ Jesus. The Lord will never leave you to fight your battles alone.

Fully clothed Christians may lose a skirmish every now and then, but they will always win the war! Times will come when every one of us will experience some difficulty and no friend, no family member and no amount of money can help us.

However, the time will never come when God Almighty cannot or will not help you!

At the end of Bible School year, during graduation ceremonies, the entire Institute (faculty and students) sang and marched to "Onward, Christian Soldiers!" We deceive ourselves if we sing this song and expect to do no fighting.

The name El Shaddai describes God's absolute power to deliver His people. Human plans and methods may fail, but Jesus never fails! Victory, however, is not the absence of pain, trouble, trials, heartache or difficulties. Face your problems squarely and press on in life, and be determined to do the work of the Lord. Run your race; finish your course.

The idea behind a victorious Christian life is to know that the outcome of the conflict is in God's hands, the place of power! When facing overwhelming situations — whether at work, at home, or in school — you must remember that God promised to be with you to deliver you. The odds are not against you, they are against the enemy — for one with God is a majority!

The more imminent and threatening the problem, the greater the blessing will be! Acknowledge the mighty hand of God in your afflictions and He will deliver you out of them all! The fastest runner does not always win the race. The strongest warrior does not always win the battle! The Lord gives us skill for battle and strength for war.

God planned for believers to be completely clothed in the same armor that is given at conversion. You will never outgrow the armor that God designed specifically for you. Each of us has been equipped with a measure of grace that is unique to the plan and purpose for which we were individually created. The same powerful weapons that Jesus used to defeat the devil when He was on earth has been provided for the Church to launch an indomitable attack against the enemy. Neglect your armor — Bible study, prayer, fasting, and so forth — and you will become weak, powerless and puny.

Do not try to wear someone else's armor. Do not try to walk in someone else's shoes! Christians grow and mature differently. Our situations and our experiences are unique to our purpose. Paul's ministry was *primarily* to the Gentiles, and for this reason he ended up in Gentile territory. His life experiences were specifically designed to bring him into the purpose for which he was called.

Being "strong in the Lord" and in His mighty power means that the Lord gives you strength. At eighty-five Caleb said, *"As yet I am as strong this day as I was in the day that Moses sent me: as my strength was then, even so is my strength now, for war, both to go out, and to come in,"* (Josh. 14:11). This kind of endurance comes from total obedience and surrender to the Lord!

Christ fought the greatest enemy of mankind, Satan, but He never carried a manmade weapon; He used the sword of the Spirit, which is the Word of God. He could have had legions of angels to protect Him, but He did not. Jesus never had a bodyguard. All His days on earth, Jesus was clothed in the same armor that God the Father has provided for the Church to be victorious!

If you want to be fair game for the devil, then take your spiritual armor off!

Insofar as God's tests are concerned, without them we would never know what we are capable of doing. Neither would we grow and mature spiritually. God's ultimate aim is to make us more and more like Christ (I John 3:2). This is an ongoing process which will not come to completion until we see Jesus, face-to-face. Not to worry! The spiritual weapons of our warfare are mightier than any manmade weapons!

The conclusion of the matter is this: as you thoughtfully examine each piece of armor, you will recognize that they are designed by God to safeguard you. Each piece is required to work as a whole for your total victory! Regardless of their circumstances, those who have on the whole armor of God as the Scripture commands will be invincible and victorious!

The anointing of God, Spirit of God and the power of God operating in the life of the believer are all supernatural in origin! We are equipped by God to accomplish extraordinary, miraculous, and inexplicable things for His glory! The armor of the Lord gives us the ability to function in the supernatural and the preternatural realm – going *beyond the ordinary* course of nature.

The *people that do know their God shall be strong, and do exploits* (Daniel 11:32). God wants to manifest His miracle power to the world through you, to the end that they might be saved.

God is going to perform miracles in these last days through the Church that will be impossible to explain; they will have no natural explanation or cause. To bring about these results, we must be clothed in the same armor that Christ wore.

God is all about doing not that which is natural, but all things supernatural! Born-again believers are equipped to function in the supernatural power of Almighty God to win every battle; defeat every foe! This power is ministered to us by the indwelling Holy Spirit through Christ our Lord.

The conclusion of the matter is: Submit yourself to the Lord. Serve Him wholeheartedly. Put on the whole armor of God! Utilize your weapons of mass destruction! Why? So that you will be able to stand firm against all the strategies of the enemy!

We have received orders to penetrate Satan's territory, take back what he has stolen from us and advance the Kingdom of God.

Keep your "war clothes" on. Rise up and go forth! Proclaim the Gospel of Jesus Christ to those who have never heard that Jesus saves!

We do not have to run on to see what the end will be. The end is that we win!

SOURCES CITED

Amplified Bible, Grand Rapids Michigan; Zondervan Publishing House (1987)

Back to the Cross, Watchman Nee, Christian Fellowship Publishers, Inc, New York (1988)

Biblical Mathematics, Evangelist Ed. F. Vallowe, Columbia, South Carolina: Olive Press (1998)

Dake's Annotated Reference Bible, Lawrenceville, Georgia: Dake Bible Sales, Inc. (1963, 1991) KJV

Lectures in Systematic Theology, Henry C. Thiessen, Grand Rapids, Michigan: William B. Eerdmans Publishing Company (1979)

Life Application Study Bible, Wheaton, Ill: Tyndale House Publishers, Inc. (1996) NLT

Matthew Henry's Commentary on the Whole Bible: Old Tappan, New Jersey: Fleming H. Revell Company

Nelson Study Bible, Nashville, Tennessee: Thomas Nelson Publishers (1979, 1980) NKJV

New Living Translation, Wheaton, Ill: Tyndale House Publishers (1996, 2004)

Ryrie Study Bible, Chicago, Ill: Moody Bible Institute (1986, 1994) KJV

Smith's Bible Dictionary, Thomas Nelson Publishers

Spirit Filled Life Bible, Nashville, Tennessee: Thomas Nelson Publishers (1991) NKJV

Unger's Bible Dictionary, Merrill F. Unger, Chicago: Moody Press (1988)

Vine's Expository Dictionary, W.E. Vine, Tarrytown, New York: Fleming H. Revell Company (1981)

Wiersbe's Expository Outlines on the New Testament, Victor books (1992)

CPSIA information can be obtained at www.ICGtesting.com
Printed in the USA
BVOW08s2005160415

396521BV00007B/18/P